handcuffs

handcuffs

bethany griffin

LAUREL-LEAF
BOOKS

Copyright © 2008 by Bethany Griffin

All rights reserved. Published by Laurel-Leaf, an imprint of Random House Children's Books, a division of Random House, Inc., New York. Originally published in hardcover in the United States by Delacorte Press, an imprint of Random House Children's Books, a division of Random House, Inc., New York, in 2008.

Laurel-Leaf and the colophon are trademarks of Random House, Inc.

Visit us on the Web! www.randomhouse.com/teens

Educators and librarians, for a variety of teaching tools, visit us at www.randomhouse.com/teachers

The Library of Congress has cataloged the hardcover edition of this work as follows:

Griffin, Bethany.
Handcuffs / Bethany Griffin.
p. cm.
Summary: When sixteen-year-old Parker Prescott is discovered in a compromising position with her ex-boyfriend, she is forced to reevaluate her life and redefine herself.
ISBN 978-0-385-73550-6 (hc) — ISBN 978-0-385-90529-9 (glb) —
ISBN 978-0-375-89121-2 (e-book)
[1. Interpersonal relations—Fiction. 2. Dating (Social customs)—Fiction.
3. Coming of age—Fiction.] I. Title.
PZ7.G881327Han 2008
[Fic]—dc22
2007043849

ISBN 978-0-385-73551-3 (pbk.)

RL: 6.0

Printed in the United States of America

10 9 8 7 6 5 4 3 2 1

First Laurel-Leaf Edition

Random House Children's Books supports the First Amendment and celebrates the right to read.

To Jamie

who never let me forget I was a writer

handcuffs

She runs out of the room crying.

Let me start over.

My mom runs out of the room crying.

Um, let me start over.

My mom gets up from the couch, lets out a little gaspy sob, the kind that lets you know someone is crying even when they aren't doing the big boo-hoo routine. She wipes her eyes, violently, like she's going to fling the teardrops away, pushes her hair back from her tear-streaked face, looks at my father, looks at me, and then she exits the room.

My dad glares at me like I'm the Antichrist and gets up to follow her. Leaving me there on the couch holding my

Christmas stocking, wearing my dorkariffic red pajamas, surrounded by wrapping paper and crisp white boxes with carefully folded sweaters in tissue paper.

The door doesn't even slam. It makes a little *dink-dink* sound. Then it's quiet except for the *blam, blam, blam* of the television as Miracle Child test-drives his new video game. *Blam, blam, blam, ka-pow!*

The key is still in my hand. I imagine throwing it across the room, breaking a window with the force of my rage and disappointment. I imagine letting it drop from my nerveless dead fingers with an anticlimactic clink as it hits the glass coffee table. I picture the guilt as my parents lean over my coffin and see that I am still clutching the key in a death grip, my fist wrapped around it, my fingernails painted to match the plush purple velour of the lining.

I am the one who should be crying. I am the one who should be running out of the room, with people chasing me and trying to console me. I am not a terrible ungrateful little bitch. Usually. In this case, I got set up.

Let me start over.

It really, actually happened like this.

ꙮ   ꙮ   ꙮ

"Look, look at all the presents!" Preston, my ultrahyper brother, sprinted down the hallway. The Christmas tree rocked back and forth as he dove headfirst into the heap of gifts.

We've done Christmas morning the exact same way forever and ever. The week before Christmas, the sibs and I put our gifts for Mom and Dad and for each other under the tree. I wasn't truly expecting much from my brother and sister. Little brother shopped at the grocery store with a ten-dollar bill Dad gave him. That made my share of the loot two dollars and fifty cents' worth of grocery store–bought lip gloss or Cheetos or whatever seemed like a good present to him. Now, my sister—well, let's just say my birthday present still hasn't been delivered. She thinks I'm dumb enough to wait patiently for my box from Amazon.com, and I have, but so far, nothing.

Christmas morning is supposed to be about wonder. After we go to sleep, my parents put out all the big presents, piles and piles of them in every shape and size. Even though we're all too big to believe in Santa, and have been for years, my heart still missed a few beats when I went downstairs and saw the tree and all the glittering gifts underneath.

Even if we were still young enough to believe in magic, I doubt we could after the year we've had. Another reason Christmas now sucks is that sweaters and shoes aren't really thrilling; it's not like it was when I was little and I got a heap of toys that I'd been putting on my Amazon wish list since September. This year I was supposed to get a new computer, a gorgeous little refurbished notebook from Dad's work. I guess that's out of the question now that Dad no longer has a job. On top of all that, my sister didn't show. I don't like things to change. I like tradition. She won't be coming over for dinner, either, because her rich in-laws guilted her into abandoning us. You'd think Mom would have cried about that, and you might imagine that Paige would be the official Christmas traitor, but no. Not quite.

"Parker, catch!" Preston lobbed a present right at my head.

"Honey, honey, some of these might be breakable." Mom hadn't put in her contacts, so she was squinting through this old pair of glasses that sit crooked on the end of her nose.

My brother stopped throwing the parcels and began to sort them, making neat piles in front of each of us, with a pile for Paige, too. Skipping out on Christmas does not mean you don't get any gifts. No way.

The heaps weren't as big as when we were kids and you could be buried under an avalanche of dolls and puzzles and games, but they weren't shabby, either. We went back and forth opening, and it got weird taking turns because there are usually three of us in a circle.

Preston happily ripped into his video games and racked up an addition to his already-superb collection of athletic shoes. I got mostly clothes. Some I loved, some I would never wear. My mom thinks she gets my style, but she's usually a few steps behind. She's always trying to buy me things with plaid or flower prints. She says I should wear bright colors while I'm young. But I like basic jeans and solid-colored T-shirts and classic sweaters. Maybe a cute oxford with stripes. I mostly just like to blend in.

Some of the excitement disappears when you stop getting toys. And I'm not one for showing lots of emotion. Some people—well, mainly my sister—say I'm an ice princess. But my lack of visible excitement isn't that terrible because my brother jumps up and down and makes enough noise for both of us. Still, I couldn't keep from worrying that my parents, the way they were watching me, wanted something more.

I remembered a Christmas long ago when Paige and I got a Barbie Dream House to share, and that made me wonder why, even when I was young, I would want some silly Barbie crap. It's all so artificial. Who wants the Barbie sweater set with the faux fur leopard collar when you can have a cute sweater for your very own? Not that you'll look like Barbie when you wear it, unless you happen to be my gorgeous sister. Paige was always playing wedding with her Barbies, and last year she staged her own real-life dream wedding. Is that what she was thinking? Who wants the Barbie dream wedding when you can have your own dress and your own cake and a blond groom with hair that isn't plastic?

I truly liked the life-sized real-girl sweater. I smiled at Mom, held it up so she could see how well it would fit.

"I love it," I said loudly, so that she could hear me over Preston trying out his video game. I hope Paige's life-sized real-girl marriage makes her equally happy. Happier, really, since this sweater says *Dry-clean Only*, so I won't be wearing it that often. My mom isn't particularly supportive of the dry cleaners in our area. She is more of the "why bother dry cleaning when we can wash it on gentle cycle?" type.

Mom wasn't particularly supportive of Paige's getting married either, since Paige and West were so young and silly—but she and Dad do adore West, so she gritted her teeth and cleaned out the Prescott family savings account to make sure Paige had a beautiful dress and fresh flowers and all that. Nothing but the best for her perfect first daughter. The happy, outgoing daughter who can thaw ice with the power of her warm smile is opening presents someplace else, so all my parents have today is the unsatisfactory daughter. I try to give them the enthusiasm they crave, but I don't like being stared at, and clapping my hands with glee does not feel the least bit natural. When did Christmas morning get so hard?

The pressure to open each present and look surprised and happy is what got me into this mess—you know, making my mom cry and everything—in the first place. That and my dad's being laid off from work, and my overactive imagination, and Mom's resourcefulness. All of these things transpired in a way that was sure to screw me over.

I put on the red pjs with the little elves on the legs of my own free will. I thought my dad would eat it up. He's kind of the holiday decorating guru. This is the first year I can remember when he didn't get outside and fling lights all over our house. Because of the for-sale sign in our front lawn, I think. He didn't want to venture out there into front-yard territory. He gave up on the annual light competition with our neighbors, gave up in defeat.

"It hasn't been the same since the Henessys moved away, has it?" Mom asked a few days ago. Dad never answered. "The restraining order expires in February," she continued. "I was thinking we could invite them over for a cookout"—her voice faltered—"once it's okay for us to be in the same yard with them again."

Dad still didn't say anything. Great idea, Mom, I thought, let's invite Paige's stalker over for some burgers. I mean, it's not like once the restraining order expires Kyle will stop being a psycho or his parents will forgive you for pointing out to the world that their son is a crazy, potentially dangerous guy who used to climb the tree outside our house and look into Paige's window. In the end I didn't say anything either. Mom was just trying to remind Dad of Christmas lights and traditions from years past. She's like me, still trying to ignore the fact that things have changed.

I don't think Dad even noticed the jolly-elf pjs. He just sat there beside the slightly lopsided Christmas tree and smiled each time Preston or I ripped into a package, but it was a little smile, not enough for Christmas morning. I wanted to make him really smile and laugh and get down on the floor to help us rip open the gifts, but I couldn't think how to invite him to do this when I wasn't smiling or laughing or rolling in the wrapping paper myself. I was watching him when he reached up and touched an ornament. It was a frame shaped like a gold star, and it sparkled around my fifth-grade picture.

"This is my favorite ornament," he said. It felt warm and fuzzy, felt extremely great to know that Dad's favorite ornament on our tree was a photo of me wearing a pink shirt and a big goofy grin. There's a picture of Paige in an angel frame on the other side of the tree. I didn't rate the halo, probably because I look completely unangelic. Dark hair will do that to you.

I'm a crazy mix of my parents' DNA, with Dad's dark hair and Mom's blue eyes. Very cold blue eyes, like a Siberian husky's. At least, that's what my ex-boyfriend says.

After the day I've just had, I think I should go find the aforementioned ex and have sex with him in his basement. Yikes, that comment didn't go over well, even in my head. Now I need to explain about my ex and his basement, and the reason he's an ex.

Preston grabbed another box, and the *crinkle crinkle crinkle* reminded me of the wrapping paper, purple and silver foil, he had used when I was exchanging presents with him. This was when he was the real thing. Official. Or enough of a boyfriend that we were exchanging presents. The *crinkle* then was from me kneeling on the discarded paper as I reached for the last present. A guy buying you presents signifies something, doesn't it? I mean, not love, but something?

And as I leaned forward, he eased the zipper down on the back of my dress, slowly, so slowly—I didn't know if I could keep my balance, if I could keep from falling face-first into his parents' designer-decorated tree with the yards of ribbon and the enormous bows that fluttered against my cheek as I tried to breathe. I mean, that was the sort of moment when falling over would be bad.

He is able to move really slowly and make you die wondering exactly what he's going to do. When the zipper was just below my shoulder blades, I felt his tongue on my neck. Just the tip of it.

The crinkle of wrapping paper and a little bit of gaspy heavy breathing. Is that what Christmas has become for me? Newly single and slightly turned on by the sound of tissue rubbing against shiny crisp foil?

So I sat under our nondesigner tree in the middle of our dollar-store-wrapping-paper shreds and watched Preston try to tear open a DVD. He had cowlicks all over his head. Preston has the biggest brown eyes ever, and even though his face is really pale, he has like ten dark freckles right across his nose. Funny how he couldn't seem to get past the little line of tape they put at the top and bottom of the DVD case. Needed fingernails, I guess.

"Time for the stockings!" Mom said, grabbing two of the three from the mantel.

Preston jumped over the footstool and practically tore his from Mom's hands. She laughed and handed me mine, and then sat down next to Dad. He took her hand and held it for a few minutes. My mind was in slow mode, a precaffeine present-induced daze. So I just focused for a moment on the way they were sitting there. It was really sweet, and it was totally weird. They've been fighting lately, yelling at each other. But all that seemed to be forgotten as they sat together in front of the Christmas tree watching me. Mom acted nervous. Her leg kind of bounced up and down. Weird. The stocking is the final spurt at the end of the present frenzy. It isn't anything exciting. Unless, unless. Here's where the imagination kicked in.

I reached my hand in. First present, wrapped in paper scraps from the bigger packages, was a tube of Chap Stick. Cool, I guess. Next was a bottle of salon shampoo. I like the one that smells like coconuts. Then some gel pens. I really liked those in middle school. I can still use them for taking notes in history class. Mr. Leonard is big on time lines. Gel pens. Kid stuff, but it's just a stocking, right?

A tube of too-red lipstick (I'm more of a gloss girl), a roll of Scotch tape (dropped in by accident, I presume?), and something small and cold that snagged in the foot of the woven stocking.

My fist closed around it. Preston was jumping up and down waving some kind of cheap little MP3 player that still had an orange *Clearance* tag stuck to it. Our Miracle Boy adores gadgets. My parents were staring at me hungrily, waiting.

I turned it over in my hand. The rounded top, the grooved side. A key.

2

I remember Paige's sixteenth birthday party with this complete sense of awe. Every kid in school was there. Well, not every student enrolled in Allenville High, but everyone who mattered. It was one of those occasions where, as a skinny thirteen-year-old, I couldn't help saying over and over to myself, My time will come, my time will come.

Paige looked really good in a hot-pink shirt and these flared jeans. Her hair was that silky sexy golden blond, and her wide slanty blue eyes were lined with this light shimmery blue stuff that just made them glow. She was happy and laughing, greeting people, the center of attention. I couldn't believe all the good-looking older boys who were there.

My mom did an Asian theme. She hung these cool little

lanterns all over the yard. During the party she stood be-hind Paige and smiled proudly. Every once in a while she walked around to make sure everyone was happy and no one was spilling Pepsi on our leather couch or sneaking off to make out or anything like that. And every time she saw my sister she smiled this radiant smile that lit her face up like one of the glowing pink lanterns, which were illuminated with votive candles. I know because I had to light them all.

We ate outside at these long tables, and there was soft music playing. I was beside the fountain. It made a tinkling sound. I remember picking at a scab on my knee and won-dering why Paige got the head-turning blond hair and I got the dark hair.

The only time Paige acknowledged me that afternoon was when our ex-neighbors, Kyle and Marion Henessy, came over and wanted to hang out with her. I guess Mom invited them, because Paige couldn't get rid of them fast enough. She pushed them toward me. I stood up, waiting for her to say something after "Hey, Parker, here are Kyle and Marion. You guys can hang out with the Ice Princess." But then she turned and left me to sit with the other party rejects. Kyle was almost the same age as Paige and her friends, but of course they didn't want to hang around with him. She walked away. He stared after her. I remember asking him a question, but he was still watching her and he didn't notice me. He was on the edge of being a freak even then. We just didn't know it. The kid sister and the guests who were only invited because our moms are friends. Real cool.

But the party itself was perfect. Someday this will be me, I thought.

Then came the gifts. Paige had the ability to open them slowly, read each card, smile at the giver so that he or she felt special for a moment, basking in her golden attention.

She was opening the last one, picking at the tape with her perfect pink fingernails, when the Volkswagen pulled up.

It was unforgettable. Paige looked up, squinted, trying to see who was driving, and then when she saw that it was Dad, she screamed. A real toe-curling, bloodcurdling scream.

Everybody stood up and clapped. The boys threw confetti, and West Thompson, the captain of the football team and my future brother-in-law, managed to get some of it in my eye. He was throwing like a maniac. Paige walked down the steps and over to the car slowly, like a sleepwalker. She opened the door, but she didn't get in. She walked around, ran her hand reverently over the candy-apple finish. She wiped her eyes. She was crying. It was amazing.

I wasn't jealous of her, except that she was sixteen and I was a scabby twelve. She was beautiful and I was awkward. She had the coolest car I had ever seen. My time will come, I told myself. Four more years. It seemed too long to have to wait.

I didn't get a sixteenth birthday party. I turned sixteen in November. Last month. Two months after my parents borrowed a bunch of money from my grandmother. Half a year after my dad lost his job. My mom took me to the Chinese restaurant that I adored when I was ten years old. I had sweet and sour chicken.

Dad gave me a check for a hundred dollars sandwiched in a card that said *Sweet Sixteen* in glittery letters. It's still in my jewelry box under the silver bracelet Grandma sent last Christmas. The card and the check. I was afraid to cash it. My parents had been fighting about checks bouncing all that week. It was the first time I'd ever heard them yell at each other.

So back to this morning, Merry Christmas and all that. I closed my fist around the cold metal key and pulled it out of the stocking. I remembered the look on Paige's face, the glow from the paper Chinese lanterns, the candy-apple red of the car, the tan leather interior that smelled so good.

I imagined myself, Parker Prescott, wearing the mirrored sunglasses that make me look like I am cool and collected and don't give a shit about anything, behind the wheel of an amazing car. Parker Prescott, perfect at last.

The key came free of the stocking, cool in my hand. I opened my mouth, but nothing came out. Then I stood up—it seems in retrospect that it should have been in slow motion—and I ran to look out the front window at the driveway.

Nothing there but the Century 21 sign, FOR SALE, the one with the additional sliver of sign over the top that says REDUCED. Mom's car was in the garage, resting happily beside Dad's Jeep. The driveway was empty.

"I told you this was a bad idea." I heard my dad saying this as if from far away.

"Parker." My mom sounded weird. "It's a key to the Jeep, honey." I opened my hand. In my palm, there was this scrappy piece of paper, a handmade coupon. My mom's big loopy writing on her work stationery. *This coupon good for 10 hours of Daddy Driving School.* There was a little cartoon of a kind of lopsided SUV and a grinning man who looked nothing like my dad. I could've made a kick-ass coupon on the computer, could've put Dad's picture right on it, but of course neither of my parents can do more with a computer than print a document or send an e-mail. And here somebody— my mom, I guess—took the time to make this. Under my anger I felt sad for all of us.

How was I supposed to know? A key to my dad's Jeep in my stocking as a gift?

"Daddy wanted to spend time with you. Daddy and I thought . . ." Mom trailed off, as if unsure of herself. My mother, who used to know everything, who always bought the hippest sunglasses and looked ten years younger than the other moms when she picked us up from after-school activities. She's the one who chose the paper lanterns for Paige's party, who made things look great, like some kind of professional party planner had put it all together.

"Parker, how could you think . . ." My dad sounded mad, and I only realized later that he was terribly hurt.

"The Jeep?" I held the key up. Yeah, that's what it was, no doubt now. It was silver, slightly squared off. Dad was too cheap to upgrade to the keyless entry, and that was way before our money problems started.

"How could you think that . . . ," Dad said again, and this time it struck a nerve.

"That you might love me as much as you love Paige?"

"Parker!" Mom said again.

"That something cool and magical could happen to me?"

My dad started to say something, but then the tears welled up in Mom's eyes.

ᔐ   ᔐ   ᔐ

She runs out and I'm left here with Dad, the gifts, and a little brother who is oblivious to anything that isn't animated and hurling fireballs. Dad glares at me like I'm a form of life lower than pond scum as he follows her out of the room. I tell myself that ice princesses do not cry, and miraculously my eyes stay dry. Probably because I'm numb from

15

the shock. Anger and hurt are lesser emotions, so I can push those away, ignore them.

A key to the Jeep. Daddy Driving Lessons. My mom crying on Christmas morning. Sometimes I wonder if I belong here at all. If their life would be merrier without me screwing things up.

Nobody notices when I leave the house, even when I reach under the Christmas tree to grab my new red and white scarf. I need it. It's cold outside, and I'm always frozen on the inside.

So now I'm back to the basement.

My boyfriend lives there. Correction, ex-boyfriend. He's like the troll under his parents' house. Except he looks pretty good. For a troll, I mean.

I knock on the door. The side door. But before my hand connects for the second knock the door swings open.

"C'mon in, I'm watching something."

I should probably explain about my ex.

"Take your shoes off, Parker."

I probably should explain, but I don't have the energy.

His TV is on, his laptop is defragging, there is a CD playing over speakers angled throughout the narrow bedroom. He's wearing headphones, but the cord is dangling, not plugged into anything. Kind of like me.

"What's up, Parker Prescott?"

"I hate the way you say my name."

"I know." He raises one eyebrow at me.

"You got any other girls coming over here today?" I ask this and am amazed at how hard it is to ask something as if you don't care when you care so much that you can hardly get the words out.

"You know I don't."

"How'm I supposed—" I stop myself midsentence. There's just no point. He plugs the headphones into something, turns a knob, nods, then lets the headphones fall down around his neck. They are the big bulky kind, not the sleek little ones that go in your ears. My parents seem to believe that I am a computer genius, but beside him I am nothing.

"Trouble in paradise?" he asks, looking at me.

"You could say that."

"You could tell me."

"I could."

"I could listen."

"You might."

He laughs and unplugs the headphones so that I can share his musical experience.

"You like this CD?"

"You know I do." This is true even though I don't remember ever hearing it before. Because I like everything when he's around. Even though he might be getting ready to tell me why he hates this CD, the fact that I heard it here, standing awkwardly beside him while he leans back in his black leather office chair, makes it official: I will love this song until the day that I die.

He knows this. I know he knows this.

"You look good, Prescott. You can sit down, you know."

The only place to sit is on his bed, which is about a foot from the desk where he's working. The bedspread is purple stripes alternating with dark charcoal stripes. I know it well.

"I got this scarf for Christmas." I sit gingerly on the edge of the bed.

"Red looks good on you." He eyes me for a couple of seconds. "Kandace Freemont got this red and white Santa robe for Christmas. Like a Santa suit, but it wrapped around with a white belt. She showed up here wearing it. Wasn't wearing anything under it at all."

My stomach lurches. He isn't looking at me. I don't know why he's telling me this. He's always done this. He'll reveal things or make comments about other girls just when I start getting comfortable with him, with us. Things about other girls that I don't want to know. But I need him. I left the family trauma to seek comfort in his basement. And this is what he offers me. It's sad, really. I'm sad, in just about every way that it's possible for a person to be sad.

"Guess you liked that," I say. This is how it always goes with us.

"I've seen better, and I've seen worse."

"What happened?" Don't tell me, don't tell me, don't tell me, don't—

"I sent her home."

"Yeah?" Why can't I breathe? Why is it so hard to breathe in this damn basement? I feel something close to hope, the best feeling I've had today, and hate myself a little for being so pathetic.

"If she'd only had a hat. With a Santa hat it would have been hot. Without it, it was just sleazy." He looks away, hits a button on the computer, and then turns back to me.

"Didn't you enjoy that?" I say this coolly, as if I don't care.

He swivels his chair so that our knees are touching. Is he trying to make me jealous? Right now I am nervous and jealous and sad all at once, and it's not a good combination. I kind of want to go home. Then he says,

"I'd like to get you sleazy, Prescott. Kandace Freemont already is. There's a difference."

He leans forward and closes his eyes, and I let him kiss me. That's a lie. I twine my arms around his neck and kiss him hard. Possessively. Exactly what he wants.

But I don't close my eyes. Closing your eyes implies trust.

His parents are pulling up in their silver minivan as I leave by the basement's side door. They wave, I wave. I walk just a little bit faster, hoping they won't notice my sudden hurry. I don't want them to offer to drive me home. I mean, if I wanted a ride I would be in his Saab right now. But I love to walk, really. Which is perfect because I don't have a car. I realize, embarrassed, that they probably wonder why I'm here. They probably think I should be with my own family on Christmas, not slinking out of their basement.

His Saab is sitting in the driveway. He never parks it in the garage. I look over at it and am glad I'm walking home. His car was the scene of our most ferocious fight. The fight when he squeezed my arm and I cried, not because of the squeezing, but because of the look on his face. I know I should be avoiding him, not the car. The car didn't make me cry. But it's hard sometimes to be sure of things. It's easy to avoid the car and impossible to stay away from him.

As I walk I think about our conversation. "Why would Kandace Freemont get a Santa robe for Christmas?" I wondered out loud as I was putting on my shoes. See, sometimes I bring up the hurtful things too. It's like when you can't stop worrying at a sore spot, making it hurt worse than before. It's all pretty sick.

"She said it was from her grandma." He was sliding the Killers disc out and replacing it with some Pink Floyd.

"Damn, she really skanked up her grandma's gift." The nerve of Kandace Freemont, coming over here wearing a robe and nothing else. Pulling the robe open in front of him. Her grandma probably thinks she's using it when she gets out of the shower. A red and white Santa robe is exactly the sort of gift my grandma would send, if she hadn't sent me a bath set with talcum powder instead. Who the hell uses talcum powder, anyway? It's like crushed-up chalk, and it doesn't even smell good.

"Some girls are like that," he said. I couldn't tell if he approved or not. I didn't kiss him goodbye.

Heading home, I can't help glancing at the house to the left of his, where a hot senior girl named Erin Glasgow lives. I remind myself that I don't have any reason to feel threatened anymore. Doesn't matter if he sits out on his deck so he can see Erin lounging by the pool. I don't have to care about him anymore. He's my ex-boyfriend, and that's not a boyfriend at all.

Erin is actually pretty cool. She was in my chemistry class last year. I skipped the intro to chemistry course, which is why I was with upperclassmen, and woefully unprepared. Erin helped me out a couple of times with stuff that my sophomore brain couldn't quite grasp. It was lucky, I guess, that before finals they moved me out of chemistry and put me in comparative religion. Kyle Henessy was one of the seniors in my chemistry class.

"It may not seem fair to you," Mr. Dawson, our assistant principal, said as I sat in his office. "Kyle did something wrong, and you didn't. We take sexual harassment very seriously here. But he's a senior and you're just a sophomore. You have plenty of time to take chemistry, and he needs it to graduate."

When I went back to the chem lab to gather my books, Kyle had his head on his desk and Erin Glasgow was trying to comfort him. And so my sister's irresistibleness screwed up my sophomore schedule as well as Kyle's entire life. Too bad Paige isn't kindhearted like Erin Glasgow, who I can't bring myself to hate, even though I find myself despising most girls if the ex even glances at them.

"**P**arker, come on in, honey," my mom calls.

Yeah, right. She knows I hate coming into a movie that's halfway over. At least, she *should* know. I feel a rush of irrational anger. Paige is sitting between our parents and Preston is on the floor. They are all sharing a big bowl of microwave popcorn. So happy and content. What do they need me there for, anyway? I thought they would be upset that I walked out and missed the big Christmas dinner event. Did they even miss me?

"She has to check her e-mail," my sister says from the living room. "Seriously, do you think it's normal for a sixteen-year-old girl to be on the computer as much as she is?"

"She isn't like you," Dad says. For a moment I wonder if he means something good or something bad. Then I look in at Paige, sitting in front of the TV. Paige had a social life, Paige had tons of friends. How could they compare me to her and see anything good?

I grab some chips and a bottled water and head up to my room to fire up my PC. The Dell desktop that was top-of-the-line like two years ago.

My in-box is empty. I imagine the AOL voice saying, "You have no new messages." The voice of social inferiority. I go to Hotmail and click to open a new account. Apparently, to open a Hotmail account you have to have a regular e-mail account. I use my other screen name, P216P, to create a dummy account. Like I said, my parents act like I'm a computer genius techno-nerd, but mainly I just push buttons and see what happens. Of course, I've done it enough that I usually push the right ones.

I have to find some way to make him remember and pay attention and realize the things that keep me up at night, the things that tie me in knots and make me want to hyperventilate at the same time. And so I type my masterpiece. Everything that I know he wants me to do to him and with him, with my hands, with my mouth, every single little thing I can think of, I tell him I want to do. He'll know it's me because I'm giving him all of his desires, regurgitated. Everything he's whispered in my ear. Everything I rejected when he became my ex-boyfriend. He has to know this is from me, right?

I get up and walk across the room. Open the bottle of Aquafina only to screw the top back on and pace again. I go back to the screen and add two more juicy little details. My fingers are sweaty. I wipe them on my jeans, and before I can lose my nerve, I hit Send.

Refresh, Refresh, Refresh, Refresh. Ten excruciating minutes for his reply.

Is this a dude? Sorry, I'm not into dudes.

"I'm afraid to break it to you, Park, but I'm thinking we're going to have to get dates for tomorrow night."

"Yeah?"

"I'm out of money with no child support check until next month. You want some gum?"

I shake my head. Raye knows I never chew gum. It transforms me into a cow. I put the gum in innocently enough, to freshen the breath after a mall burrito or whatever, I chew it discreetly for a while, and before I know it I'm deep in thought and gnawing at it like a heifer. A mad cow.

Raye knows this, but she still offers. Raye is kind of a pusher.

"I have a little bit of Christmas money."

"And you have that check for one hundred dollars in your jewelry box."

Rachel Tannahill is my best friend. She knows things about me that nobody else knows.

"You keep saying that about the child support, people are going to think you have a bunch of babies running around," I say to change the subject.

"With a body like this?" Raye flashes white teeth at me. She wears her dark hair short, with all these wild edges that look even wilder because of her big dark eyes. She's one of the few people on earth who can wear any color of eye shadow, even purple, and still look cool. Raye's dad left her mom for a younger woman five years ago. Her mom turned around and married a dentist. To show her colossal disdain for her ex-husband, Raye's mom just has his child support check deposited into a checking account for Rachel Tannahill. I have to say, the loot went a lot further before Raye developed an astronomical car payment. Guess I should chip in some gas money sometime.

We walk into the Gap, my favorite place to buy solid-colored V-neck sweaters. Raye walks straight to a circular rack of shirts and starts flipping through them, but I feel like I'm attached to the planks of the hardwood floor. The first thing I see as I scan the store is Marion Henessy, my ex-neighbor. She's standing in a fairly long line of day-after-Christmas shoppers. It's funny how I pick her out immediately, even though I'm not looking for her, or anything else, really. Just wasting time. Marion turns and sees us and her mouth scrunches up like she's tasting something sour.

She's stocky and not very tall, and her hair is curly. When we were little she used to wear it in these two long pigtails. Now it's medium length and kind of blah. What my sister would call unstylish.

The customer in front of Marion signs a credit card slip and walks away.

"Can I help you?" the guy behind the counter asks. Raye has abandoned the rack of shirts and is standing beside me now.

"No." Marion sounds like she's ready to cry. "No, I'll come back later." She gives me a venomous look, holds the bag of stuff that she must've been returning close to her chest, and stomps out the door. The salesguy blinks a couple of times and then turns to the next customer.

"Boy, she really hates you." Raye is as mesmerized by Marion's clumsy stomping retreat as I am.

"Yeah, she can really hold a grudge."

"I like this shirt," Raye drags me over to the rack where she was browsing and picks up a hot-pink T-shirt with long sleeves, very punk chic.

I reach out and touch the sleeve. It's a nice soft cotton.

"Marion can't seem to understand that the thing with Paige and her brother has nothing to do with me, or with her, either." It makes me so mad, the way she treats me like a leper or something.

"I heard they had to put Kyle into a center for depression a few months ago, that he was completely suicidal before they hospitalized him," Raye says.

"No way. That didn't happen."

"How do you know?" Raye puts down the shirt. I pick it up.

"I would know. I would've heard."

"From who, Marion? She won't speak to you, and she's not going to put anything bad about Saint Kyle on her blog,

28

that's for sure." Marion has this blog that's a big deal around our school, even though Marion herself is not.

"I just think I would've heard." I hold up the shirt she put down. "You don't like this?"

"I already have a shirt that same color. You want it?" I hold the hanger up and away from me and look at the shirt, thinking about how much Marion cares for Kyle. They're like a different species than me and my sister. Paige wouldn't care if I fell off a building and got a concussion, unless blood splattered on her and messed up her outfit.

"I don't think I own anything hot pink" is what I say.

"You should get it, that color would look good on you."

"Yeah?" I look at the price tag. "We really need to go." I put the shirt back on the rack, remembering that I have no disposable income. None. "We should go down to the food court." I suggest this but don't leave the store until Raye glances at one last shirt and then turns and walks out. I'm two steps behind her. I take a deep breath.

"I visited the basement yesterday." I've been putting off telling her this, but all of a sudden I need to talk.

"No!"

"Yeah."

"I thought he told you not to come over again unless you were willing to . . ." I grab her arm and she laughs. "Just because you don't want to do it doesn't mean I can't say it, Parker!"

"Whatever." I put my hands into the pockets of my jeans and shuffle my feet around a little.

"So did you?"

"It doesn't matter."

"Are you back together?"

"No."

"So you didn't?"

"It was Christmas, Raye."

"What does that even mean?"

I shake my head at her and we walk along in silence.

The mall is a sad shrine to materialism. The wreaths are crooked, the boughs of holly are falling down, and the HAPPY HOLIDAYS sign over the entrance is askew. The mallployees were perhaps too overwhelmed on Christmas Eve to do more than ring up the pathetic last-minute shoppers. Now there are lines and lines of people returning crappy gifts. I wonder if the Things Remembered store would like to have a key returned. Piece of crap probably came from Wal-Mart, anyway. Or the hardware store. It's in my pocket now, jingling around on my vintage Hello Kitty key chain.

"You have that dreamy look on your face."

"I don't."

"You do. You're thinking about lover boy."

"I wasn't. But I am now." I feel my mouth curving into this goofy grin that feels pretty good.

"God, Parker. You should just marry him and move into his basement lair."

"Maybe I will." I smile at her. She knows he makes me crazy. She knows why we broke up. There isn't any reason to go back over it now. Not here in the middle of the mall between the hordes of preteens flocking to Limited Too and the chunky post-teens flocking to the Great American Cookie Company.

"So how about it, you want to go on a date? There's this guy I've been checking out, and he has a friend." Raye has access to a much wider pool of boys than the rest of us because her dad lives in this gated community all the way across town. So the boys in her dad's neighborhood go to a totally different school, and she's always meeting guys who ask her out. Once I spent the night with her at her dad's and some guy from down the street turned and looked at me like twice, but he never asked me out, which is good because I would have said no. Probably. It's obvious that even with a wider assortment of possible dates, I would never get asked out even half as often as Raye. She always looks guys right in the eye and smiles really slowly. She could have a different date every night of the week if she wanted.

"Don't they all," I say.

"What?"

"Don't they all have some single friend?" Meaning guys, and Raye's guys in particular.

"Correct me if I'm wrong, but aren't we both single at the moment?"

I nod, unwilling to proclaim my newly bereaved status aloud, though I did break up with him, sort of, by default.

"And are we not short on funds?"

I can't help picturing the hot-pink shirt. It might be nice to own something bright like that. I nod.

Raye and I have had this strategy since we were fifteen. That's when my parents first started letting me out of the house for dates. Seriously, I couldn't wear mascara until I was a freshman. Paige was drinking vodka and doing it in the back of some college guy's BMW and I had to sneak eye shadow into the school bathroom and try to apply it really fast while Ms. Rolland yelled for me to hurry up so the other girls could get in and pee.

So now that I can officially wear makeup and go out with boys, the strategy is as follows: One weekend night is reserved for us, Parker and Raye, to hang out, watch a movie, eat mall pizza, whatever. While we were dating someone, the other weekend night is for boys. Movies, popcorn, and big soft mall pretzels on the guys' dollars. What could be better? Especially since I don't have an abundance of dollars anymore.

See, this date is kind of a friendship necessity thing. Raye went through a really bad breakup at the beginning of the school year. I mean, as much as I've second-guessed my decision to walk away from the basement, and despite the three and a half times I've slunk back down there, I did keep some dignity. Raye got totally dumped and cheated on. The girl her slimeball boyfriend Ian cheated on her with wasn't even the girl he dumped her for. It was ugly, really ugly. So I'll probably go along on the planned excursion to meet this guy she thinks she might want to go out with. I'll probably go for Raye, with no other reason, but what happens next makes it definite.

Raye grabs my arm and says, "Let's go into the sunglasses place."

"What?" We never go into the Sunglass Hut. Raye is a pretty bad liar sometimes. I look into the sunglasses store, because I'm the kind of girl who has to look when someone says not to look, and there reflected back at me is my ex-boyfriend walking beside Kandace Freemont. I guess Raye was trying to get me to dive in there and avoid them or something.

"Hi, Rachel," Kandace says. She doesn't say anything to me, just stands back kind of behind him. He and Raye circle each other warily, two cowpokes with itchy trigger fingers. Raye is always suspicious around him. I guess I would be suspicious too if I saw my best friend reduced to quivering jelly by some guy. And now, since the breakup, I suspect it's going to get worse. He's bringing Kandace Freemont to the mall. He's crossed some kind of invisible line now, and Raye is unlikely to forgive him, ever. She's like that sometimes.

"Hey, Kandace, what're you guys doing here?" Raye sounds bored but she looks concerned. Am I that big of a social retard that she thinks I'll foam at the mouth or something?

"We're shopping for hats," he says. Raye gives him a dirty look. She doesn't like it when she asks someone else a question and he answers. Though in the past it was his answering for me that she objected to.

"I think the Santa at Sears got drunk and left his hat in the Dumpster. If you hurry you can get there before they pick up the trash," I say.

He flashes me a smile so sudden and sincere that it makes my heart stop. Kandace and Raye don't know what the hell we're talking about, and that makes my heart beat faster. Stop. Start. Stop. Start. God, he keeps me so off balance.

"You must really like that new sweater, huh?" Oh my God. I'm wearing the same sweater from last night. This morning it just seemed like the only thing in my closet with any appeal. Because it's new and pretty is what I told myself. Because he said I looked good when I was wearing this sweater and because it was pressed next to him for nearly ten minutes is what I know to be the truth. Again they are looking at us like we are speaking a foreign language. And then he does something unprecedented.

"Parker wore that sweater last night," he tells Kandace. She glares at me. She has been working so hard to ignore my existence, and now he has forced her to acknowledge me. He's such a social sadist.

"Look, I really need a cappuccino and a cheesecake brownie." Raye grabs my arm to pull me away.

"Prescott," he calls after me, "I liked your e-mail. I know you aren't a dude." I can feel my face burning. Raye is pulling me away. I don't look back because I don't want him to see me blushing. Raye doesn't ask about the e-mail, but I see her frown, her eyes turning down at the corners.

"Cappuccino," Raye says soothingly. "Cheesecake brownie. You can even have one of those awful cookies with M&M's on top that you love so much." She doesn't say anything about the basement or ask me about the e-mail. She went through a breakup. She knows how crazy it can all get. She won't even ask me about it later. I hope.

"Do you think Cute Cookie Guy will be there?" My voice sounds fine. My voice sounds normal. Doesn't it?

"Cute Cookie Guy will totally be there."

"Did you notice?"

"That he was wearing that ratty corduroy jacket you despise?"

"No, Raye."

"That Kandace Freemont wears bright red lipstick to the mall?"

"No, Raye."

"That Sunglass Hut had Ray-Bans on sale so you can play cops and robbers in your trailer-park bedroom?"

"No." Loud sigh. "Raye."

"What, Park?"

"He was explaining things to her. He never explains himself."

"That's because he's an absolute tool."

"No, Raye. It's because he can't stand idiots. He doesn't like to have to slow down for people."

"Because he's an absolute tool. And Parker, I don't think he's hanging out with Kandace Freemont for her intelligence." I push my hair out of my face and feel myself sagging, deflated. He was with me last night. He kissed me. He got my e-mail and read those things that I said I wanted to do with him. And yet he's here today with Kandace. There is no way to deal with this unless I admit that I am in serious pain, the kind of emotional breakdown that you can't hide, not even if you're an ice princess.

Raye is determined to medicate me with sugar. She pulls me along and I follow her because I can think of nothing else to do. There is no line at our cookie place, because it's off in the corner and not as flashy as the other cookie place. They don't have smoothies with protein infusions, but they do have frozen mocha-mugs, though these come in paper cups rather than mugs and have mucho-mocha fat grams, and chocolate shavings.

"I'll take three cookies." I try to ignore Raye's words, though they are bouncing around in my head.

"Rough day?" Cute Cookie Guy is always sympathetic. If he wasn't so obviously gay, I would run off with him, bear his children, and get fat eating cookies all day.

"Terrible day, terrible week, terrible life," I say. He puts twelve cookies in a brown bag and rings me up for three. Cookie Guy rocks.

He hands me the bag. "At least you have a good metabolism."

"Tell me about it." Raye is practically shoving me out of the way, because she's addicted to iced cappuccinos. Raye wears size six jeans and I wear size four. This means that I can borrow her jeans and she can't wear mine. This is fair because she has a bank account and I don't.

8

Three hours, two phone calls, one quick glance at Marion's stupid blog, and six cookies later, we are on our way to the movies. Raye has a cute date named Josh, if you like the clean-cut type. My blind-date guy is tall, which is good, but kind of droopy, which is bad. He is down and depressed, which is okay (Parker likes the moody guys, all right?), but he's moody because his girlfriend broke up with him, which is bad.

He keeps staring at the front of my new sweater, which I have realized might be a bit tight. If I liked him this might kind of be good, but I absolutely do not like him.

Clean-cut guy drives an SUV. Me and Droopy sit in the back. Raye keeps the conversation going until we get to the theater. The real theater, not the one at the mall. These guys are a class act.

So Droopy doesn't say anything until we get out of the vehicle, then he comes around to help me down, and he asks,

"Do you like fish?"

"Um, like fried fish?"

"Do you like *to* fish?"

"What?"

"I really like to fish."

"Like, catching fish with a fishing pole?"

"Yeah."

"Uh-huh." I am imagining that whore Kandace Freemont in the basement. If his parents are out, then they will be on his bed. It squeaks. Great, now I have visual *and* audio. If the family is home, they will be on his floor, on the striped quilt. So much for his not liking sleazy.

"You know what," I say, and as I am opening my mouth I'm already kicking myself, but I just plow on and say, "there are a lot of challenges in this world, but I don't have to try to outwit a fish, because I have all the confidence in the world that I am smarter than the average fish." Raye is looking at me and kind of stomping her foot. Clean-cut guy is looking at me with a little half smile on his face. Droopy is staring at my chest again.

We get into the ticket line. Raye is quizzing Josh about the types of candy he likes. Reese's Pieces get a yes, Sour Patch Kids a no, Junior Mints a sometimes. Raye doesn't like Sour Patch Kids either. They should live happily ever after. I am trying to keep my mind out of the basement when I notice Droopy has dropped out of my peripheral vision. What's he doing now, checking out my ass?

Raye and Josh, tickets in hand, sprint to the candy line, intent on those Reese's Pieces, and I am left staring at the ticket guy, who has six piercings just in the side of his face that is turned toward me. (Eyebrow, nose, weird chin thing, and three earrings.) Freaky.

"How many?" he asks. I glance behind me. Droopy is intently studying the coming attraction posters.

"How many?" The ticket guy is getting impatient, and he's a little intimidating, with all the barbells stuck through his face and the lank midnight black hair. Droopy, on the other hand, is not moving forward. I get the message, loud and clear. My blind date is rejecting me; he's forcing me to pay my own way.

"One," I say. The ticket guy prints my single lonely ticket. I have to pay with my last wrinkled dollars and eight quarters.

Cheap ass suddenly becomes aware that he's in the ticket line and asks for one ticket. I don't know whether I should wait for him. Obviously we aren't exactly on a date, are we? I could walk ahead to show him I don't really need his lousy company. I feel all jangled-up and confused. Droopy does not go to the refreshment line, and I can't afford even the cheapest, smallest item they sell. There is exactly thirty-five cents in my purse and a few sticky pennies that don't count because they don't fall out when I turn my purse upside down.

For some ridiculous reason, I feel my eyes start to tear up a little. I feel crappy that I can't afford anything to snack on, and even more crappy that Droopy didn't consider me date-worthy. What's wrong with me? I take a really deep breath and force the feeling away, because there is no way I'm going to sit here and cry in the middle of this action-adventure spy thriller, with Kandace probably in his bed and my feet stuck on the floor thanks to the adhesive nature of spilled cola drinks, when I can't even afford a syrupy fattening soda of my own. I take three deep breaths and then wipe my eyes with the back of my hand.

Raye has horrible taste in movies. Not that she was really ever planning on watching this one. I look over at the end of the previews, prepared to bum just a couple of Reese's Pieces, but she is already locked in an embrace with this Josh guy. My brain is in slow mode, and they catch my eye for like two seconds more than I'm comfortable with. It's weird, seeing something like that from another perspective. His tongue, her tongue. Different when it's my best friend and not some person on TV. Or me on the striped blanket on my ex-boyfriend's floor, trying to be quiet. Anyway, I guess Raye likes Josh.

On-screen two people hit each other until one guy, the bad one, I think, falls down. I glance at my watch, but I can't see it because the probably-good-guy is running through a cave now, and there's no light. I'm guessing that the movie is about half over. I feel a stab of annoyance that morphs into anger. Anger that Raye's being a total slut. But I know that's not fair, because I want her to get over Ian and move on. Because if I am jealous that she went out with Ian for nearly a year, and jealous that she is finally able to kiss some new guy and forget about missing Ian, I wouldn't be a very good friend, would I? So I'm not jealous, and I'm not pathetically sad, and I'm no longer stuck to the floor because I kept wiggling my feet until they pulled free.

As I sit through the movie I concentrate on being really still between the kissing session on one side and my anti-date on the other—oh, and trying to follow the movie, since I invested all my money in watching this film. I don't use the armrests at all. By the time the lights come back on I'm almost used to having my elbows smashed up against my rib cage. Almost.

After the last explosion we file out of the theater, and Raye suggests we drive to the park. She wants a more scenic place to make out with Josh. To give them privacy I walk with Droopy down to the fishpond. It's a koi pond, like with those really big fat goldfish.

"So would you like to fish here?" I ask him.

"No," he says.

Then he moves in and tilts his head, and his whole face comes closer and closer. This is not possible. No way. He's not trying to kiss me. Or at least he shouldn't be, but, well, he is. I take a step back. I mean, really. I'm not saying I would have kissed him if he had paid for my movie ticket. It isn't like the price of a movie ticket will guarantee you a few minutes of putting your tongue in my mouth. But he didn't even pay for my ticket. I don't *like* him. He's weird and he's boring and he stares. The not-paying thing was just like the ultimate in disdain, so even if I had liked him he would have ruined the date. Plus, since he and Josh are both from Mr. Tannahill's neighborhood, the price of a movie ticket should be nothing to him. Disdain.

I do let him press his mouth against mine, just to see how it feels. Just to test myself. Nothing.

I pull away from him. I have proven that I'm impervious to the thrill of pressing up against random guys. This is good because I haven't turned into a complete and total slut like my sister, but it's bad because it proves that I'm still hung up on my ex. I'm not tempted to kiss some weird guy just because he's leaning over and staring into my face. That's kind of a relief. With the genes Paige and I share, who knows what could happen.

"Raye tells me you just got out of a serious relationship," I say in a tone that indicates I care.

I would have sworn it was impossible, but he droops even more. Then he starts in on his life story, and after half an hour, which I deem plenty of time for Raye's mouth to get to know Josh's mouth, we head back to the SUV. I seriously hope they aren't doing it or something.

Oddly enough, Raye and I stopped talking so much about sex like three months ago, and even though I've told her a little bit, well, mostly I've been happy not to discuss certain things. I mean, she knows things and I know things, but we stopped sharing the really private things. There used to be all this endless speculation. You know, what do you think it will be like? And who do you think we'll do it with? That kind of stuff. Raye was really into Ian, the cheating dumping ex. I'm pretty damn sure she was pretty damn intimate with him, and look how that turned out.

Josh drops me off at my front door, and Raye says, "I'll call you later," in her breathy voice that means she really wants to talk.

I go up to my bedroom and check my e-mail. Nothing. Since I don't feel very sleepy I reach under my bed and pull out the big sketch pad I bought last year for geometry class. Mr. Lopez was desperate to help us understand why accurate measurement is so important. A squared plus B squared equals C squared and all that. So he made us design our dream houses. Mine was four thousand square feet and, get this, had an ice-skating rink in the basement. I don't even like ice-skating that much, but the girl next to me was putting a bowling alley in hers, and bowling is just way too loud for me.

I never could quite get the lines right, even though I

used the ruler, and Mr. Lopez still thought it was outstanding. He hung it up on the wall of the classroom and wrote *Outstanding!* on it with his big red marker.

I really liked the way the pencil felt in my hand, which was weird, 'cause I hadn't used a pencil since fourth grade when they started letting us use ink pens. The softness of it felt right, especially when it had just been sharpened. I took that yellow pencil and the notepad home with me and stored them back under my bed.

I even did a drawing of my real house, kind of for practice and kind of in case we have to move so that I can remember everything about it. Downstairs there's the big eat-in kitchen, the dining room, the oversized family room, where my family gathers to watch TV. Upstairs there are four bedrooms, all with decent-sized closets—though none of them quite big enough to suit Paige—and my dad's tiny little study that is right at the top of the steps, where he sits and works crossword puzzles when Mom says he should be updating his resume.

I look at the huge expanse of empty white paper for a few minutes, and then I start sketching the façade for my dream house. Mr. Lopez still has the final copy, but I have the drafts. They're floor plans, completely open so you can look inside. I figure the house could use a front. My house would definitely have a privacy fence, and maybe a stained-glass window.

Making a drawing to scale is really hard. When I realize that the front door is two stories tall, and I totally didn't mean for it to be that way, I shut the sketch pad and push it back under my bed.

Raye never calls and it's really quiet in my room. I know music would just accentuate the loneliness of everything, like trying to cover the quiet up, when it's always, always still there.

I pull the sketch pad back out and turn to the back part, the secret part, where sometimes I try to draw people. I close my eyes and imagine my ex-boyfriend, and when I'm done, it doesn't look like a camel or a bear or George Washington, though it doesn't look like him, either. I got the mouth right. I stare at the mouth for a long time before I put on my pajamas and get into bed.

They say bad things come in threes. Like the Prescotts: Paige, Parker, and Preston. Except if I had been the boy they wanted, my parents wouldn't have produced a third child. Anyway, here are Parker's Very Bad Three:

1. Broke up with the love of my life
2. Made my mom cry on Christmas
3. Went on pseudo-date with "I like fish" guy, aka Droopy

You would think it might be time for something good to happen.

But then I start to think. Stuff started going wrong around here a long time before this.

Kyle Henessy started following Paige around and freaking everybody out.

Paige talked Mom and Dad into getting a restraining order against Kyle, throwing his sister and staunch defender, Marion, into a murderous rage that has not cooled, even though it's been nearly a year, and putting Kyle (this is unverified) into some kind of treatment for depression.

Dad lost his job.

Yeah, it's really time for something good to happen.

"I've missed you, Parker Prescott," he says into my hair. When he kisses me he bites my bottom lip, and my stomach clenches up so hard that I almost start to cry. Maybe it isn't my stomach.

I lean back into him, willing myself to relax. "Why are you here?" It's only four days after Christmas, only three days since I saw him in the mall. He didn't call, just showed up. It's Saturday morning, and we are sitting in my father's office. It's this small room right at the top of the stairs that's just big enough for the desk where my dad sits to fill out bills and, before he lost his job, to talk on the phone to his boss. Besides the desk and the office chair, there's a love seat and a bookshelf, and that's pretty much it.

He is on the black leather minisofa (for some reason Dad won't call it a love seat) and I am sitting in Dad's high-backed leather office chair with the tiny little wheels.

I was working on Dad's computer when he knocked, and I went back to it after I let him in, to minimize everything I'd been working on. Raye laughs at me for being so secretive, but I just don't like people reading over my shoulder.

Before I could look up he grabbed the arms of the chair and pulled me forward, so that I am right in front of him, where he can kiss me, if that's what he wants, and if I let him.

"Where else would I be?" He grins. I bite back any and all comments about Kandace Freemont.

"You never even came over here when we were together," I say.

"Your family was always here doing family stuff. You know how I feel about the whole family routine. Anyway, you always came over, then. If you don't come to me, I have to come to you." I kind of like the sound of that, like he needs me. It makes me feel, well, elated. I douse this crazy, out-of-control feeling by turning to him and saying,

"You know, you don't have to talk in really short simple sentences with me." It's a jab. A direct reference to Kandace and her stupidity. I need to talk about her because I can't stop thinking about what might've happened between them.

But he laughs. I've turned my anguish into a joke and he thinks it's funny.

"Are you jealous, Parker?" His voice is so warm, his eyes intent. This is how it used to be before I freaked out and messed everything up. I would so love to go back in time and not let myself get scared. I would love for things to be like they were before.

"Should I be?" Damn, how does he always get me to

walk into his trap? The pain that shoots through me is real. He puts his hand behind my head and caresses me softly, like he's massaging my neck, but so gently it's really just a stroking motion.

"There is nothing between me and Kandace Freemont." He says this as he looks directly into my eyes. "There is something between you and me. There's something about you, Prescott, that I can't get enough of." I hold my breath. Is he going to say it?

He kisses the side of my face very softly. Then he kisses me again.

"Are both of your parents gone?"

"Yeah." He kisses me again, more deeply. I relax into him just a little.

"Little brother?"

"He's at a birthday party."

"Really?"

"Yeah, Ernie Libman's little brother. His dad works with my mom."

"Ernie Libman's little brother's having a birthday party. With cake and ice cream and all that?"

"I guess." I let him unbutton the top two buttons of my shirt, and then I shift so that my chair rolls to the side and his hand falls away. He overwhelms me, and I'm not sure what I want. I pull away from him, so that maybe I can focus.

"You think they'll have a pony or a clown or something?"

I push my hair back. "I don't really know."

"So what do we have, like half an hour, an hour?"

"We have all day. My parents will just be here part of the day."

"Do you want to have some fun?" What kind of question is that to ask the girl who is panting with lust for you?

He pulls a pair of handcuffs out of the pocket of the oversized black jacket that Raye believes I hate. The jacket I secretly think is sexy as hell, in some weird, perverse baggy-and-faded way. Real handcuffs, shiny metal cuffs linked with a chain. Something in me surges toward him, opens to the challenge in his eyes.

"What did you have in mind?" My voice is steady. I don't want him to think that I'm some silly Kandace-like girl giggling at his every word, but I do need to keep him interested. In me.

He puts one cuff around my wrist, and it is so big that it makes me feel tiny and delicate, like I'm made of porcelain. It tightens to grip my wrist and even bites into it a little. He runs his hand up my arm and shivers run through me. Then he pulls my other arm back around the chair so that they nearly meet. I have to wiggle around to get comfortable, and while I'm doing that, he snaps the other cuff. It's cold and harsh.

"Do you trust me?" he asks.

"No." I want to. I've always wanted to trust him, more than anything. But I don't.

"Good."

He unbuttons my shirt the rest of the way. Making eye contact the entire time. It's weirdly exciting, staring into his eyes and feeling his fingers carefully opening each button. I catch my breath, and in that second I hear the front door slam and the *creech creech creech* of athletic shoes on the stairs.

My mom throws the door open. My heart totally stops and I'm sure I've stopped breathing. I watch her like a person in a coma, a person who is already halfway dead. Mom is wild and disheveled, and I will learn later that the stain on her shirt is my brother's vomit. There's a towel in her hand. I don't notice the shirt because I'm looking at her face. I do notice the towel because it falls to the floor and just lies there. It's been several minutes. My lungs are collapsing. Finally, I gasp and take a long slurping breath. I'm alive. The horror begins to take over as my body goes back to breathing on its own. The whole thing seems to be in some sort of crazy slow motion.

"Jane, where's that towel? The interior of the Jeep is going to be— Oh my God." Dad is standing behind Mom in the doorway of the den.

My shirt is still on, pushed back and then scrunched above the elbows. My bra is just loose enough that it has shifted forward. They can't see anything, but they have to realize that he can.

I can't keep from looking over at him even though I'm about to faint. I would pretend to faint if I thought it would make them stop looking at me like this. He is balanced between the mahogany desk and the wall, where he stumbled when the door opened. He is very, very still, and his face is whiter than usual. He slides the tiny key to the handcuffs out of his pocket, moving delicately, holding it between his finger and his thumb.

"Oh, Parker," my mom breathes. Her eyes move past me to him. "You should leave," she says.

"Parker . . ." He reaches for me. But I'm in this weird position where the only place he could touch would be my face or, well . . .

"No," my mother says.

"Get. Away. From. Her." Dad's voice is shaking. I can't

look at my dad. Mom is angry, and I can deal with that, but when I look really fast, I see that Dad's face is totally ghostly pale, and I feel sick to my stomach.

Mom snatches the key out of his hand. For a second I imagine all the madness that would ensue if there were no key. Ha-ha-ha-ha-ha. Yeah, it's like I've gone crazy or I'm delirious or something, and this will never be over. This weird part of me that has given up hope for the future wants to ask him if we are back together now, but I am mute. I watch silently as he slinks past Dad. I see my father take off his glasses, which he never normally does. My mom wraps her arms around Dad and pulls him away into the hall.

There is absolute silence, then a loud squeak as my ex hits the fourth step from the bottom. The dreadful squeak that is the reason all of us Prescotts hop over the fourth step. The reason I didn't hear my mom coming until it was too late and her shoes were creeching right outside the door.

The screen door bangs shut. Mom and Dad come back in and we all stare at each other for a minute. The door creaks open again. She leans forward and unlocks the handcuffs. Her hands are sweaty, and I pull away from her because I feel as gross as her gummy hands. I want her to stop looking at me with the horrified expression. I want them to leave me alone so I can start working on pretending this never happened.

We hear two footsteps on the hardwood floor downstairs. Someone is in our house. The part of my brain that's still working recognizes our neighbor Mr. Bronson's quavery voice.

"Jane? Chris? Your son is out on the front lawn throwing up."

I'm in my room. It's been nearly an hour. I can't sit still. I walk over to my bed and pick up the little stuffed Siberian husky he gave me right after we started dating. I look at myself in the mirror. My cheeks are flushed. He says my eyes are cold, but right now they are just freaky, pupils dilated, glimmery. The way he looks at me makes me see myself differently, like there might be something attractive about me. It's a good feeling to have.

I run a brush through my hair. Raye's short hair has cool wild edges. Mine is wild in its own way; thick and just a little curly, it hangs past my shoulders. The combination of pale eyes and dark hair is striking. That's what my parents always say, that I'm striking. When they say it, it doesn't mean anything, except that I don't look adorable like Paige. Sixteen long years of wishing for pretty, but what I see doesn't bother me so much, not when I see myself through his eyes. If striking is what he likes, that's good enough for me.

In my mind, I keep replaying every second we were together. The desire in his eyes, the intensity, the chemistry that crackled between us.

I go over to the window and run my hand over the cool pane. From across the room I hear the click of incoming e-mail and I dive across my desk to hit the mailbox icon, but it's just my lab partner sending me notes about this project we're supposed to do over the break.

Back to my door. I ease it open just a little.

My parents are fighting, but I can't hear what they're saying. Dad's voice makes me kind of shudder as I remember his face, the way he couldn't quite look at me. I push that thought out of my mind and go back to my own audacity.

Parker Prescott, the plain little good younger sister. Not so plain or good or boring anymore, huh? I would have let him do anything to me, I tell myself. I should be worried about this. I should try to keep my self-control. I shouldn't let him take me over so completely, but he already has. Is it wrong to fight something that feels right and good? Should I just give up? I look at my bed with the fluffy pillows and imagine curling up and sleeping for a long time, like a fairy-tale princess or something. Snow White. I feel so tired and out of control and confused.

The phone rings twice, and suddenly I'm not so sleepy. I hold my breath. It would be too much to hope for that I might retain phone privileges. Mom already took my cell when she escorted me to my room. Would he dare call my house line? Is he thinking about me?

Mom shoves the door open.

"Raye is on the phone. She's been calling your cell. I think she's worried about you. You can talk to her for long enough to tell her you're grounded and to cancel whatever plans you might have," she says coldly.

"How long am I grounded?" I hold my breath and hope for a week. This is something I do when I know things are bad, I just hope for something—not that they won't punish me, because I know they will, but for a punishment I can handle. Like in eighth grade when I got a B on my midterm in math, or last year when I forgot to tell them that I was going to Raye's after school and they got all worried, but I only ended up grounded for like one day. I realize that my fingers are actually crossed, and it would be funny, acting like a four-year-old, if my situation weren't so hideous.

"Indefinitely." She hands me the phone and turns away quickly, like she can't stand the sight of me. I don't look her in the eye, because I don't want to see her disgust and disappointment. And I don't want her to see that beneath my shame, there is an undercurrent of excitement, a thrill from doing something so un-Parker-like. It's a much better feeling than humiliated remorse, so I try to hold on to that, but it's impossible when I look at my mother.

"What's going on?" Raye sounds breathless. "I've been calling and calling. I wanted to tell you that Josh invited me to some kind of dinner party his parents are having. Do you think I should go? If I go, will it be like saying I want to be a couple with him? 'Cause I don't know if I'm ready for that. Do you think he's cute? I mean, I know you said you did, but—"

"Raye, I can only talk for a minute, to tell you I can't talk."

"What?" Raye sounds suspicious.

"I'm grounded forever and my mom is coming to take

the phone back in just a few minutes." I hate this; I would rather tell Raye face to face so I can see her reactions. This is really hard.

"What happened, Parker?" I hear curiosity and fear, and I know that she is worried for me. I want to make it sound thrilling, like it was before Mom walked in and it got so horrible, but I know Mom is right outside the door.

"We got caught," I mutter.

"What?"

"My parents came home early, and we got caught."

"Who? Oh my God, Parker, was it him?"

"Yeah." I hear my mom exhale in the hallway, and clutch the phone as if somehow I will be able to keep talking to Raye if I hold the receiver tight enough.

"Doing what? Don't tell me you were—"

"No, Raye. Not that, it's just . . ." Why is it so hard to explain to her? The door opens and Mom is on the threshold with her hands on her hips. "My mom is here to take the phone. Look, don't expect to see me socially for a while. I'm in big trouble."

"Parker, you can't leave me hanging. Do you still have e-mail?"

"For the time being." Mom and I are eyeing each other across the room.

"You have to e-mail me."

"I will see you at school Tuesday. Have a nice evening." I say this woodenly, hoping that my strange response will convey to her that I will e-mail as soon as it's safe. How I wish for a sleek, inconspicuous laptop. The Dell sitting on my desk is so obvious. Next thing I know Mom will be carting it away and I'll be truly stranded here in my frilly little-girl bedroom.

"Sit down," Mom says, so I do. My mom's hair is so

pretty and blond. I'll bet she never had any problems in high school. She's still a knockout except for this line between her eyes that she always gets when she talks to me.

"Your father and I, we don't want you to see that boy again." I glance up to examine her face and then back down because her eyes are so cold. This is bad. Does she not know that I can't live without seeing him again? They can't keep us completely apart, but they could seriously get in the way of our relationship. If we even have a relationship.

"Oh, Mom," I say, my voice calm. It might be repentant enough to satisfy her. I hope.

"It isn't like we haven't done this before. We've raised a teenage girl before. We just didn't expect this from you."

I stare at her. "What do you expect from me?" My voice is flat. I hate being compared to Paige, but I can't lose my temper now. I have to be contrite. I must show her how sorry I am.

"Parker, don't start with all this middle-child baloney."

I don't know what bothers me more, that she would say some kind of crap like "baloney" in a serious conversation with me or that she would automatically think I was going to play the middle-child card. And she is totally discounting the middle-child card, which I generally hold in reserve for emergencies, though if there was ever an emergency in my life, this has to be it.

"Mom, do you really know me at all?" I stare at her, and she looks down.

"Parker, what honestly is there to know?" My mouth drops open. I've never felt my mouth drop open before, wasn't sure it could even happen to a nonanimated person. For the second time since the Handcuff Incident, I truly feel like crying. I mean, if your mom doesn't think you are some kind of awesomely badass individual, how lame are you in the eyes of the rest of the world?

"Honey, maybe you could show me a little bit of yourself. Right now, it's always Parker and Raye, or Parker with that creepy boy. It's never just you talking to me and Daddy, or spending time with Preston and Paige." My mom is so blind. How can she call him creepy? Even the teachers at school treat him with deference. They see that he's special, but Mom can't see it, or she can't appreciate the elusive thing that makes him so irresistible.

Another click. I'm hyperaware of my computer. I almost always am, but Mom is oblivious to the fact that I just got an e-mail. I don't let myself breathe. Don't let her realize I have one last line to the outside world, I pray, though who would be listening to my prayers right now? I can't imagine God would care if I get e-mail or not. I keep staring at Mom's feet. Her red shoes clash with my girly pink carpet.

"I'm going to ask Paige to come over and talk to you."

"*Paige?*" I hear my voice rise, it's almost a shriek. Great, now I've lost control of my voice. I can't even believe she is suggesting this. The last time I saw my sister, besides on Christmas when she was being the good loving daughter, she had a beer in one hand and a Long Island iced tea in the other, and, even worse, she was wearing a hot-pink tank top. In December. What a role model.

"She's already been through much of what you're going through. She knows the danger."

"Mom, she doesn't know anything."

"And you know it all."

That isn't what I'm saying. The stupidity of her saying that goes right through me. When have I ever even suggested that I know everything?

Another click. I pretend I don't have a computer; I'm so focused on not looking over there. It's a very good thing that I turned the volume down. Mom would freak if my computer announced I had mail right now. A second message. The first one is almost surely from Raye, but the second one? I force my eyes not to stray over to the computer. I force myself to look at her, look at my feet, back at her.

"Do you want something to eat?"

"I couldn't eat anything."

"Good, I'm glad you feel some remorse. This is the first sign of it I've seen."

Remorse? I'm too excited to eat. It's a sick kind of excitement, but still, I feel like I'm becoming something else, someone people might notice. A person willing to take risks. I'm sure the bad feelings will overwhelm me later, when I can't stop ignoring all the implications of what's happened, when I'm wondering if my parents will ever see me the same way and if he'll ever call me again and all that. For right now I'm just going to savor being bad.

Mom gets up and leaves. No mention of exactly how long I'm going to be grounded. Probably better not to ask.

I peer out the door again to make sure she isn't coming back, that Dad isn't coming to speak to me. I don't want to see him right now. I can hear him say, "Jane, I can't go through this again." I know they're thinking about Paige, they always are. Mom's disembodied voice answers; she sounds soothing, nicer than she was with me. I creep across the plush pink carpet in my fuzzy pink slippers.

I have two messages. I squeeze my eyes shut for a moment, and then I look. A message from Raye titled *WTF?* And one more.

I scan his quickly and my heart sort of leaps. The words are there. *I love, I love, I love . . . your sweet lacy bra.* Not exactly what I wanted to see after those words. The entire message goes like this:

Park

Can't stop thinking about you. You were so hot today. I
love your sweet lacy bra. I wish you were here right now.
Next time, you and me at my place. No parental interfer-
ence. Did I mention that I can't stop thinking about you?

Not much. It doesn't say that he wants to get back together with me, just that he wants me. And that I already
knew. I mean, we went out for long enough that I know he
wants me in that way. What I need to know is if he wants me
to be his girlfriend again.

I push my hair back from my face and focus on the rele-
vant information: He e-mailed me. He's thinking about me.
I can survive anything knowing that.

But he has to realize how bad this is for me, doesn't he?
I think about how white his face was. It shook him up, getting caught. But I know deep inside that he'll blow it off, act
nonchalant. My relationship with my parents is in serious
jeopardy, and all he cares about is my bra. I feel the annoyance build up for half a second until I remember Kandace
Freemont, waiting to steal him away from me. He e-mailed
me. That's all that matters.

I pad downstairs, stealthy in my fuzzy slippers, to see if
there is anything left to eat. Except I forgot that Paige and
her husband are always coming over here looking for free
family dinners. They live so close they could walk, if West
weren't so lazy and Paige weren't so afraid that a little wind
might mess up her hair.

Mom and Paige are sitting at the table. West has his
chair pushed back so that he can see the TV in the other
room. He's not really into hanging out with my parents, that
whole family dinner thing. His family eats in fancy restaurants

and at the country club, not around a rectangular dining room table like my family does. If one of my parents asks him a question he'll smile with his perfect white teeth and say the right thing. Otherwise, he'll stay glued to the TV.

After the incident I put on my pajamas. I mean, it seemed too anticlimactic to sit there wearing the same clothes. I should probably burn that shirt. Mom and Dad will never be able to look at it again without being reminded of what happened. I'm wondering if my pajamas are too revealing. They have cute little low-slung pink pants and a skintight T-shirt, and I mean, who wears a bra with their pajamas? I'm wondering if I should grab a robe or something. If they see me like this they might once again start thinking about me and sex, a combination that I do not want in their minds.

They're talking about me, of course.

"Was she handcuffed *to* something?" Paige likes juicy details.

"No, he had her hands behind the chair," Mom answers. I'm not even surprised. They gossip together, the two of them, about everything. It doesn't even make me mad, but it does put me on the same level as Paige's friends, the ones that are interesting enough to speculate about.

West gets up, going for another Mountain Dew, probably. You've never seen a guy suck down the Dew like my sister's husband. He catches sight of me standing back from the doorway, not hiding or anything, Mom and Paige just haven't noticed me.

He doesn't say anything, but he looks me over. Really. There was a time (when I was maybe fourteen) when I thought that West was a superb specimen of manhood. He's tall and has kind of sandy brown hair. He was *the* most popular senior when I was a sophomore. Paige, believe it or not, wasn't a cheerleader or anything, but she nabbed the most popular boy anyway. In all the years I've known him, he's never acknowledged me with more than an innocent hair ruffle. But right this minute, here in my kitchen with my mother and my sister, he is totally checking me out. Even though I know in my mind this is gross, it feels really cool to be the girl who walks into a room and instantly gets checked out. I could get used to this. I almost like it.

"I don't know what she sees in that boy," my mom says.

"He has sex appeal," Paige says. "Too much sex appeal for Parker."

What's that supposed to mean?

"Oh, Paige, you don't mean that." Mom is still determined to think of him as creepy. "I just can't believe that Parker would do this."

"Mom, she's probably just grateful to have a boyfriend." And what is *that* supposed to mean?

"Parker." Mom's voice gets louder as she catches sight of me. I don't think she's even embarrassed to have been caught saying those things about me. "Why don't you get something to eat and go back upstairs? Your father does not need to see you tonight. He has a job interview tomorrow." She's looking at me like everything is my fault, even Daddy's not having a job, and even though I know that's not true, that there are a few things I'm not responsible for, my stomach still drops to my shoes.

Dad has a job interview? That's huge. I glance into the living room, but Dad is hunkered in front of the TV with the remote, and he doesn't make eye contact with me. I spoon a glob of macaroni onto a plate and grab a Pepsi and then my cell phone. It's right there in the drawer. Mom will never miss it, and if she does, how could she be any angrier at me than she already is? That's the thing about hitting rock bottom.

There is a loud screeching noise, like a hungry robot, coming from the kitchen sink.

"What did you put in the garbage disposal?" I hear Mom ask over the noise.

"The Batmobile," Preston answers calmly. I remember him playing with that this morning before they went to the birthday party. It was a long black metal car. Sounds like it's being destroyed, and in the process breaking the most useless appliance in our house. I hope I don't get blamed for this; I was probably supposed to be watching him.

"I think he bought that car in the Henessys' moving sale," I hear Paige say as I walk out of the room. I hear her footsteps on the stair behind me, but I figure she's going to the bathroom or getting something out of her old room until I turn and there she is in my doorway.

"So you got yourself in trouble today," she says, smirking.

"Yeah." She looks kind of like she wants to laugh, but she doesn't.

"You got busted." Paige is totally enjoying this. She can't stop smiling.

"Yeah."

"Mom and Dad are so pissed. They're very disappointed in you."

"Yeah." I hate hearing that; she has to know that hearing something like that, obviously a direct quote and probably from Daddy, tears a person up inside. But I act like it doesn't matter. As much as she loves my disgrace, my coldness always gets to her. She's starting to look a little bit pissed herself.

"I'm trying to help you, Parker. You don't have to do the Ice Princess thing. You can talk to me."

"How?" Just seeing her perfect blond hair makes me feel annoyed, and that smug look on her face makes me want to be as rude to her as I can manage.

"By talking. I don't think you ought to bottle this up. Don't you want to tell me about it?"

"*What?*" I cannot believe she is asking me this. She wants me to tell her about it?

"Do you remember the time you told on me for kissing Brett Sanders out in the backyard?" She's looking straight at me like I'm on trial or something.

"I didn't tell on you for that," I answer, trying to keep my cool. I've heard the long boring litany of all the guys Paige was with. Yeah, Brett Sanders was possibly hotter than West. She should make a freaking photo collage or something, because she can't stop thinking or talking about them. She'll never stop rubbing in how popular she was.

"You did tell on me, because you were jealous. That's why I want to know how it was for you."

"So you can go tell Mom and Dad?"

"Just so you'll know how I felt getting caught. I can't believe you're still being such a little princess, even now." Her voice oozes disgust.

"What?" Why am I even talking to her? She's just here to enjoy my misery.

"Mom and Dad catch you in the act but you're still better than me, is that it?" Everything she says confuses me more. Better than her? Me?

"What are you talking about, Paige?" I realize that she's twisting things. Somehow everything always becomes about her. Even this thing that is so totally about me. Even though she's mad, she still takes a second look at herself in my full-length mirror. My big sister.

"Did you know that Marion Henessy turned all of her Barbie dolls into Paige and Parker voodoo dolls and then she beheaded them?" she asks out of nowhere. "Well, actually, she only beheaded mine. She torched yours."

Now she has my attention.

"Oh my God, how do you even know that?"

"She took a picture and sent it to my Gmail address. Can you believe it? I was going to e-mail her back and say that only I could be Barbie and that she should use some ugly old Bratz doll for you, but West said I shouldn't respond." She laughs like this is funny. I think she really is trying to be funny. We used to play with all of them together, Bratz dolls, Barbies, this stupid army action figure that I think belonged to Kyle. We always fought over the Barbies; nobody wanted the other dolls.

"Thanks, Paige." It's hard to manage a sarcastic tone when you're totally freaked out. "She burned the Parker Barbie?" I can't stop myself from asking.

"Melted its face right off. That girl is as crazy as her brother. At least he was never violent."

"How did you know which one was me? If they were both Barbies, I mean?" This conversation is surreal. She's telling me all this and still looking at herself in the mirror.

"She had it all labeled, like *Paige Prescott, death by beheading. Parker Prescott, death by bonfire.*"

I shudder. Paige is acting like this is no big deal, but I think it's terrible to have someone hate you this much.

"Well, I don't know why she torched my Barbie. I never did anything to her."

"It's your fabulous luck being my baby sister. Anyway,

how is it my fault her brother wanted to watch me with binoculars and stuff?"

I've never quite figured that one out, but somehow I suspect that she is at least a little bit to blame, and Marion Henessy thinks she is totally to blame and will do anything she can think of to try to get back at both of us.

Paige's reflected image shakes her head at me sadly and runs her hand through her glossy golden hair. It does sort of look like Barbie's.

"If you want to talk about getting in trouble or you want any advice, you have my number."

"I'm grounded from the phone."

"All right, Princess Parker. You know Mom will let you talk to me if you tell her you need to. Just call me, okay? And put a little more conditioner in your hair. It looks dull. Try some Paul Mitchell."

She should totally start an advice column.

The Coming of the Ice Princess:

So, once upon a time there was this little girl who liked to be neat. She liked her clothes to match and to be clean and she liked her toys to be put away in the toy boxes. One of this little girl's first memories is of her mother having a miscarriage.

She remembers her mother falling on the floor, holding her stomach, and she remembers that there was a lot of blood.

Mrs. Prescott (as we will call the mother) had one miscarriage after another in her quest to have a son. Then, when her little girls were five and nine years old, Mrs.

Prescott had a pregnancy that lasted longer than the others. At thirty-three weeks she had her little boy, but he was so small that he had to stay in the hospital for months. The littlest Prescott girl was in kindergarten. Her father got her up each morning and helped her get dressed. Wearing neat, clean outfits that matched, particularly with matching hair ribbons in her dark hair, made her feel safe and secure, and close to her mother, who was often in the hospital with the miracle baby, as everyone called him.

At the age of ten, the girl's sister got up on her mom's desk in the middle of her office in front of all of her coworkers and did an entire song-and-dance number, complete with a flip at the end. Family legend states that it was not two weeks later that the girl's mom got a fabulous promotion. I remember vaguely that someone asked if the little one sang and danced too. The little one ducked her head and held on to her mother's skirt.

I guess I—er, I mean *she* didn't change much when she got older.

Paige was the center of attention. Preston got over most of his initial health problems, but he has severe ADHD, which keeps Mom busy all the time. I never caused any trouble, not before this week.

There's something about being the younger sister of the most popular girl in school that makes your fellow students, or at least those that I met my first day at Allenville High, think you are a colossal snob. I don't know. It's kind of hard to jump up and yell, "Hey, everybody, I'm not a snob!" Especially when the reason they think you're a snob is because you're so quiet. It's a dilemma.

Allenville is a magnet school. It gets two types of students. Well-to-do students from the surrounding middle-class neighborhoods who have decent-to-good grades, and really smart kids from everywhere else. Our house is in the Allenville school district, so I guess that makes me one of the well-to-do students. Which is pretty funny when you think about it. Ironic or something.

The ex-boyfriend wasn't around my freshman and sophomore years because he was at a private prep school. An honest-to-goodness boarding school in New England. He got kicked out. There was speculation for weeks over what heinous crime had earned him the axe.

They put him in my advanced British literature course, where he settled in the back of the room kind of hunched in his seat with his legs crossed at the ankles. He was wearing a long black coat. He'd been in private preps for so long he didn't realize that the trench coat went out with Columbine. It was ultimately hot on him.

All the girls were panting over him. I was hot for him too, but I didn't know how to break out of the cool quiet calm façade that I had built around myself, so I just observed while every creature with breasts threw herself at his feet. Although some (Kandace Freemont) were aiming a bit higher than the feet. He was polite but sarcastic. He was quiet. He had a mysterious little smile that drove me crazy.

The rejected ones swore he was a homo, but he didn't have that vibe. Being uninterested in some whorey girl doesn't make you gay. It just makes you discerning, right?

So he was in my fifth-period class. When they moved him in, the rest of the boys dropped off my radar. Unfortunately, I didn't drop off theirs.

Sometime, someplace, some genius realized that my pale skin holds a blush exceptionally well. Let the games begin. It became a challenge to see who could make me blush first. I think the thing that bothered me most about the constant torment of the guys who called themselves the

Gruesome Twosome and their little psycho friend was that they initiated their torment in front of him. These guys had it in for me.

It really big-time sucked.

They didn't torment me around Raye, and I never mentioned it to her. I mean, Raye and I met in middle school when she saved me from some kids who were teasing me. But that was a long time ago, and I didn't want to tell my best friend that I was still such a loser that all the boys still wanted to embarrass me. Since we'd become best friends I liked to feel somewhat equal to her in coolness. So I didn't tell anyone. I just tried to ignore it and hated every minute that Ms. White wasn't hovering over me in advanced British lit, shielding me from oncoming humiliation. Until October 13.

I remember the date because it was Friday, therefore Friday the thirteenth. I didn't have plans for either weekend night, but that didn't mean I was interested in anything the Gruesome Twosome could think of to tempt me with. And the little weirdo they had picked up was even nastier than the original two. As soon as he caught sight of me coming into the room his beady eyes would light up, and I knew he was searching his tiny brain for the dirtiest and most perverted thing he could think of to say to me.

We had a sub in advanced British lit, and he was really interested in current events, so no hovering at all. In fact, I'm not sure he ever looked up from the Friday newspaper. Didn't Ms. White know that I needed her to be there every day?

They had a theme going. You could call it creative, but it was probably because they weren't so good at thinking stuff up. They needed a bit of inspiration. The subject for that day was tea bagging. If you don't know what that is—and I didn't before it became one of their topics—it's, well . . . They were talking about . . . What they were doing was . . . speculating on how much I would enjoy having their balls in my mouth.

"So, Parker, would you just slide them into your mouth and suck on them?"

"Wouldn't it feel gross? Squishy?"

"What happens when you get a little hair in your mouth, do you like that? Huh?"

I was staring at my notebook because there was nothing I could say to make them stop. On TV you could have a comeback so good it would stop everyone in their tracks. In real life you would be lucky to spit the words out, and even luckier if they heard you over their own laughter.

"I'll bet she loves it." The little one was standing right in front of my desk kind of gyrating toward me. I glanced up and several girls were watching, but they looked away, unwilling to help me. This is one of those awful classes where I don't really know anyone. And no one has ever tried to get to know me. Probably because they don't want to get picked on too.

"Is it the salty taste you like, Parker? You want that, huh? You love it?" Maybe it wouldn't be so bad if they didn't always say my name. Then it would be a little less personal, less like they were imagining me actually doing these things and, judging by the fast shallow breathing, getting into it. I wondered what kind of damage a sharpened pencil could do. I was so mortified I didn't want to look up. Was afraid I'd glance toward them and see some telltale sign of how into it they were. Less than five minutes until the dismissal bell, I told myself.

The boys in the back row were listening. I could tell because several of them were leaning forward, laughing silently at me. The little evil one leaned down on my desk, so close I could smell something decaying on his breath. "So you like to put balls in your mouth, you like to suck on them, do you? Would you like me to—"

"Back off." At first I didn't know who said it.

"What?" The little asshole almost died of shock. No one had ever said anything to him before. His Chihuahua eyes bulged with disbelief.

"I said back off. Get away from her, you little pissant." Then I recognized his bored drawl and I could see the toes of his scuffed black boots even though I was still afraid to look up. What if *he* was going to say something perverted now? What if he was judging me over all those things they said to me and my inability to defend myself?

"What's your problem, man?" Gruesome Twosome Guy Number One sounded irritated but also a little nervous, like a person who knew he had been doing something wrong and had been expecting to be called out on it.

He laughed. "You wanna pick a problem? I have several. How about you acting like Parker Prescott would give you the time of day, much less touch your shriveled, diseased, and probably microscopic balls? Is that a good enough problem for you?" His voice softened and I knew, even though I was still staring at my notebook, that he was saying this for me. "I know you guys get a rise out of trying to heat up the Ice Princess, but let me tell you dumb fucks something. Making a girl blush is nothing." I risked looking up really fast. He wasn't looking at me. He was standing in front of me, keeping them back. He was protecting me.

"Parker Prescott is beautiful, in a way that you three

don't understand." His voice went low. "If anyone is going to thaw her, it's going to be me." I felt a flush of embarrassment. He knew about the Ice Princess thing. He knew what people said about me. And yet there he was protecting me, watching me with something like fascination. There was something dark in the way he said the thing about thawing me, something that made me forget to breathe, but there was also a certain softness in his voice that made me curious about what he saw when he looked at me, curious about the interest that I thought I detected in his eyes.

In my bedroom prison I glance at the right-hand corner of
the hulking computer screen where it tells the time. It's just
Thursday morning. Who knew Christmas vacation could be
so long? I've never been grounded like this, not during the
holidays. I mean, this is the part that usually flies by. The
first week you're always looking forward to the big present
stash, the second week you're totally loving the break and
totally dreading going back to school. But not this year.

"Do you want to play Tetris?" Preston asks.

"I guess so."

We play Tetris for like half an hour. When he doesn't get
the blocks in the places he wants them, he gets agitated.
Then, because he's so jumpy and pacing back and forth, he

misses where the other blocks should go. I beat him every time, even the last few times, when I'm really trying to let him win.

"Will you draw me a castle?" he asks.

"What?"

He asks me some crazy stuff sometimes.

My miracle brother trots into the kitchen and comes back with this big pink sheet of construction paper with the outline of a castle and, get this, pink cotton balls glued to the turrets.

"Why did you make it pink?"

"Kristi likes pink."

I don't ask him who Kristi is. Or if she was the reason he glued a row of Rice Chex above the purple door. Sometimes it's better not to ask him things. My parents are always in his business, like, Who did you talk to today? And, Did you make any new friends? Did you remember to go to the bathroom?

I never ask him any questions. I find this a more restful way to interact with such a hyper kid, and I think he appreciates it.

"Wow, this door folds down." I bend it down a couple of times. Pretty creative.

"That isn't a door, it's a drawbridge. I want to do a not-pink one. Will you help?"

"Yeah." I mean, it isn't like he asks for a lot. When he's focused he's easily pleased. I walk up the stairs, get my sharp pencil, and carefully ease a sheet of drawing paper from the pad I keep under my bed.

We get a couple of rulers and start designing a castle. Preston has an Elmer's glitter glue stick. He keeps popping the cap off and then putting it back on.

"You aren't going to start gluing stuff to this, are you?" Sometimes he makes garbage collages with all kinds of stuff that he glues to construction paper. They're weird and occasionally gross. He smiles at me. Somehow it feels peaceful and nice working side by side with my little brother. Then he says,

"Draw the murder holes."

"The what?"

"And the arrow slits."

"What?"

"They gotta be angled so that you can shoot arrows out and not get shot by the people outside." What are they teaching kids in school these days? I carefully sketch some narrow windows, hoping they look like arrow slits or whatever.

"Um, okay." Here we go. "What's that marshmallow for?"

"This isn't a marshmallow. This is a vat of boiling oil. We'll pour it on our enemies so that they can't attack our castle. Are you gonna make me a grilled cheese sandwich for lunch?"

"I guess." With just those few references to medieval torture and violence, our loving sibling moment is over for now. I stand up and stretch and head for the kitchen. "Will you take this pencil up to my room?" I ask, half expecting him to say something like Why? because it's just a normal pencil, my parents have them all over the place in case we get the urge to do math homework in any room in the house, but he nods and runs it upstairs. Sometimes I think that kid may know me better than anyone else in this family.

In the kitchen, as I put the cheese and bread together and turn on the stove, I find myself staring at the phone. If I were completely lame, I would say something out loud, like How come you never ring? I would start a conversation with it. But ice princesses don't talk to phones about their problems, if they have any. Problems that is, not phones. Ice princesses need communication as much as anyone else.

Then, as if I made it happen with my amazing mental powers, the phone does ring. I stare at it stupidly. I look at the caller ID. It's Raye. I shouldn't pick it up, but I really want to talk to someone from the outside world. I hit the button and put the phone to my ear.

"You know I can't have phone calls," I tell her. I'm unreasonably annoyed because she isn't the one I was hoping would call, and she's wasting stolen moments that I could conceivably spend talking to him. If he would just call me.

"Are you home alone? Preston won't tell on you."

"Yes he will. If she asks him he'll tell her the truth. And she will ask. She knew I talked to you yesterday." Raye called yesterday to tell me all about her latest date with Josh. It's good to know that even though the world passes you by when you're grounded, your best friend will call and update you on things outside the house. But that doesn't make me any less frustrated that she's the only one who ever calls.

"Well, this is important, Parker. Have you talked to the world's biggest asshole yet?" God, I hate it when she calls him that.

"You know I haven't, I would've told you." I would've e-mailed her or stolen a phone and called her. I would've been jumping up and down if I had heard from him.

"Well, guess what, Park. He's talking about you." Raye sounds pissed. I can almost see her shaking her bangs out of her face. "And Kandace Freemont is talking about him. You're featured on Marion Henessy's blog."

"No." I feel a stab of dread. This is Marion Henessy,

enemy of the Prescotts. The one who mangles Barbies while pretending they're me. I'm used to being discussed on her blog, but I always hate it, and I particularly hate the idea of us being talked about, me and him, and if Kandace is in there too, this cannot be good.

"Yes. With, looks like around thirty responses, and half of them are anonymous."

"That's bad." My heart sinks even more. Anonymous posters always write the most hateful things, because they don't have to worry about a counterattack. I balance the phone between my shoulder and the side of my face and listen to Raye while I put the grilled cheese on a plate and cut it in half from corner to corner. Two big triangles, his preferred grilled cheese shape. Preston slinks into the kitchen and sits down in front of the plate. I pour a glass of milk and try to smile at him since he's watching me with big eyes. He can sometimes tell when I'm upset, but he returns my smile and takes a big bite.

As soon as I know he's okay I run upstairs to turn on my computer, nervous. I have to know what they're saying about me, even if afterward I wish I didn't know.

"Being a feature on Marion's blog sucks," I say as I wait for her stupid site to load.

"Depends on how you look at it," Raye says.

"Yeah." I know what she means. There are losers who try all year, any lame stunt they can think of, to get on Marion Henessy's blog. Any publicity is good publicity, you know? But I am not one of these people. It's my bad luck that in the Allenville High School social scene, Marion is the voice of relentless gossip that she smears across the Web with no thought for anyone else's feelings or privacy. She's just a sophomore, and slightly fanatical, but she's good at finding scummy stories to entertain her readers. I vote her most likely to grow up and work for a tabloid faking pictures of the devil seen in the clouds or Elvis working at Burger King. Marion is a big fat attention hog and a liar. She used to be my friend, but things changed, even before Paige had her brother taken to jail in a real police cruiser, in handcuffs. They didn't keep him, of course. The way Marion carries on, you would think her darling brother was rotting away in prison.

The short and sweet version is that Kyle, who maintains her professional-grade Web site, used to stalk Paige. Night-vision goggles and everything. Scary shit. My parents filed a police report. Then, not two weeks later the police were driving by and found him in the tree next to our house with a pair of binoculars around his neck. The judge issued a restraining order, and here we are. I used to hang out with Marion when we were younger, but now I don't even think we were friends back then. Just little kids who thought they should be because they lived next door to each other.

I have her blog bookmarked. I would bet that everyone who goes to Allenville does.

The Social Siren by Marion Henessy

(This is the name of her stupid blog.)

January 2
Fellow students of Allenville High, Kandace Freemont is available on the Allenville dating circuit once again, according to Ellen Birch. A tearful Kandace confided to her friends that she had been ditched for Parker Prescott, aka the Ice Princess. Anyone have a comment about this development only two days before we go back to school?

Anonymous says: Kandace Freemont can come to my house, I'll dry her tears.

Ellen says: I have never seen Kandace so upset. Kelsey call me about tomorrow.

Kelsey says: what a jerk

Mathwhiz says: what's up with trigonometry?

Marion says: keep the posts on topic Michael, I mean math whiz, or you will be deleted!

UbErKyLe says: does any one have a pic of Parker Prescott? Does she look like her sister Paige? What's she like?

Marion says: Hey dummy we have a picture of them in our own house, from the Bahamas cruise where you got that sunburn.

UbErKyLe says: a recent pic. Since she's grown up.

Anonymous says: Parker is kind of aloof, kind of cool.

Ellen says: If by cool you mean a little bitch. I'm sorry this happened to you, Kandace.

Anonymous says: Kandace is hot, hot is better than cool.

Hip-anonymous says: I would rather abuse myself on a nightly basis thinking of Parker Prescott than have Kandace Freemont spread-eagled on my bed right now.

Anna Anonymous says: Wasn't there a post awhile back that said Parker Prescott had a nose job?

Anonymous says: spread-eagled? I like the way you think, hippo.

Marion says: hey guys my mom reads this blog!

Bigboy says: maybe you're abusing yourself too much hip guy

Marion says: about the nose job, I quoted another student who speculated about Parker's perfect nose. I guess there was a shadow in the shot from her middle school yearbook that made her 7th grade nose look bigger than the little nose she is wearing now.

Kandykat says: Thank u guys for your support. It really hurts to be rejected.

Latisha says: what exactly did he say?

Girliegirl says: he's an a-hole you're better off without him.

Kandykat says: he said, I'm sorry, but I've got this thing going on with Parker. I'm kind of obsessed with her or something. I don't mean to be a dick but I guess I wanted to make her jealous by taking you out.

Anono says: R they back 2gether?

Girliegirl says: did you and he? U-no

Kandykat says: you can email me, I won't discuss it here. It was amazing, tho

Anonymous says: Kandace you are an idiot. Shut upp!

Ellen says: I hope Parker is reading this right now.

Girliegirl says: Parker is too good for this blog.

Anono says: what do you have against Parker? She's very quiet.

Marion says: too smart for her own good.

Ellen says: there's something about her.

Raye says: WTF do you guys have a problem? Marion?

Marion says: Hey everybody, it's Rachel! Oh, sorry I forgot you were friends with the little Ice Princess.

Raye says: you don't forget anything Marion. Why are you being such a bitch?

Marion says: C'mon Rachel, we're only joking.

Anonymous says: I heard the ice princess got thawed!

Ellen says: thawed, LOL

Raye says: You guys are idiots

Kandykat says: I want him back

That's the last entry. Kandykat typed it four minutes ago.

I minimize Marion's poisonous bitchfest and put my head down on my arms. I would love to punch Marion in her smug face, but she and I both know that ice princesses don't fight using their fists. She and Paige gave me that stupid nickname years ago. She knows I can't do anything to her, even though I'm so mad and frustrated that tears are building up. My eyes feel grainy and weird. I blink a few times, trying to convince myself that there were no tears to begin with. I begin to type.

Every time I look at her lame blog she's saying something about me and it makes me feel like throwing up. But throwing up won't help anything. The one thing I know about Marion is, the best way to get to her is through her brother, those two are tight. And the one thing I know about Kyle is, he has one major weakness, and it's this gorgeous blonde with no heart. Paige Prescott (Thompson). It will totally freak Marion out if I can prove to the world that Kyle is still obsessed with my sister, and I know he is because he drives past our house several times every day. I've seen him.

I navigate the Internet on autopilot until I find a free anonymous e-mail site that is truly anonymous, no AOL screen name to trace it back to. Then I hit the notebook icon. Raye and I played some Internet pranks last year, just messing around with some of Marion Henessy's blog disciples. Raye finally decided it was immature so we stopped, but the anonymity was kind of a rush. I didn't want to look immature, but I didn't really want to stop, either. There's a link directly on Kyle Henessy's name, where he commented on the blog. It takes me to a Write Mail page. I title my message *Paigey Waigey* and the text part is pretty simple:

:how much would you pay for pics of Paige in a bikini? How about naked?:

I don't put my siggy on it, of course. After I hit Send, I pop open my Pepsi and stick a straw in the can. It's doing that fizzy bubbling action that only a canned soft drink will do, and it stings the back of my throat as I suck it down. As far as I can tell, I'm providing a public service, keeping a pervert off the streets and glued to his computer screen. I do have swimsuit shots of Paige, right here on this computer.

I take a deep breath. I feel like I could have a heart attack right this second. From throwing up to a heart attack. Marion's blog is going to find a way to kill me, unless I kill it first.

I check the pictures from Florida. They are in a folder on my desktop. I had to help Mom send them to my grandma after our last vacation to visit her. It would be truly amazing if Kyle got any more jazzed up about those photos than Paige herself. They're pretty good shots. The angle makes her legs look like a runway model's, impossibly long and slender. The idea of that pimply nerd-freak getting himself all lathered up over them is kind of amusing, and if Paige knew he was looking at her, she would vomit until she died.

Everyone thinks Paige was so damn scared of Kyle Henessy, but I know the truth. She wasn't scared, she was disgusted. She was embarrassed that he followed her around everywhere.

I think of all the things Marion has said, rumors that she's started about me, the way she scrunches up her face when she sees me like something smells bad. I think about Kyle making my family afraid in their own home and about

Paige acting like she's the queen of the world, talking on and on about herself while my mother hangs on every word. It's enough to fill my eyes with tears, this anger. If I were a volcano, I'd be, I'd just . . . I put my head in my hands and breathe in and out slowly. I'm not used to feeling like this.

Revenge on Kyle, Marion, and, in a roundabout way, my sister at the same time. In exchange for the pics I'll get him to do something about his sister's blog. Destroy it. Take it down. Whatever you do to kill a blog. It's the center of her world, so without that blog, Marion Henessy will be nothing. As I typed the anger drained out of me and now I feel strangely calm.

A few hours later I hear the garage door creaking open and hear my parents talking as they walk in through the kitchen. I hear the TV come on. Don't they realize Preston has been watching TV almost all day? He turned it on right after he helped me clean up after lunch and has been watching most of the afternoon. I don't think it's good for him to watch TV all day, but it's hard to keep up with him when he isn't in front of the television. I worry about this, sometimes, when there aren't a million other things to worry about. I sit on my canopy bed, scrunch up my knees under my chin, and try not to think about anything. Tomorrow is the last day of Christmas vacation.

I wake up freezing, so I know my parents are gone. They have this timer on the heat that turns it down whenever we're not home. Only it isn't programmed to know I'm still on Christmas break. At least I know I'm alone in the house. Preston has ADHD camp today, which isn't a camp at all, just a program held at his school for part of the day where ultrahyper kids run around wearing helmets. It's nice to get a break from making grilled cheese sandwiches, but kind of lonely too. My family is kind of ignoring me this week. They don't want to think about me, don't want to see me, and I think it's best to lie low. We'll be back to family dinners and having intrusive conversations once school's back in session and we get our schedules ironed out. Once the thing that they witnessed fades from their minds and they're able to see me as just me again, without the handcuffs.

I put on a sweatshirt over my pajamas. Tie my robe on over the bulk of the sweatshirt and head down to adjust the thermostat. Seems like a good idea to grab a yogurt smoothie while I'm downstairs, and as long as I'm in the kitchen I kind of slide a certain drawer out. No luck, my cell is gone, probably in Mom's purse. Three days ago I snuck downstairs and put it back in the junk drawer, unwilling to test my luck any further. Stealing it had been useless because I didn't have the nerve to call him, no matter how bad I wanted to. I was like some old-fashioned girl, the kind my parents wanted when Paige was in fifth grade and they kept telling her not to call boys, that she should wait for them to call her. By the time she hit puberty Mom and Dad had given up on that notion. But somehow, even though I went to where his number was stored, I couldn't make myself push the button. So the possession of the phone was not worth the risk of having stolen it. My parents are still mad and hurt and disappointed, but who knows when they might relent and let me out of the house for good behavior? I am hopeful but not overly optimistic.

I grab the regular phone, which is resting neatly in its cradle, where the phone has remained, when not in use, since Paige moved out. When she lived here, you would have to hit the Find Handset key every time you wanted to order a pizza or something, and half the time the battery would be dead.

I turn it on and get a dial tone, but when I start to dial nothing happens. Finally, I hit Mom's work on the speed dial and it goes to a recorded message. "This number has been set to receive calls only; no outgoing calls can be made from this number." I didn't even know this phone could do that! It's my rotten luck to have a dad who reads every single page of every instruction manual. He can even call from his cell and enter a code to get all of his messages. Too bad all that instruction reading didn't help him keep his upper-management job. He was in charge of telling people where to take semi trucks or something. All I know is he was always calculating supply orders and gas mileage on big spread-sheets, then writing reports that he e-mailed to someone named Harold.

What happens if I have an emergency and need to call 911? What happens if I desperately need to get in touch with Raye? What happens if I need a Hawaiian pizza? I feel all deflated, like the balloon that Preston brought home from the infamous birthday party. It's a green balloon that's been losing helium all week; now it just droops in the corner of his room, saggy and pathetic. I am so expendable that my parents don't even care if I die. I sigh, knowing I'm being silly. But it is obvious that they don't care if I get hungry for pizza and can't get it. I mean, I know we can't afford pizza, but if I were *starving* . . . I guess the computer is now my only connection with the outside world. I feel like a prisoner. I head upstairs to take a look.

My in-box contains a long message from Raye detailing all of her problems with Josh and why she isn't sure if she wants a long-term relationship with someone who doesn't go to school with us. It's hard to rub your ex's nose in your new-found happiness if he doesn't even know you have a fabulous new boyfriend. As a single grounded person I can't offer much in the way of advice. And then there's the message I've been waiting for. Not just one, but three of them, all neatly in a row. For a minute I'm scared to open them.

Message one
Subject: *parker, please*
Message: I

Message two
Subject: *Parker, Please*
Message: Need

Message three
Subject: *PARKER, PLEASE*
Message: You

I Need You. Yeah, my heart soars when I read this, but it's too bad that suddenly I can't get Kandace Freemont out of my head. *It was amazing,* huh? I can imagine. I don't want to, but I can't help it. Kandace Freemont has a body any girl would envy, and the evidence shows that guys aren't too reluctant to pant over her, to use her, to . . .

Trying to shut off the imagination. The anger stays for several minutes, because it's always there, but then the longing for him comes back even stronger, and I put the anger away, push it deep down and ignore it.

Still ignoring the fact that I have feelings (I do this sometimes, try to shut them off), I minimize his e-mail and check the dummy account I set up last night and find this message from Uberdork Kyle.

Who is this?

I type in *your worst enemy* and hit Send. Melodramatic, I know, but hey, when you play silly mind games you have to play them stupidly, right? I stare at the screen—*your mail has been sent*—feeling dumb and shaky. Why am I doing this? I didn't really think he would even respond, and suddenly I want to take the whole thing back.

There is yet another e-mail from Raye in my in-box. She's all confused because she says she likes this Josh guy about half as much as she liked Ian. I know how she feels. I doubt I'll find anyone I like a fraction of the amount I like my ex, and yet he's an ex. What's wrong with me?

The phone rings and I jump. Incoming calls seem to be working, which can only be good, right? Caller ID says *Unknown*, but I'm pretty desperate for someone to talk to, so I hit Talk and say, "Hello?"

"Mrs. Prescott? This is Albert at the electric company."

"Um," I say, confused. Why would the electric company be calling us?

"If you remember, Mrs. Prescott, you told me last week that you would be sending half of your past-due balance. This was on December twenty-second. You said right after Christmas, do you remember this?"

"Um . . ."

"Mrs. Prescott, your account is seriously overdue. If you don't want us to shut off your utilities you will have to pay part of this bill."

"My mom isn't home right now." I want to get this guy off my phone now, I do not want to talk to him or hear about this at all.

"What?"

"My mom isn't here."

"Why didn't you tell me that to begin with?"

"I tried to tell—" *Click*. I put the phone back on the charger and sit down at the kitchen table; then I get up, run upstairs for a pair of socks and back downstairs to put the thermostat back on freezing. My hand is still on the thermostat when I see the Volkswagen pull up. Four years old and it's still a gorgeous car. I hope Paigey-poo isn't going to try to get me to share my feelings again.

The doorbell rings. She's always forgetting keys and things. I go to the door and find West there, not Paige. I feel relief that I'm not going to be interrogated, followed by irritation. What does he want?

"Hi, West."

"Hey, Parker." He pushes past me and goes straight for the kitchen. I follow him, curling up my toes as we go over the cold, cold tiles in the hall.

"Something wrong with your heater?"

"No, it's on a timer. It goes off when nobody's home."

"Oh. Where's the ketchup?"

"What?" He came here for ketchup?

"I'm making hamburgers for lunch and I need ketchup and cheese slices."

"Cheeseburgers, you mean." He gives me a kind of mad look. "I mean, if you put cheese on them, they'll be cheeseburgers, technically, not hamburgers." This clarification does not make him any friendlier. In fact, he looks downright pissed. I lean into the fridge and pull a big plastic Heinz bottle from behind a gallon of milk. "Here's the ketchup. Are you gonna just take it?"

"No. I'm going to pour some in my hand and rush home to put it on my *ham*burger." Somebody should tell him that to be sarcastic you have to say something that makes sense. Duh. He's so irritating and I'm not in a good mood. That phone call has me feeling more worried than usual about our money situation, and now dumb inconsiderate West is stealing all our food.

"I don't think Paige would like you to drive her car with a handful of ketchup," I answer, unable to stop myself. Seriously, somebody needs to put this freeloader in his place, but it probably won't be me. He still intimidates me a little, and if nothing else, he is married to Mrs. Popularity herself. I guess he thinks I don't have anything more important to do than deal with this burger emergency or whatever. His rich parents probably don't keep ketchup around because, you know, you can't put it on caviar. "We don't have any cheese slices, only this shredded stuff." I pull the bag out and show him. He takes the bag of Six-Cheese Italian Blend and stares at it for what seems like a long time. He doesn't look very happy. "Isn't there a convenience store right by your apartment? They probably have American cheese slices."

"I don't like to go to the grocery store," he says, "and the convenience store only has something called 'cheese food'. I don't think it's really cheese."

I stare at the bag of cheese in his hand, wondering if it's real cheese or another substitute that poor people like us buy. Too lazy to go the big supermarket, too snobby to eat imitation cheese. What an amazing guy my sister snagged. For some reason my parents think he's the perfect son-in-law, and even my brother likes him. He ruffles my hair. Stupid oblivious West has no idea that his free-food emporium is about to have the power shut off.

"You know," he says, as if we were having a conversation, "I think I'm going to trade in the car for a truck."

"Really, you could get a trade-in on that thing?" He had a Mustang. Well, he still has a Mustang, but he backed it into a parked dump truck. Then later he drove right off the road and into a ditch. The only place it isn't smashed is on the driver's side. Our parents keep expecting West's parents to buy him a new one, but so far they haven't. Sometimes he shows up in his dad's Jaguar, but mostly he just drives around in Paige's car. I think it maybe says something about them as a couple that they both drive red cars, though his was flashier than hers. Before the wreck and then the other wreck.

"I meant the Volkswagen." He puts a banana in his pocket. Then he turns to go and says, "Stay out of trouble, Parker!" West smiles at me with his big white teeth. The smile that made all the girls swoon, once upon a time. Does he think he can charm me out of even more food? With our ketchup, our shredded cheese, and our last banana, he heads out to my sister's shiny still-new-looking car.

The phone rings again. I peer cautiously at the caller ID. I'm miserable enough right now without hearing how they are going to come and repossess our couch and fine us a hundred dollars because Preston broke the handle on the reclining part or something crazy like that. Do they repossess couches? Ours is kind of new, so I'm betting we still owe somebody for it.

The caller ID reads *Chris Prescott*. Mom said Dad didn't need to see me or talk to me before his big job interview on Tuesday, and he had a second interview this morning, so I tried not to get around him, to distract him or remind him, or whatever. I've been avoiding my father, and I hate that, because he's one of my favorite people in the world. I put the phone to my ear.

"Daddy?" My voice shakes a little, I'm that nervous. I hate talking to him now, he makes me all uncomfortable and scared I'll say the wrong thing.

"Hi, Parker, is your mom there?"

"No, isn't she at work?" Um, why wouldn't Mom be at work? I'm so confused.

"She thought she might come home and check on you if she wasn't too busy."

"I guess she got too busy." Mom used to work part-time, but she's been working all the hours she can get lately, trying to cover our bills. They fight about it and talk about all the things they should've done (save money) but it's too late now.

"I wouldn't be surprised. Anyway, honey, would you tell her that I'm sticking around here for a few hours? I want to meet the corporate manager and he's not going to be in until after lunch."

"Okay, Daddy."

"You guys have dinner without me, okay?"

"I'll tell her." It's good, I think, that he sounds so okay talking to me, like maybe things could go back to normal between us.

"And Parker, keep the doors locked. There are crazy people out there." I know he's thinking of Kyle Henessy back when he used to lurk around. If the neighbor kid you've known all your life is capable of criminal behavior, what might some stranger do?

"I will, Daddy, I will." We say quick goodbyes and I sit down again. The hand that's holding the phone shakes just a little. Yeah, I'm cold, but I'm suddenly really nervous too. Think about it. Daddy not home until after dinner. Mom too busy to come home and check on me. Last day of Christmas break, and I'm spending it alone and freezing in my own house.

I know a place where it's warm, and where I won't be alone.

I sent him an e-mail, but I doubt he's online and I don't have any way to let him know I'm coming over, so when I walk up to the side door that leads into the basement my stomach starts dancing around. He comes to the door wearing Levi's and no shirt, and that makes me feel kind of light-headed, walking inside with him. It takes me back to our third date, the first time things really got hot between us.

We were on the floor, on the striped comforter, and he was propped on one arm, kissing me. I heard the front door open and his little brother go pounding up the steps. His mother called down to the basement for him to help her carry in some bags. I panicked, was desperately trying to button my button-fly jeans. Those things are easy to open but a bitch to refasten from a horizontal position.

He put his hand on my arm. "Don't worry about it," he said softly, and buttoned his own jeans, gave them a little adjusting, and ran out without even pulling on a shirt.

I huddled in the corner of his room, mortified. I was sure his parents knew exactly what we had been doing. And maybe they did, because they never called him to run up and help with anything again. I hoped that he didn't say anything to them, like "Don't ask me to carry in groceries when Parker's here," or more likely, "Leave me alone when I have a girl over, okay?" Part of me is uncomfortable imagining what his parents must think, but another part of me doesn't care. This is what he does to me.

"I needed to talk to you," I tell him, feeling incredibly dumb. Why else would I be here?

He breathes out hard and reaches for me. When I step back, he grins at me and ushers me in ahead of him.

"I thought you were under house arrest."

"I am. I escaped." I stand there, unsure what to do with myself. Finally, I decide to put my hands in my pockets, but my jeans are pretty tight, so then I don't. All this thinking and I'm still standing here not knowing what to do with my hands. He ties all of me in knots, including my brain.

"I'm glad to see you." He's playing shy with me now, staying just out of reach, watching me.

"We need to talk," I tell him. I take off my hat and gloves, take a step over and put them on the striped bedspread. Finally something to do, and then the task is done and I have to turn to look at him again.

"We talked before." He sounds irritated, almost mad. He means after the breakup. At least, I think that's what he means.

"I know."

"You walked out on me." He's right, and I'm so upset

with myself for this, and yet it seemed like my only choice. The only way to retain some control of myself and the situation. I need to have some control.

"You pushed me too far." Does he know what I mean? Is he aware how it was all going too fast and crazy?

"I know. I guess I did and I'm sorry. Look, if you want to talk, come with me."

He grabs my hand loosely and pulls me behind him, out of his house into the January chill. I move closer to him instinctively; my gloves and hat are still lying in his basement.

"C'mon." He breaks into a run, has to be freezing out here with no shirt, but his enthusiasm is contagious. I stumble after him. He pulls me into his neighbors' yard, not Erin Glasgow's but the one that belongs to the older couple who live directly behind him. A frosted glass enclosure wraps halfway around the wooden deck. Cobalt blue tiles line the area around a sunken hot tub. He drops my hand and pulls the cover back. Steam rushes out and blinds me. I feel trapped between the vicious cold and the pull of the humid warmth. And now I see. He will have this discussion, but it will be on his terms, and we will be together in the steaming hot water while we talk.

"Let's get in. We can talk all you want here."

"What about your neighbors?" I look up at the back windows nervously. I'm not ready to go through the whole getting-caught thing again.

"They're in Jamaica for a month. I know where the key to the house is, if you want to go in."

I look up at the huge house, terrified that he'll try to get me to trespass into another person's private space.

"No, I don't want to go in."

He laughs. "Don't worry, my mom is watering their

orchids. We have a key and permission to watch their enormous TV and use their hot tub. We aren't trespassing, relax, Park." I breathe out and let the tension go. Does he do this to me on purpose?

"I don't know if I can."

"The hot water will help. It's, uh, soothing." I look at him. "Soothing" doesn't sound like something he would say, but I don't ask him because I get distracted. He's unbuttoning his pants.

"I'm freezing, Parker. Let's get in and warm up."

"This isn't what I wanted. . . ." I am not going to take my clothes off, I tell myself. No way.

"Parker." He pulls me into his arms. "I promise I won't push you any further or faster than you want to go. I'll set the rules right now. No touching in the hot tub unless you initiate it, okay? You can trust me."

"Right." I half roll my eyes and he laughs. There is a long silence. He pushes the button and the water comes to life.

"Well, we'd better get in or we're going to die of hypothermia," I say, like I've wanted to get in the hot tub all along.

"That's my girl." And that approval in his voice, the warmth, is what gets me. I pull off my sweater and fold it neatly, putting it on the cedar bench behind me.

He's already sinking into the water, completely naked. I peel off my jeans quickly and fold them because I just can't stand to leave them in a heap on the deck. After a very long hesitation, I put my foot in.

With the cold wind rushing right through me, the water feels like it might boil my skin off. Through the steam I see him watching me.

When you think about it, your panties and bra are about the same as the average bikini, so I shouldn't feel too self-conscious, but I can't stop the thought of my parents' stunned expressions in Dad's office, and picturing them makes me feel all gross and embarrassed, and not at all what he wants. He wants someone comfortable with her body, someone who feels sexy, and I'm not that person.

I take a deep breath and plunge into the heat. My body feels boneless, like I've melted and become part of the water. The cold against my face and the tops of my shoulders feels marvelously cruel, burning away last week's loneliness and my parents' shock. True to his word, he doesn't lay a finger on me, though our thighs are just barely whispering against each other.

"Do you want to get back together?" he asks. I feel a quick burst of excitement. Hope. I've been so lonely since we've been apart. I don't know how to answer. He has pushed his hair back with a wet hand and it curls damply against his face. He looks vulnerable.

"We aren't good together. We make each other crazy," I say, because I need him to talk me into it.

"I won't argue with that."

"Look, you have to tell me what happened with Kandace. Don't hold anything back." I look at his face, look away from his face, look at his face. I need to know, but I dread what he's going to say.

"You walked away from me, Parker."

"I know. But I have to know where you've been before I consider walking back in." He leans back and rests his arms against the sides of the hot tub.

"Did you know that I noticed you my very first day at Allenville? That was surreal, going back to regular school. Penbrook was quiet. There were hardwood floors, and of course, there were no girls. At Allenville it was all giggling and flirting and silliness. Then there was you. You were so aloof, so beautiful. I think I fell for you that first day. You met my eyes, but you didn't react to me, so cool."

"Did you sleep with Kandace Freemont?"

"Okay, okay, Park. You want complete honesty. I felt pretty bad, pretty rejected by the way things ended with us. She was there, and she was willing. I didn't, we didn't go the whole way, but we got a good start."

"Oral?" He doesn't meet my eyes, and my stomach drops. I knew this was a possibility. I knew they probably had. I wish I could stop tormenting myself like this, I really do.

"She offered."

"And?" Now I have to pretend like I want to know, even though I don't, not exactly. It wouldn't be cheating exactly, and yet if he wanted to get back together with me, why would he do something like that?

"I wanted to. Really, I mean, really I wanted to. But it felt wrong and I kept thinking about you."

"You were thinking about me when you were with her." This is both good and bad. I want him to think about me, but I don't want him to be with her at all. Still, it's better than nothing.

"Well, yeah, thinking about how hot it is with you even when we're just kissing. Thinking how I was a jerk when we had that last fight."

"She said you were amazing on Marion's blog." I just can't seem to let it go.

"I wasn't amazing. I drove her home and told her I'd see her later, nothing really happened. Did you see what I wrote about you?"

"Let me think." Our thighs are pressed tightly together

now, the only physical connection between us, but that connection is alive, and it's present in all my thoughts.

"Did it go something like"—I take a deep breath—" 'I would rather abuse myself on a nightly basis thinking about Parker Prescott than have Kandace Freemont spread-eagled on my bed'? 'Hip-anonymous'?"

"You do know me too well." He fakes a goofy accent, leans forward, but I don't move in to kiss him, and by his own promise he can't press his lips against mine. Our eyes are level, though, and I see that challenge in his again. "It's true, you know. Do you want to see?"

"What?"

"Are you curious, Parker?" He's taunting me, and even though I know it, I can't stop myself from blushing. I would be lying if I said I hadn't been curious, hadn't wondered about the darkest, most private things that guys do, but some things are better kept secret. I lunge out of the water to stop him, even though I know he's just teasing. I put my hands against his shoulders and push him down, and somehow I slip forward. My body rests for a moment on top of him and then we sink down back into the water together.

I am balanced on the end of his knees, I feel him. He has gone stone still. His knuckles are white as he holds the beveled edge of the hot tub. I know that with one movement, I could change everything between us forever, that's all it would take.

I think about him for a second, not sex, just him, how much I love him and how much it hurts to love him. Then I propel myself back across the hot tub, out of his reach. I don't feel like I did before, powerful because of his silly promise to me. I feel angry. I want to hurt him. The good feelings have been replaced by frustration. Maybe because I don't believe his bullshit story about Kandace. Just because it's what I want to hear doesn't mean it's true.

"Parker, I am sorry I pushed you so hard before. I'll wait as long as you want." Somehow things have changed in the last ten minutes. He's looking at me differently, like he can't keep his eyes off me. Can I believe him? Should I? I want to. I glance at my watch. Good thing it's waterproof.

"I really need to get home." I want to curl up under my pink bedspread and stare up at the ceiling for about a week, and try not to think about this or about him.

"There are towels in that bench, the seat folds back." He jumps out and hands me a towel. It's a huge fluffy one, though I'm not properly appreciative of the cottony softness since I am now freezing to death. Not exaggerating here, I am facing certain death if I don't press myself against him and force him to share his towel. Unless we share our body heat and our supersized towels we will surely die.

Wrapped with him in his towel, I use my own to wipe every drop of moisture from my body before I shimmy into my jeans. My panties are dripping and it feels terrible in the cold. My bra is soaked too. Miserable.

"I don't want you to walk home in the cold," he says.

"I don't want to get caught with you. If my parents show up, I can pretend I just went out for a walk to clear my head and ponder the error of my ways." I'm starting to worry, but somehow I can't focus on my parents' beating me home when I'm standing here with him.

"They might wonder why you smell like chlorine and why you're soaking through your clothes. Let me take you." He's right. They probably would wonder about that, especially since they don't trust me anymore. And because it's pretty hard to explain why I'm dripping wet and my hair is frazzled from the steam. I should definitely ride with him. He'll get me home faster.

It's easy enough to follow him and climb into his shiny black Saab. It's hard to keep from touching him. He pulls smoothly out of the driveway and turns left. Timid little mouse that I am, I put my hand on his thigh, very lightly. He stops at a light and then turns left again. I jerk my hand back, unsure of my instincts. He gives me a little half smile that I can barely see because he's looking at the road.

He parallels right in front of my house, pulls me to him, and gives me one of those "I know your parents are watching out the window" kisses. Very showy and dramatic. More head action than tongue action, which isn't his style at all. A weird show since there isn't an audience. I know I should stop him, that if anyone is looking I'm in more trouble than ever, but somehow I just can't.

"I'll see you at school tomorrow." I disengage my face, disengage my throbbing lips from his perfect, perfect mouth.

I slam the Saab's door behind me and run up the steps of our red brick colonial, the steps where I fell chasing Paige and busted my lip when I was four. I keep my head straight so that I don't have to look directly at the Century 21 sign.

I unlock the door and then relock it behind me, remembering Daddy's warning, and run upstairs to my bedroom. I need to take a shower before my parents get home. Need to get rid of the evidence.

"Where have you been, young lady?"

It isn't the words so much as the surprise that halts me in my tracks and makes my heart nearly stop. What is she trying to do to me after Daddy already scared me with his talk of crazy people? Paige is lying on my bed filing her nails. She blows on them and smiles at me.

"Out." Crap. She knows I'm grounded. She could get me into serious trouble.

"Oh, Parker, I invented the 'out' line. Can't you do better than that?"

"Not really. With a big sister like you it's hard to really be original." She smiles like this is the world's biggest compliment, and I have to admit, she knew how to handle Mom and Dad. She never got grounded indefinitely, and she was a million times worse than me. If her goal was to freak me out, then she succeeded, but that last kiss is still throbbing through me, and I just don't care about my silly vain sister right now.

"I have to say, those handcuffs were original." She stops talking but keeps filing. Then, "Your boyfriend thought of that, huh?"

"Yeah. Paige"—I still do not want to discuss this with her—"um, I didn't see your car."

"West dropped me off. He's going to pick me up after the game, that way we can drive home together. He's watching football with Joe and Tyler."

"Very romantic." I roll my eyes and then change the subject. "Hey, when do your college classes start?" College students, I've learned, have much longer breaks than us poor overworked high school students. Paige is supposed to be taking classes in communication or public speaking or something. Mom and Dad say she has no idea what she is doing with her life, but they want her to have a college degree anyway. Mom always tells us that at least Paige settled down with a nice boy. She doesn't seem settled to me, but what do I know?

"A week or two." She scrunches her forehead up. I don't think she knows. Paige isn't much on academics. Mom had to go with her to help her register for classes last summer.

"West was here today borrowing cheese and stealing our ketchup. He says he might trade in your car." I'm wondering how she will get to school. The campus is all the way across town, and there's no way she would take a bus or anything like that.

"West wants a nicer car, like a BMW or something."

I glare at her. I'm the sister who doesn't even have a car, who would never, never scorn the Volkswagen, if I were lucky enough to have a car like that. "But West is loaded, right? Why can't he just buy a BMW if he wants one?" And they can just give me the Volkswagen if they don't love it anymore.

"West's *family* is loaded, but they have this thing about making your own way in the world. It totally pisses West off that they won't help us get a house. He doesn't like living in an apartment." She shakes her head and I can tell she doesn't want to think about any of it. She's always ignored anything stressful or negative. I'm the one who can't stop worrying; she's the one who can't be bothered even with mild concern.

"Hey, is this my comforter, the one from my bedroom?" The room that our parents keep exactly the way she left it?

"Yeah, I've been trying to tone down the pink princess theme in here."

"Good idea. This is such a little-girl room, especially the canopy bed." She laughs. I don't much like her making fun of my Disney Princess–style room. Really, it isn't officially Disney. As in, I don't have any licensed products. It's just pink and frilly with a canopy bed. You know, the type of things parents buy for their young daughters.

"Do you remember . . . ?" she begins, and I know where she is going. Disney World, when I was seven. It was one of the big happy family trips we took with the Henessys. Mrs. Henessy arranged for all us girls to have breakfast with the Princesses. Mr. Henessy and Dad had taken Kyle deep-sea fishing or something equally manly, so it was just Paige, Marion, and me. We had these little autograph books that we were supposed to get the characters to sign.

My mom handed me my book and this great big pen with a feather on the end of it. A quill. Paige and Marion got identical pink books, but Mom got me a yellow one that had Cinderella on the cover. I guess she did that so Paige and I could tell them apart, but I wished I had the glossy pink book too.

I remember being superexcited in that giddy way that you get when you're really little. Then the Princesses came in, and they were all beautiful, and I looked down at my plate and wouldn't look up. Marion and Paige had a great time getting all the Princesses to sign their autograph books, but the only one I got was the Little Mermaid, and that was because she felt sorry for me and came over and signed even though I wouldn't look at her.

I hate the word *shy*. I don't ever use that word. Shy was what I was when I was seven and my one Princess signature got smeared across the pastel yellow page because I dripped tears all over it, because I was afraid and couldn't lift my head no matter how much I wanted to. That's how the shyness works. You want to talk, but you can't. People look at you with scorn. Being an ice princess is infinitely better, even if some people think you're a total bitch. A snob. Reserved. Those are choices a person makes, to be reserved, to be quiet, or to be a snob. Shy isn't a choice.

"Remember what?" I know where she's going but I don't want to reminisce with her.

"Oh, just Disney and all the fun we had. Do you still have that dumb pink autograph book that you stole from me?"

"Paige, that was like ten years ago."

"Remember you hid it under your dresser and Mom found it when she was vacuuming? But then you stole it again, didn't you? It's probably still in here someplace, and your room looks exactly the same." She stretches out her fingers and admires her work with the emery board.

"There isn't much point in changing it, is there? Not when we're going to be moving soon," I say. My voice is low and kind of shaky. She knows I hate talking about any of my episodes. That's why she loves to bring them up. "I have to take a shower." This conversation is over and I want her to leave.

"Yeah. You have hot tub stink all over you."

"You would know." Being a little sister totally impairs my ability to formulate a decent comeback. It's sad. "Are you going to tell Mom and Dad?"

"That you snuck out and spent your afternoon with sexy-pants in some hot tub? Nah, but I think you're in way over your head." I know she's probably right, but then, most of the time she acts like I'm still twelve years old.

"Probably." I step into the shower. I hope she will get out of my room while I'm gone, but of course she just lies there getting tiny little nail pieces on my comforter.

I usually hang my bathrobe on the hook on the back of the door before I take a shower, but it isn't there when I get out. Paige really distracts me sometimes.

I ignore her, still sitting there, as I drip my way to the closet wrapped in a lime green towel. Paige's clothes were always in a haphazard heap. I keep mine hung neatly in the closet. Of course, her wrinkled clothes still looked completely hot on her. They always do.

"Damn." I turn toward her, ready to hear some comment about how I fold my underwear and color-coordinate all my socks. "You really are growing up, aren't you? No wonder sex-on-the-brain is so into you."

"Whatever." As usual, I blush, but I love her surprise. And more, I love the reluctant admiration that made her say it aloud.

Finally, I can tell she's getting tired of tormenting me, and she stands up to leave my room when she hears the front door squeaking open and Preston shouting, "I'm home!" at the top of his lungs.

"You got lucky, you know." She looks at the clock on my nightstand. "If it were me, they'd have gotten home ten minutes ago."

Yeah right, I'm so lucky and she's unlucky. There are a million ways I could refute this, but she won't listen, so I don't say anything.

I'm drying my hair when Mom calls for me to come downstairs. She's thrilled that Dad made it home in time for dinner. I'm thrilled that I made it home for dinner twenty minutes before they did. We used to eat dinner together all the time, before Dad lost his job and started sitting with the newspaper and circling things. Eventually he just moved with his paper to the living room to sit in front of the TV, and the rest of us started eating wherever we could find a comfortable place to sit.

I take a deep breath, relieved. I really did just get here in time. The realization that I could've been in deep, deep trouble right now makes the never-ending dinner experience easier to bear.

Dad is telling us about his job interview. "It's just a delivery job, but it has management potential," he says between bites of some kind of mushy casserole with crushed-up Doritos on top. I've been trying to skim the Doritos off the surface and avoid the greasy ground beef.

Preston is actually picking the Doritos off with his fingers. He sees what I'm doing and puts a couple of big Dorito chunks on my plate. Mom raises her eyebrows but she doesn't say anything. The fact that Preston is sitting still at the table is unusual. I think it's possible only because he's focusing all that energy. While his body remains still his fingers are picking, picking, picking.

"Delivery?" Paige asks.

"Yeah, it's kind of a boutique take on an old idea. You remember, Jane, how they used to deliver milk in the old days?"

"I guess." Mom frowns. She wants to be supportive of Dad, but he's just such an idiot sometimes, so trusting. You can see the frustration on Mom's face.

"Well, this is sort of a special delivery service where you can preorder certain items and have them delivered regularly."

Preston is sucking the orange cheese powder from the orange tips of his fingers. When he goes to put another choice bit on my plate, I block him with my fork and shake my head.

"Sounds like a good idea, Daddy." Paige's teeth gleam in the soft light of the dining room chandelier. She's eating the casserole mush like it's five-star cuisine. She really wants to get on Mom and Dad's good side for some reason.

"I thought so too, sugar. Only problem is they haven't started their business in this area. They're actively looking for someone who can run the business and handle sales."

"You did all that at your old job, Chris." Mom is smiling, but she doesn't really look happy.

"Exactly. I got the feeling I was exactly what they were looking for."

"That's great, Dad," Paige says. I can't help wondering if he's exactly what they're looking for because he was willing to listen to their spiel. And because he's so close to being desperate. I sigh.

Mom glances at me, and then looks back at Dad. "So what's the problem?" she asks. Her perfect eyebrows are almost up to her hair. Not a good sign for Dad and the lousy job he's describing.

"What?" Dad rubs Dorito powder across his forehead. His hair is brown, and the overhead light shows how thin it's getting. His white dress shirt is pushed up past his elbows, and his black pants have nice creases. The man for the job. How could those people not want to hire him?

"You said there was a problem." Mom dips her napkin into her ice water and starts scrubbing the side of Preston's face.

"There's a start-up fee involved. An investment to get the business going. It's more than we have, and possibly more than I have in my 401(k)."

"Well, something else will come along, Chris." Mom wipes the Dorito residue from Dad's forehead with the same napkin she used on Preston. At least she didn't use spit to moisten it. Dad scrunches up his face.

"I'm still trying to think how we can manage it, but I don't know." He puts his elbows on the table. He sits there looking hopeful and pathetic at the same time, wanting to cash in his retirement money to pay to deliver milk and bread to suburbanites. It makes my heart hurt for him. You shouldn't have to pay money to get a job, even I know that.

"Did you take Preston to the indoor amusement park?" he asks Mom after another long silence, changing the subject.

"He went with his day camp today," Mom tells Paige, because I think I was supposed to know this already because she told me yesterday. "All those rambunctious kids, it reminded me of you. Do you remember, Chris, the first time we took Paige and Parker to Disney?"

"Parker and I were just talking about that trip." Each of Paige's smiles is even more dazzling than the last. Both parents turn toward her and look hopeful. They want Paige to hang out with me. They fantasize about their daughters being best friends. Even this little thing makes them hopeful. They want these things from us, but they only get them every once in a while from Paige. With her big smile and her sparkling blue eyes, she can fake interest in anything they want to talk about. That's why she's their favorite.

After a hesitation, when I guess he's remembering, Dad chuckles and says, "Oh yeah, Paige was so excited when we went on the roller coaster, remember? She was whooping and hollering, and if I remember right, she peed in her pants. Parker just sat very still. She wouldn't put her hands in the air, and she never laughed or even smiled. She just sat there with her little body shaking and her little mouth pressed into a line. It was so funny."

"That trip was really nice," Mom says. "It's too bad about the Henessys." She scoops up some dishes and carries them into the kitchen, and Dad follows her with some glasses.

"See?" Paige turns to me and smirks. "That's why you should retain your precious virginity."

"What?" She's such a complete bitch, even if my parents don't see it.

"If you can't even let go and enjoy a roller coaster, how're you going to manage an orgasm? Really, Parker."

"At least I didn't pee on myself. And how do you know I'm still a virgin?" I hiss this so that Mom and Dad won't hear. I'm not an idiot.

Preston has his entire face in the Doritos bag now, crunching away at the little broken pieces that are always left on the bottom.

Paige gives me this big smile and hisses back, "Because your guy wouldn't still be around if he'd already had you. Once he realizes you're frigid, he'll drop you and move on. Ice Princess."

I pretend that I don't care, but that last one hurt because that's kind of what I'm afraid of. I know older people make that stuff up to scare you, those stories where a girl goes too far with a guy and then he takes off and never speaks to her again. But like all made-up stories, it's probably based on some truth, and I figure the girl the legend is based on is probably someone exactly like me.

Paige and Marion gave me the nickname. Back when Marion lived next door and she was still trying to balance being my friend with worshipping Paige. That must've been hard for her. It was during summer vacation, and even though Paige was in middle school, Mom made her go next door when she was going to be gone all day. So Paige was sitting on Marion's vanity stool painting her toenails. Marion found a picture in some book of this superthin dark-haired cartoon woman who had icicles for fingernails, high cheekbones, and an expression of cruel disdain. The pages after it were stuck together, so I never knew what part the ice princess played in the story. Whatever terrible fate or frog prince was waiting for her, I'm betting she didn't rate a happily-ever-after. Paige was fascinated by the stupid thing.

I wasn't sure at first whether I liked getting so much attention or not. Then I got a good look at Paige's face and knew this was a bad thing that I wanted to be over. Like all their teasing, they'd get tired and forget about it when I didn't respond.

"Where did you get this?" she asked, laughing.

"It was in a box of old books my mom keeps in the basement," Marion told her.

Kyle came in wearing a too-tight Spider-Man undershirt and blushed bloodred when he saw Paige sitting there. I just sat quietly and waited to see if anyone was going to braid my hair. That was what we were doing before the whole dumb ice princess book was introduced. I guess that it should make me mad or something, but it's been so long that I just can't remember anything besides waiting to see if they were going to gossip with me about girl things, not knowing that the picture in the book would ever be important to me.

"Mom said to, um, ask you if you wanted to come downstairs. She said to come downstairs for a minute," Kyle stammered. He was trying to look at Paige without letting her know he was staring and it got him all confused and nervous. Paige and Marion left the room, still laughing. I took a good long look at the ice princess. Other than the weird icicle fingernail thing, there were worse things you could be. A troll or a goblin, for example. The ice princess had very wide cold blue eyes.

"What does *frigid* mean?" Preston asks.

I give Paige the finger. It feels superbly awkward, sticking my middle finger up right there at the long rectangular table. I immediately wish I had thought of a less lame response. It's kind of tough, though, because sometimes I worry that maybe I'll freeze or do something wrong. You know, during an intimate moment. Obviously, ruining my self-esteem is Marion's entire reason for existing, and Paige is always willing to do her part to make me feel like crap.

"It means 'cold,' honey," Paige says.

I know I'm not frigid, because he can melt me completely, but I am always so nervous about losing control. What if my sister is right and I can't relax enough? What if my mom is right and he only wants one thing?

Cinder block upon cinder block upon cinder block. That's Allenville High to me. Faced with the criticism of being elitist, the school decided to officially stop painting. I guess they couldn't hide the three computer labs, the state-of-the-art science and tech department, or the vast two-story library. So they haven't even touched up the worn pea-green of the institutionalized hallway walls in the last decade.

It's a strange situation, being part of a geeky magnet school. The popular crowd is nearly feverish in their attempts to make Allenville as snobby and social as any other place. They've got a big GPA to overcome.

Raye isn't here yet. She's running late. That's the thing about having to bum rides. You're always at the mercy of other people. Like my parents and, you know, fate. For instance, if something happens—like last night Raye broke up with Josh because he just wasn't Ian, and then she sat in her little blue Honda and cried and she left the lights on and ran the battery down—then I have no way to get to school.

After Raye called to report this my mom was seriously irritated. She started to tell me about the meeting she had to get to before nine and how she needed to prepare a presentation and write a memo.

"It's okay, Mom. I can get another ride." I reached for the phone, trying to hide my nervousness. Would he be irritated if I called him this morning? Was he driving some other girl to school, would he come and get me if I asked?

She pursed her lips. "I can take you."

My dad came downstairs. "You need a ride to school, sweetie? I'm not doing anything today. I can take you."

"Well then, you need to hurry, Chris. She already has enough tardies from stopping with Raye for croissants." She never talked to him in that tone of voice before he lost his job. Or maybe she did and I didn't notice. I felt bad for Dad in his paisley bathrobe, and more annoyed at Mom than usual, with her day planner and her stupid high heels. I don't know who she thinks she is. She still can't pay the electricity bill.

"Oh, okay. Let me just grab my glasses. Do you want a croissant?"

"No, Daddy." He should know I don't do breakfast, but he always asks. My dad really is a great guy. I hoped he wasn't thinking about how disappointed he was in me. I started to feel nervous. What if he said something? I didn't think I could handle a direct confrontation. I didn't think I could handle him saying he was disappointed in me. I realized that he was looking at me, that he had retrieved his glasses and was standing in the doorway waiting. I forced myself to look at him and smile.

"Anything? We can stop." He stepped back into the bathroom and came out without the ratty robe. I guess he was wearing it over his normal Dad outfit, khakis and a polo shirt. I don't think he can stand to be out of bed for five minutes without putting his polo shirt on. Anyway, he's always wearing the robe over his clothes. Maybe that's why he doesn't notice that it's freezing cold in our living room. Mom once said that Dad really thinks his robe is some kind of swanky-type housecoat that he ties with a sash and when he wears it he imagines he is both wise and comfortable. Like Sherlock Holmes with wire-rimmed glasses. About this one thing, I suspect she's right.

"Chris, you barely have time to get her to school." Mom was on edge this morning, and I wished she'd just leave us alone.

He wiped his glasses on his shirt and ushered me into the garage. It was quiet in the car. I realized that this was the first time we had been alone since it happened. It was not a good thing to think about.

"I should've brought that cup of coffee," Dad said, kind of to himself. As if the coffee that he left on the counter was something he couldn't live without. I hoped he wasn't going to start in again, wanting to stop and get me something to eat. I hoped I could get through the ride to school, that traffic wouldn't be bad and we could just cruise into the parking lot and be done with this. I realized as we turned, getting closer and closer to school, that I was scrunched down in the seat, almost hiding behind the thin diagonal strip of tan seat belt. I forced myself to sit straight.

"Do you want to pick a CD?" he asked. Paige and I used to always fight over what music to play, but it doesn't really matter to me anymore.

"That's okay, Daddy."

My dad looked sad suddenly, like the one thing he thought he could do to brighten my day was let me pick some music to listen to on the way to school.

"Daddy," I said.

"What, sweetheart?"

I took a long breath and adjusted the strap on my backpack. "I love you." He smiled at me as I climbed out and slammed the door of the Jeep, and I felt truly great for a minute, and then the look on his face in his office came back to me, and the good feeling sort of faded into nothing.

I was still climbing the front steps of Allenville High School when the warning bell rang, so as I walk down the hall, I'm more focused on being on time than anything else. Of course I scan the hall for him, my ears hypertuned to the sound of his voice, but I don't really expect to see him until lunch. Our paths just don't cross that often.

I'm hurrying because even though I like croissants as well as the next person, I also like to be on time.

There's a puddle beside my locker. Last year the air conditioner units started leaking and there were puddles everywhere. I really hope we aren't forced to have classes in the gym again. That pretty much sucked.

I turn the combination and swing the door open, and there in the open wall cavity that is my locker is a big pile of slushy melting ice. It's one of those moments when you just don't know what to do. The slush is soaking into my books, but I have no way to get it out of my locker, no place to put it. I feel violated.

Somebody opened this locker, which is supposed to be my private space, and they dumped a bunch of ice, which they knew would melt. Why? Who would hate me this much that they would want to destroy my calculus book, and my careful notes on eighteenth-century literature, and a few early copies of my secret drawings of my dream house? I mean, they weren't secret in the beginning, but I just kept working on them and trying to make a pretty stained-glass window. Now all that hard work is a glop of pulp. I feel like a glop of pulp myself, formless, drippy. The icy cold water has splashed and is running down my leg. Perfect.

Yeah, I know that it has to be connected somehow to the whole Ice Princess thing. I'm alone and humiliated, standing there as the last few kids scamper to class. The tardy bell rings. An office aid comes by with a clipboard, checking the halls for cutters. He seems surprised when I wave at him, motion for him to join me in front of my still-open locker. I take a deep breath and pull myself together. I won't give whoever did this to me the satisfaction of seeing me upset. But after a minute I don't even have to try to act normal, because the whole Ice Princess thing kind of takes me over. My face feels frozen.

"What should I do about this?" It's such a relief to ask another person for help, and this guy looks capable. He's tall and skinny with reddish brown hair and these black-rimmed glasses. He's holding this clipboard, and he has really nice hands with long fingers. For an unreal moment I imagine him touching me with them. I imagine enough that I start to blush. I hope he thinks my blush is due to my mortification over the prank, not from imagining him slipping his hands under my shirt.

"Holy crap!" he says. I laugh when he says it, actually

forget myself and laugh out loud. He stares into my locker and shakes his head. "Who did this to you?" I feel my fake smile sliding away from my lips. I don't want to be a victim and I don't want this guy, or anyone else, to consider me one.

"I don't know." I am now totally studying my shoes.

"Well, let's grab a garbage can and scrape the ice into that. Do you think it was Marion Henessy? She hates you."

I glance up at him, surprised. He looks kind of embarrassed and shrugs. "I read the blog when I'm bored sometimes, and I was at my grandparents' house for three days over the vacation. Let's just say I was very bored." I can't believe this, it's like everybody in our school reads that stupid thing. Great.

"Oh yeah, me too," I tell him seriously. "Not the grandparents, but I read the blog sometimes." He's looking at me, kind of running his eyes over me. I put my shoulders back a little. I mean, I have been totally slouched since he first came over to investigate. I don't want him to think I have exceptionally poor posture or something. I guess this is my version of nervous flirting. Some girls would giggle and push their hair back or something, but I just try to stand straight and look okay. It's a nervous reaction, though, not serious flirting.

"You ever post on there?" he asks.

"I did a few times, but Marion deleted them."

He positions a black rubber garbage can in front of my locker and starts scooping the ice out with his big capable hands.

"Do you think I'll get in trouble for being out of class?" I don't mean to be so anal about it, but I do wish he would hurry, because, as I have mentioned, I don't like to be late, and because, as I have not mentioned since I don't want to draw attention to negative possibilities, I do not want to be standing here peering into my locker when the bell releases everyone for first period. I have already had enough *thawed* comments to last me a lifetime.

"You won't get in trouble." He smiles at me shyly. Is he flirting with *me* now? I gotta get control of this hormonal fluctuation thing. I may be sending the wrong vibes to unsuspecting guys everywhere. He puts my soggy books into a second rectangular garbage can and picks one up with each hand. I follow him. We reach the office just as the bell rings.

One of the football players is waiting to talk to the principal, sitting in one of the overstuffed chairs that everyone knows are really there for the parents.

"Whoa, it's the Prescott girl," he says. I know, I know, Paige's little sister. Paige was pretty popular with Allenville's sports teams—football, basketball, tennis. You could say that guys with balls adore my sister.

"You can call me anytime, Prescott. I like hot tubs, too."

I die right there in the middle of the office, standing there between the attractively geeky office aide and the stocky football star (both seniors, I think) with the contents of my locker dripping onto the floor.

How does he know about my personal life? What does he know? How? Did I already say that? I stand there for a really long time while the office aide reports to the principal. I wonder if I should try to care about what they might be saying.

The counselor, Ms. Miller, calls me into her office. Before I go in, the office aide touches my shoulder. With his very nice hand.

"Hey, my name is Mason. If you have any more trouble around here, let me know."

"Thanks, Mason." He's being so nice to me that it almost freaks me out. I move my mouth in a way that I think is a smile. I know, normal people don't forget how to smile, but it just doesn't come naturally to me right now.

I go on into the counselor's private chamber. Two weeks ago, I sat here doing my mandatory ten-minute "What colleges are you applying to?" session. That was when Ms. Miller looked into my file and suggested that I should consider community college. So somehow Ms. Miller realizes I'm poor. Because it can't be my grades, I have very good grades. There must be something in that file that says *Parker Prescott's father lost his job. Parker Prescott has thirty-seven unpaid lunch charges* or something like that.

For over a year I've been collecting glossy college brochures from all over the country. I would really like to go to a nice private college. If I were in a private school with gleaming hardwood and quiet hallways, I wouldn't do anything to get myself kicked out.

"Do you know who might have done this, Parker?" Ms. Miller asks, as if I am somehow to blame. I try to focus on her instead of thinking about colleges, instead of thinking about hot tubs and being an ice princess and slush melting. Ms. Miller is tan, like the tannest person in the world. She's seated at her desk, and the assistant principal is standing behind her just a little bit to the left of her chair. Compared to Ms. Miller, he looks like a white skeleton-man. She must go to the tanning bed every single day, go through a gallon of tanning lotion a week.

"I don't know, but I think it could be Marion Henessy," I say in my quietest voice. I so do not want to be here. I need to get out of here and start finding out what's going on, whether—my stomach clenches up here—my ex-boyfriend has been running his mouth. His perfectly shaped mouth with the soft lips. There's only one thing that I can be sure of, and that's that these administrators aren't going to help me figure out the important stuff.

Ms. Miller and Mr. Dawson give one another a look and I am reminded of last year when Paige was a senior and Kyle was also a senior, and Paige filed the restraining order against Kyle. It made things kind of a nightmare here at school. Classes had to be changed. We weren't supposed to even pass each other in the halls. The administration was both exasperated and annoyed and they did not try to hide it. So I'm pretty sure they aren't going to do much for me now, and I'd like to just get out of here and go to class.

"Why do you think it was Marion?" Ms. Miller asks.

"She wrote some things on her blog last week. She used the word *thawed*." They look at me blankly. I nudge the black rectangular garbage can that is sitting in front of me with my foot. It sounds almost like a glass of ice water shaking back and forth. "The ice is, um, thawing," I say stupidly, waiting for her to get it. "Like, melting."

"You know that a student's personal blog is outside of school jurisdiction, right?" Mr. Dawson asks me. "Unless someone brags about it online, if they actually were to say they did this, then we might be able to do something, since the, er, prank was on school property."

"The Supreme Court hasn't really ruled on Internet posting as freedom of expression in relation to schools, and what she says on her blog could technically be called bullying," I say quietly. I looked all of this up a long time ago when Marion started the blog from hell. I found a ton of articles about legislation being filed against cyber-bullying, but I couldn't figure out what, if anything, had been passed.

"Be that as it may, we are discussing a prank, not Miss Henessy's blog," Ms. Miller says.

"Destruction of school property, though." Dawson sounds frustrated.

"It's going to be very hard to figure out who did this, very hard," Ms. Miller tells him. I tune them out and start thinking about the hot tub. Who knows about it and how? How could he do this to me? I feel tears start at the corners of my eyes as the embarrassment sets in. I trusted him. It takes all of my willpower to ignore the tears and focus on what the counselor is saying to the assistant principal.

"Someone must have seen something," Mr. Dawson argues. I understand that Ms. Miller thinks it's a waste of time to go after the perpetrator and Mr. Dawson can't stand the fact that something bad—a prank, as he calls it—happened in the school and he can't figure it out. And, more importantly, I realize that I'm not going to make it to second period, maybe not even to third. Finally, they find me these pitifully flaky old textbooks to replace the glossy ones that are landfill bound by now and send me off to lunch.

"Try to stay out of trouble," Mr. Dawson calls after me as I leave the office. Great, now in his mind I'm a troublemaker. He's probably making a note of it right this minute, opening the folder and writing on my permanent record. Thanks, Kyle, Paige, and Marion. If it weren't for you guys I could've made it through high school without a single administrator knowing my name.

I square my shoulders, take a deep breath, resquare them. During my lengthy office stay I've managed to get over the locker fiasco, soggy literature book and all. I mean, I know the whole thing was an hour-long discussion of the Prank, but talking about it gave me a chance to put the incident in perspective.

I mean, it sucks, and I will certainly miss the nice textbooks. The replacement ones really should be in a Dumpster somewhere, a recycling bin. But people have tormented me on and off throughout my years of school. It's just something that happens, for some reason, to me. If I let myself think about it, I would have to sit at home and be home-schooled or something, and I don't think my relationship with my mother could survive her trying to teach me, well, much of anything. She won't even try to teach me to drive. I wish I'd let Dad get me something for breakfast now. Something with a lot, and I mean a lot, of caffeine.

I have a new situation to obsess about now that I've gotten the locker thing under control. Hot tubs. I'm totally weirded out by the fact that Joe Football Player knew about the hot tub thing. How could he know? That was private. That was between me and him. And yet, since we were the only people there, he must've told someone.

First I think maybe he has run his mouth. It's very possible that he ran his mouth. Then I think, He doesn't talk to all that many people, definitely not any football guys.

My next thought is, But this is Allenville High School. If he told just one person, even innocently, even just mentioned it like I might've mentioned it to Raye, chances are good that everyone would know by now. But what if it wasn't innocent? What if somehow he's making a fool of me? More of a fool than I already am, I mean. God, I wish I had stayed in bed today. The flu, a nauseating virus that would have kept me sick and in bed, miserable and pathetic, wearing my pajamas and wishing for a quick death. Anything would be better than this.

I want to call my dad. He's not interviewing today. He could come and pick me up and take me home. We could watch daytime TV shows together and pretend he's not unemployed and I'm still his perfect daughter. But I'm not going to do it. Whatever people may think, I am not a doormat and I am not a wimp.

Who am I kidding? I've never stood up to Marion, and in my advanced lit class the Gruesome Twosome said awful things to me and all I did was pretend to be deaf. I like to think that eventually I would have stuck my deadly pencil into someone's scrotum. It was just that I generally use a mechanical pencil and I didn't think it would do enough damage. Plus, there were three of them making fun of me, which made it hard to decide who most deserved to get their balls impaled by a number two pencil. Yeah, that's why I didn't do anything. And, see, I've already told myself more than once, this ice-in-the-locker thing is the same sort of deal. Ignorable, really.

Like me. I nearly don't exist at this school, and that's okay. If I had brought attention to those guys teasing me I might have dropped to a lower level of the social hierarchy. I might have become a victim rather than a nonentity. That's why I try not to read Marion's blog. She's constantly bringing me up. People probably don't even know who she's talking about. I hope.

I'm walking down the hall, lost in my own thoughts, the same thoughts that swirl around in my head and keep me awake sometimes at night. They're all mixed up with straightforward anger. I'm a mess. When I hear a few skeezy girls whispering about me it jolts me out of the unpleasant thoughts and into my unpleasant reality. I hold my head high and make eye contact. Things like this make people think I'm stuck-up, in an ice princess sort of way, but how else am I supposed to deal with it?

In case you don't have skeezy girls at your school, skeezy girls are cheap. Not like Kandace Freemont. She's a certified whore who's been with every reasonably hot guy in the school (except for one, and I'm not going to speculate about that right now), but she is also desirable. I think I mentioned her enviable assets and her wavy chestnut hair? My guy might have a weakness for dark-haired girls. Anyway, these ladies are the type of girls who are only desirable for their willingness. Kinda ugly and kinda slutty, like fat girls wearing body glitter, you know? I don't usually have a problem with that type, but right now as I walk down the hall they're cackling and I hear one of them say something about doing it in a hot tub. I ignore them. If Raye were here she would say something to make them shut up. I walk fast and look right past them.

The next group to look me over is a group of ultra-popular girls lounging by the library. They make me feel awkward and a little bit tongue-tied. Plus, even though they're nice enough when I see them, they've never said "Hey, Parker, come to this party" or anything. If I were invited, I might go. Paige says that nobody sends you a damn invitation in high school, but I don't like to show up places without being asked—it makes me feel weird, awkward.

Sadie Collins, this major social butterfly, grabs my arm. "Damn, Prescott, I didn't know you had it in you."

"Had what in me?" I'm not dumb enough not to realize by this time that everyone knows about the hot tub, but why is this such a big deal? I guess it's because Marion is always calling me a stuck-up ice princess. I don't get why they care. See, the in-crowd makes me incapable of normal thought patterns. I know that technically they aren't any different than everyone else, but somehow, just like my perfect sister, they are.

"All I can say is way to go. Your boyfriend is totally hot." Camille Singleton elbows Zara Thorpe.

"Parker's pretty hot too. Did you have a good look at those pics?" Zara asks. Pictures? There are pictures? I am going to have a heart attack right here in front of the popular girls. I don't want to pass out in front of Zara Thorpe, she always makes me nervous anyway. She has this reputation.

Zara goes both ways. The guys totally dig it, and if you want to know the truth, she is incredibly hot. So hot I can't admit how I feel about her or even put it into words. I mean, it's attraction, but not sexual, not like I'm going lesbo or anything. She's just so comfortable with herself that everybody has to accept her. It's fascinating.

I look her straight in the eye. She has pretty eyes, but it's her mouth you notice. Okay, I look her in the eye, remind myself that I am too frozen to be intimidated by this girl who can do and say anything and not care what people think, and I ask,

"What pictures, Zara?" I can almost see myself throwing up in the middle of the hallway, right on Zara Thorpe's black shoes, that's how bad my stomach feels.

"Oh my God, you didn't know?" They are all staring at me, and I hear someone laugh, an ugly derisive laugh. I feel a sinking shame that I didn't know something, that I wasn't aware of something I should have been aware of. This is stupid, but it's how I am. "Oh, Parker, you have to see them! They are so totally hot," Zara continues, and when she smiles at me, I have to relent and smile back just a little, no matter how bad I feel.

"Let me guess, Marion Henessy?" I say. She nods, and the other girls laugh again.

"You're lucky, Parker. That one shot she got of Amanda, she looks like she's picking her nose." They all laugh again.

"I was totally scratching it," Amanda says, untroubled. She's kind of the jester of the popular girls, the funny one.

"Anyway, at least they look good. You should check them out."

"I will." The realization hits me, like the sun coming out from behind a cloud. It wasn't him. He didn't tell. No matter how bad things are, there is still that. I stand there thinking about it and they watch me. They're waiting for me to move on. I guess I've stayed beyond my welcome.

"Your boyfriend's already in the lunchroom," Cecelia Danly says. I start to correct her—ex. Ex-boyfriend. But what's the point? Cecelia Danly was the first person who ever told me (this was in kindergarten) that my initials were the same as what people do in the potty.

He's in the cafeteria. Everybody in school has seen pictures of us together. I feel light-headed and I know suddenly that I can't go in there right now.

I turn around and head back the way I came, past the giggling socialites and the glaring skeezers, past the skateboarders who are wearing black eyeliner and who mutter a few suggestive things, nothing over-the-top because there's a teacher coming down the hall from the other direction.

The guy who helped me earlier is long gone, probably sitting in advanced rocket science class or something.

"Has Rachel Tannahill signed in to school yet?" I ask the receptionist.

She looks into the red pleather-covered ledger and shakes her head. "Sorry, hon, no Rachel Tannahill."

"Okay, thanks." This receptionist cannot possibly know how much I need my best friend right now. Without her I am alone in this terrible awful place where I am forced to come and be tormented five days a week. On top of that, I'm not going to have time to eat lunch. Good thing I have absolutely no appetite.

As I leave the office I nearly collide with Kyle Henessy. I haven't seen him in a couple of months, unless you count when he drives by our house, but when that happens I never see his face, just his car and his hunched-over sinister silhouette. Kyle the stalker is wearing this stupid Hawaiian-looking shirt that makes me remember that cruise to the Bahamas, the last trip our families took together. I remember how Marion followed Kyle around making sure he had enough sunscreen, and how, even though he was only thirteen and Paige was twelve, he kept taking the sunscreen from his sister and trying to get Paige to let him rub it all over her. My parents kept whispering to each other about it, and I was listening to them, which is why I remember it so clearly.

"What're you doing here?" I blurt out.

"Hey, Parker." He isn't as geeky as I remember. His body has kind of caught up to his height, and he doesn't have any noticeable acne. Plus, his hair is clean and looks almost blond. When he was stalking Paige, and always lurking around our first-floor windows, his hair usually looked unwashed and kind of dismally brown. I'm shocked. He almost looks cute.

"Um, hi," I say, unsure how to proceed.

"You look a little more like Paige than you used to." High praise from Kyle Henessy, though a little creepy, I realize that. His voice isn't all creaky and broken anymore, and besides the shirt with the great big flowers, he looks normal. Right now Kyle is violating the restraining order (he isn't supposed to be within fifty feet of *any* members of my family), but I don't say anything about it. Not because I want to be near him, exactly, but because it's kind of unfair since he couldn't know I would be in the office. He's holding a red Allenville band sweatshirt I presume he is dropping off for Marion. Poor baby must be cold. You'd think their mom would do it, but no. She probably called Kyle at work and he rushed right over to help his precious little sister out. They're so protective of each other it's sickening.

There isn't anywhere else to go, so I head back to the cafeteria. I am resigned. Raye is not here and there is no one to help me, and nowhere to hide. I can't stay in the office, not with Marion on the way, so I trudge slowly down the hall.

I imagine that it will go silent when I enter through the double doors and walk down the ramp, but everything goes on as it was. Conversations surge, girls laugh, forks chink against unidentified objects buried deep in the meat loaf.

In fact, he doesn't even see me as I walk up behind him. He's sitting at the end of one of the long rectangular tables with Jeremy Tenant, this incredibly animated actor guy who is pretty nice-looking. They're feeding one another lines from Monty Python, which they recite in phony British accents followed by roars of laughter. Their own laughter. Nobody else is listening or laughing.

"Um, hi, Jeremy," I say.

"Hey, Parker." Jeremy stands up so that I can have his seat. "Look, I've gotta stop by the auditorium for a fitting—the costumes for *Macbeth* are in. I'll see you guys later."

"Did I run him off?" I would kind of like to be cool enough to hang out with Jeremy Tenant. On the other hand, I need some undivided attention. I need him to focus on me. Yeah, I'm glad Jeremy is gone.

"Nah, he's been talking about those costumes all day."

I sit down and stare at him. I can't help it. My stomach feels weird. I'm getting sick of being jittery and nervous all the time, but my day has been bad. I need him.

"Can you move a little closer?" He has his hand on the small of my back and is pulling me into the area between his legs so that I'll be pressed against him. I put my hand against his chest. This is the stuff I didn't like, before we broke up, the public stuff.

"Look, I don't think you have to prove anything about us to anybody today."

"You saw the pictures?" he asks. He rubs my leg with his thumb. He isn't even looking at me. I can't believe this. Did he know that there were pictures of us online, and he didn't even send a crappy e-mail?

"You saw them? Whatever everybody's talking about?"

"Last night."

He's so calm. I pull myself away from him, just a little bit, so he knows I'm upset.

"Who took them?"

"I wish I knew. It's bizarre, thinking somebody was watching us."

"Yeah."

"Don't worry about it too much, Parker. I'm sure it was just some freak job with a digital camera."

"Too many of those around here." I clench my teeth, think about Kyle and how he got caught in a tree outside Paige's window and how my parents were so completely freaked out that they called the police.

"Yeah. Aren't you going to eat?" He hands me a Reese's cup. I nibble the edges off, all the way around. He thinks the way I eat is funny.

"Don't say anything." I give him the look. I feel almost comfortable beside him, and yet I am on edge. The good feeling is just masking all the turmoil underneath that I don't want to acknowledge. I try to focus on being happy.

"I won't say a word. I wouldn't dare." He's teasing me, but in that cute way he has. I smile and look into his eyes, trying to make things right between us with the force of my will.

Right now things are weird when we're together. Comfortable and uncomfortable at the same time. I think he's too sure of me. That's why I broke up with him in the first place.

The sureness. If I were equally sure of him it would be different. Like he knows that when he calls I'm going to grab the phone and be all breathless, and that if he asks me to do something I'm going to do it. Breaking up with him was the only way to surprise him, and it did, the look on his face was priceless. But it didn't really stick, I guess.

We have advanced British lit after lunch. When the bell rings we stand up and walk side by side. "Hey, what happened to your books?"

"Don't ask."

"You think we'll have to write that essay today?"

"I'm sure of it." Before the break we were supposed to write this major essay comparing Romantic poets with rap music, but then school got called off for two inches of snow. So, major essay, here we come. Too bad I know less about rap music than I do about Romantic poets. Middle-aged teachers who try to act hip are so incredibly lame.

20

It's a strange situation, deciding where to sit in class now that we are kind of tentatively back together. I mean, do I move to the back of the room, or do I stay in the middle? Why doesn't he move to be with me? If I move, do I sit where I have a good view of him? Or do I allow him the view of me? Are the other students watching me? Are they even slightly aware of the things passing through my head, or am I crazy?

The questions just keep coming. Do I sit to his right or to his left? Should I try to pass notes to him? Of course I don't pass him lame little notes. I sit two seats behind where I used to sit, before we started talking in the first place. He's in the very back, I'm one row ahead and to the left diagonally. I rarely look at him, not even when I'm sitting in class, but all I can think about is him.

This is the last class of the day, and I am so ready to get out of here, but it's a long class. We're on a block schedule, which means I may actually die of old age before I get out of here, and the hands on the clock above the whiteboard are barely moving. The Gruesome Twosome are totally smirking at me. I guess they saw the pictures too. I don't want to think of them looking at me, and I think maybe he feels the same way. Out of the corner of my eye I see him frown. He kind of shifts in his desk, and I can tell he's annoyed by their smirks. Since we've been dating, they haven't even looked my way. The little freakazoid is staring down at his desk now. I'm aware, like I've got some kind of radar to tell who's looking at me and who's not. If I could just get that focused on the lesson. I glance at the little weird kid. Maybe he's just keeping his head down because he has a black eye and a busted lip. Who knows how he got beat up, but he had it coming.

The essay is a piece of cake, even though I don't have my notes. Even though my neat outline of everything Ms. White had to say about the Romantic poets is now a dripping mound at the bottom of the Dumpster outside the office. She writes her prompt on the board and sets a timer, and I tune out all the tension around me, forget about the other students in the classroom, and start to write. I turn the paper in just before the dismissal bell rings. I can feel the evil twins checking me out from behind. I step out into the hallway, relieved to get away.

My purse is making little buzzing noises. We're supposed to keep our cell phones in our lockers, but that wasn't an option today with the slush and all. I fumble for my phone. Finally, Raye calling me. My mom gave it back this morning so I can get in touch with her if I have an emergency—the whole reason they bought me the phone in the first place, in case the school blows up or something.

"Hello?" As I speak I turn and search the hallway for him. Is he still in the classroom? I stop and wait, just in case.

"Hey, Park, I didn't make it to school today." Like I hadn't noticed. Raye's voice is all scratchy, like her nose is stopped up. "But I can take you home. Want to meet me at Arby's?" The Arby's is right next to the school. Big sigh of relief. I had been toying with the idea of asking him to drive me home, but now I can't even locate him.

"Sure." I have to move on. This tall girl is glaring at me. I guess I'm standing in front of her locker. I look over my shoulder and then start to move my feet. Defeated. You would think after the afternoon, the walking together and the glances, that he would take the time to say goodbye. I swing my purse over my shoulder and lug my new stack of old books with me, out the side door and toward the sidewalk that leads directly to Arby's. I wish Raye were here to walk with me; I always feel self-conscious walking alone. I have to go all the way across the school parking lot to where the sidewalk begins and then across the Arby's lot.

She's hiding behind a big roast beef sandwich dripping with bright yellow cheese. "What happened to you?"

"God, Parker you have to get ungrounded. Not having anyone to talk to is ruining my life." This is good, I like being irreplaceable and important. Not good that she feels her life is going to hell, but really, this happens to Raye periodically, and with my help, she deals with it.

"Maybe you can tell my parents that." I sit down. Dad isn't really aware of little details like when I'm supposed to get home from school, but if Mom asks him what time I arrived and they realize I didn't come straight home, well, that could extend the grounding. I push the fear of further punishment out of my head and focus on Raye. "So you broke up with Josh?"

"We'd only been on four dates. I wouldn't call it an official breakup." She looks down. I think she's being too casual about this, and that means something.

"Then why did you sit in your car and cry?"

"Ian e-mailed me last night." Okay, first there was the e-mail. Then she cried and left the lights on. I wonder suddenly how she got her car started after she called to tell me the battery was dead this morning. Raye puts the sandwich down on the shiny foil it was originally wrapped in and reaches for her drink. She isn't looking at me, which I think is a bad sign.

"Really?" I pick up one of her curly fries.

"Yeah. He just wrote about all this personal stuff. It reminded me of the old days. I miss him." She wrinkles her nose. Some other emotion is hiding under her carefully blank expression. Hope? Is she getting back together with the magnificent Ian?

"He started your car today. With jumper cables or whatever." It's a guess, but her eyebrows fly up and almost hit the spiky fringe of her dark hair.

"He had jumper cables."

"So do lots of people." I say this softly so it doesn't sound so confrontational.

"Afterwards we talked. It was good. He went to school. I couldn't."

"You can't be serious?" I'm testing her a little bit, she's been so staunchly anti-Ian for so long. I need to be careful. I can't blast him if she thinks she loves him.

"I said I miss him, not that I want you to be a bridesmaid at our wedding!"

"I know you too well, Raye. I know what the look on your face means," I say.

"He'd have to come back on bended knee and kiss my feet and apologize."

I hear what she's saying, but what I'm picturing is totally different.

"Even that wouldn't be enough, even kissing your feet, not after what he did to you." Instead of Ian, I'm imagining my ex on bended knee. It's kind of enticing, and I can see why she's in dreamland with this prospect.

"At least I'm not doing Kandace Freemont leftovers." That one gets me. I mean, the shock of an attack like that from Raye. My eyes start to water.

"Hey, I'm sorry. I didn't mean it the way it sounded." She backpedals. Now it's her turn to be careful. She reaches out and puts her hand on my arm. Sometimes Raye can get overly defensive about the whole Ian situation, but I know pretty much exactly how she feels, so I'm not really mad about it.

I don't want her to think I'm crying because she snapped at me. Raye can be pretty snappy. It's just part of who she is. You accept it, or you get scorned and made fun of.

"It's been a rough day," I tell her. I didn't want to talk about today before I had a chance to work things out, but I need Raye firmly in my court and not doing that "you're my best friend so I can take my crap out on you" routine. So I tell her everything about the locker and the ice and the pictures. She takes a second to digest my information, and possibly her sandwich as well.

"Oh my God, Parker."

"You haven't been on the bitch blog? You haven't seen or heard anything?" I ask. Raye checks these things more frequently than I do.

"Of course not, I would have told you. I've been on the move all day, hiding from Mom and Dad. I just couldn't stand to see Kara after some of the things Ian told me. And this morning I needed to think." Kara Bennington is the girl Ian broke up with Raye for, and she's in Raye's chemistry, algebra 2, and English classes. Nice, huh?

"I need to get home before my dad gets suspicious." I check my watch. I've sat here way longer than I planned. "Come on, Raye." I'm starting to get nervous. I hate having to go home almost as much as I hate the thought of my dad frowning and looking away whenever he sees me. I feel trapped between life and my life, if that makes sense.

"You don't want a sandwich or something?"

I don't want to tell Raye that I don't have any money. I mean, she will insist on buying me something, and I owe her from the last three times we went out.

So I lie. "My size-fours are a little snug right now." She laughs, stands, and gives herself a little shake.

"Nothing to be ashamed of about a size six," she says, angling her cup to get the last of the Diet Pepsi out.

"I figured I'd move up to a five first." We both stand and she carries her tray to the garbage can. I didn't think she'd heard me, but she turns and says,

"The Limited doesn't make jeans in size five." I love the Limited's basic jeans and that Raye knows me so well.

"I might shop someplace else."

"Fat chance of that!" Raye laughs and I join her. Yes, I am predictable. It feels good to just be me in my classic-cut jeans and not worry about things for a minute, like whether she'll realize I'm a total loser and drop me for cooler friends. I feel like an imposter sometimes when we're laughing and I'm pretending to be spontaneous. I try to be careful with my friendships. It seems sometimes like friendship can be a fragile thing. I've been dropped before, by Marion when we were neighbors, by the popular girls in middle school. No matter how dumb it is, those things still hurt when I let myself think about them.

Sometimes I wonder whether Raye'll get so wrapped up in Ian love that I'll drop off her radar. She pulls into my driveway and I gather up the crusty dusty books and manage to hit my elbow really hard on the door of her car. My eyes start watering all over again as I stumble out of the car and up the sidewalk.

Dad is in the living room and he calls my name but I pretend I don't hear him and head straight for the computer. I pull up the Social Siren and take a look.

The pictures are black-and-white, which is weird. Like some artsy photographer was traipsing around the neighborhood snapping shots. I know that's not the case, because the pictures are digital and black-and-white is just one of the options on a digital camera. Still, it's a weird choice.

Is it wrong that the first thing I notice is that I look really good? Zara was right. Those painful crunches I do every night before I go to bed have paid off. The first shot is when I pulled him back into the water with me. He's kind of leaning back, and my body is on top of his. I might as well be totally naked since someone (probably Marion) has put little black squares over the really private parts. This makes it look like I am hot-tubbing naked with him, and Marion, out of the goodness of her heart, covered me up. Even if you know to look for them, you can barely see my bra straps in the first shot, but nobody's going to notice something like that anyway. People usually think the worst.

The second shot is the one that makes me stop breathing. It's of the two of us, wrapped in his towel. In the black-and-white shot the towel is unbelievably white. You can't see my face because I'm looking down, but you can see his. I don't know how to describe it, the look. Yearning. His cheek is resting against my hair, and the look is almost painful. How could anyone look at this and think we had sex?

If he ever once looks straight at me with that expression, I will do anything for him. Anything.

There's no mention on Marion's blog of me or any pranks involving ice. Of course, I knew Marion wouldn't post anything for Mr. Dawson to pounce on. She may be evil, but she isn't stupid. The ice incident is probably destined to remain unsolved. And the pictures? I sigh. I miss the days when my life was uncomplicated.

I go downstairs for a snack and to find Daddy. He's on his cell phone, but he hangs up as soon as I come into the living room.

"How was school today?" he asks.

"Fine." I know my dad really cares, but how could I even hope to begin explaining the Ice Princess thing to him? It just isn't going to happen. Plus, I don't want him to think that I'm unhappy or a reject or anything. He needs to think I'm happy.

"Theresa is going to show the house to a couple tomorrow." Kick in the gut. A couple possibly buying our house. This is a family house. This is my family's house.

"If they buy it, where will we move?"

"I don't know. There are some new houses going up across town, some new developments. Your mother and I are going to look at some places next weekend."

New development. I know what that means—no yard, no trees. House the size of a postcard. Raye and her mom and her little brother, Flint, lived in one of those until her mom got remarried. It was fine for them, but they didn't have Preston. My brother could make a mansion feel like a confined space, what with the running and the jumping and the yelling.

"Will I still go to Allenville?" My voice sounds panicky and I take a deep gulpy breath. There's no way I can handle a new school, don't they know that? Even with the stuff that's been happening, the fear of starting over is enough to paralyze me. I don't do well with change.

"Of course. Allenville High is a magnet school, and your grades are outstanding. You'll be able to go there no matter where we live." If I can get a ride. Will Raye drive to some crappy place across town to get me? She can barely make it to school on time as it is.

"In that case, I guess I'd better go work on this history paper if I want to keep my grades up." I make my voice cheerful.

Dad laughs, even though what I said wasn't funny. "I'm so proud of your grades, Parker. You're so focused, like your mother."

I go over to him and press my cheek against his. I should kiss him—a year ago, even a few months ago, I would have—but it feels weird now. I feel weird, almost afraid. I liked being his little girl, but I pretty much screwed that up, didn't I?

I feel bad because Dad looks so out of place sitting at home on a weekday, wearing his khakis that don't ever really fit him correctly. He's just sitting on the couch, not even watching TV or anything.

I really do have this paper to write about the Byzantine Empire. It isn't due until next week, but it isn't like I have a happening social life these days. All I have is a Dell.

Just out of curiosity, I hit my bookmark for Marion's blog. Okay, it isn't just curiosity. I want to see that picture again. His face. I want to live in that moment for the rest of my life. I think I'll print a hard copy for myself.

But the pictures aren't on the front page anymore. There's a new headline. *Allenville boy collects $1,000 prize along with frigid girl's virginity*. I say a really bad word. I say more really, really filthy words. I try to convince myself as I scroll down, my hand shaking just a little, that Marion's use of the word *frigid* is coincidence, that she isn't talking about me. But I don't convince myself of anything.

The Social Siren by Marion Henessy
What kind of a guy would date a girl only to collect a one-thousand-dollar prize for "de-flowering" her?

(I hope Marion knows *deflowering* does not need a hyphen and shouldn't be in quotation marks.)

There were some Allenville students who wondered what anyone would see in Parker Prescott. Apparently, a payday. It seems a group of guys got together and put up a one-thousand-dollar prize for the winner, the first one to get into her pants. Prize money was collected today, mostly in one-dollar bills.

She obviously just posted this. There are only three replies.

Anonymous says: I knew a hottie like him wouldn't go for her! Think he'll want Kandace back now?
UbErKyLe says: Marion we need to talk.

Yeah, that's cool, they send messages to one another on a blog when they live in the same freaking house.

Anonumoose says: he has plenty of money why would he do something like that for money?
Marion says: I doubt it was about the money. More a bragging thing. Poor, poor Parker. She thought he really liked her.

I want to punch the computer, to hurl it across the room, to smash it into a pile of twisted cords and black plastic and whatever wires and gizmos make up the insides of a computer.

I know it isn't true, of course. It couldn't be true. It's crazy Marion bullshit. But I don't feel alive anymore.

I lie down on my bed, stare up at the ceiling, and try to think of a way to get back at Marion Henessy. And I try to think of a way to figure out that it definitely, for sure, isn't true without looking like an idiot. Like more of an idiot. There is just no way.

22

"People are going to believe it," Raye says.

It's Tuesday morning, second period. I feel sick and totally dejected. No way, I keep thinking. No way no way no way no way. No one in their right mind will believe he went out with me because of some bet. No way. And yet this is just sick enough for Marion to have orchestrated it. I know it's not true. That didn't keep me from having a dream where Marion was handing him one of those enormous checks, the ones you see when someone wins the lottery or whatever, checks the size of a small school bus, while Kandace watched and clapped her hands.

We're in the library in front of one of the nice computers that the school got through a grant. At least, that's what it says on the little plaque above Raye's head. She and I e-mailed back and forth about the situation all last night. I never heard from him, though I watched my in-box and checked four times to make sure my cell was on Ring and not Vibrate, that I hadn't missed a call. Even if he didn't want to call my house and he didn't realize I had gotten my cell phone back, how hard would it be to send me a message?

After all that stress the only thing Raye and I came up with seems to be that some people are going to believe it.

"Some people always will. They believe all the ugly rumors. Do we really care about them?" I ask. She's always saying we shouldn't give a crap what anybody thinks, and yet right now she seems to care very much.

I want to tell her that I've been thinking about nervous breakdowns lately. Will that sound insanely melodramatic? It's just too much, too many things at once. I want to drop out of the world and sit in a padded room and let life pass me by for a few days. Of course, that's kind of what happened to me when I was grounded. And the bad things just kept coming.

1. The discussion on the blog about him and Kandace, like I needed to read any of that.
2. The melty ice in my locker.
3. Some weirdo took pictures of me and him.
4. And now this insane thing about a bet.

I know who my enemy is, but I don't know what to do about her, and here Raye is telling me that all the idiots who read Marion's blog have opinions that matter. I really don't need this right now.

So I got an e-mail from Kyle Henessy last night, but it got overshadowed by the other crap that's messing up my life. Plus, it was very disappointing, and I'm trying not to think about what a dumbass I am to even try something so pathetically lame. The short version is that Kyle isn't biting. No selling pictures of Paige in a bikini. No convincing him to sabotage (or just stop maintaining) his sister's evil Parker-destroying blog. I need to make an alternate plan, but I don't have any great ideas.

"You have to look at them for the next year and a half." Raye is talking. I try to focus. She's talking about our fellow students and their vile thoughts and opinions that I have to consider all of a sudden. Because they matter or something. "And most everybody in school thinks they've seen you next to naked now." I told her about the bra. I mean, you could see the straps if you looked close enough. "At least you looked good." She gives me a look that's almost dirty. "What's with the sculpted abs, Parker?"

"I've been getting ready."

"For?"

This is embarrassing, especially now.

"Him."

Raye maximizes the picture. "Looks like you're ready. Seriously, Park, what are you waiting for?"

"I don't want to tell you."

This is the part where I expect Raye to laugh at me, where I will respond by laughing at myself. But no one laughs. I do not want to talk with her about this. It's the thing that's been bouncing around in my mind since our very first date. The hope that I don't want to jeopardize by saying it out loud.

"Look, I know you two are totally back together, I know you are going to do this with him eventually. I just want to know what the holdup is."

I study my hands. Wish we could still afford to go every

week and get our nails done. I mean, I wish *I* could still afford to get my nails done. I love having unbelievably smooth nails in any color I want. I love tapping my nails against things with that neat little *click, click, click.*

"I'm waiting for him to say he loves me," I say more quietly than I expect.

Raye just looks at me levelly, over the can of Diet Mountain Dew that she isn't supposed to have open in the library.

"He hasn't said it yet?"

"No. . . ." It comes out as a whisper. Does she think that he would have, is she surprised? Am I a loser for hanging around this long waiting for some declaration from him?

"Damn. Ian told me he loved me on our third date. Right before we, well . . ." The bell rings. Not having a social life outside of school royally sucks. Of course, we didn't talk about this stuff that much before I got grounded either. Because Raye is smart enough to know that on the third date, right before whatever, he couldn't have meant it. But then, she was with Ian a long time. There must've been something there. At least she didn't feel she had to push him away. At least she was absolutely sure of what she wanted.

Here's a question for your secret diary. You know, the one with the flimsy little key. Is it better for him to lie or to not say it at all?

I want to see him and I don't want to see him. I hate school. I hate the hallway, and the lights and the noise.

He catches me between third and fourth periods. *Catches* is the exact right word, because once I see him it's like invisible ropes are holding me in place and invisible butterflies are devouring my guts. For some reason that's what I thought when I was little; I didn't understand that the fluttering of nerves was what people referred to as butterflies. I always pictured them feasting on my insides.

"Parker!" Does his voice sound weird? A little higher-pitched than usual? "Parker, why didn't you call me last night?"

"I'm grounded, remember?" He can't put this on me. He should've called. He should've sent me a message. He didn't. I'm mad and really uncomfortable. We're standing right in front of the double doors to the gym, and people are watching us as they walk past. I hold my books against my chest. Even while the anger courses through me, more than anything, I want him to make it all better.

He reaches toward me, like I'm really far away instead of right here. He pushes my hair back from my face. It's a small gesture, but intimate. I hear someone laugh behind us.

"Parker, there's no way you can believe, there's no way you could possibly think that I would . . ." The look on his face is tragic, and a little bit of my anger melts away, but not enough. There's hurt and anger and some sort of stupid shame that I don't think should be there inside me but won't go away.

"You were pretty clear from the beginning that you were planning on thawing the Ice Princess." My stomach sinks. Did I really say that out loud? When I was trying to go to sleep last night I imagined this conversation at least thirty-seven times. I never, ever thought I would confront him like this.

"And I haven't, have I?" He's standing too close to me, and his voice is a growl. I shiver at the sound of it. More of the anger dissolves. I need him. There's no way that I'm going to lose the possibility of us, lose whatever we have together, over some bullshit Marion thought up, probably just to keep us apart. I remind myself that I never really thought it was true anyway. I can't stay mad at him over suspicions that bubbled up after some stupid nightmare, not when he's standing right in front of me. I look up at him. He's only a little bit taller than me. I wish I had big brown puppy dog eyes that could tell him how vulnerable I am right now and make him forget that I sounded totally bitchy a few seconds ago.

I guess my Siberian husky eyes do the trick, because he puts his hand on my waist and pulls me just a little bit closer. His voice is still that low sexy growl, right in my ear.

"I'm gonna stick by you and hold your hand and break every school PDA rule every time I can so that everyone sees what bullshit that story is."

"I want to go back to being invisible," I say in a tiny sad voice that I immediately despise.

He puts his arm around me. "Do you see any teachers?" I look over his shoulder.

"No." He kisses me. There is no kissing allowed at Allenville, no fondling, no making out, no hand holding, even. The touch of his lips makes my toes curl in my black lace-up Doc Martens. I hate public displays of affection, or I used to. But with him here, I just don't care about little things like privacy anymore.

"So is there a bet?" I ask when I can breathe again. I can't help myself. The bell rings.

"Shit, I'm late. I'll talk to you later, okay?" He squeezes my arm and heads off. I sigh and watch him go. Why didn't he answer the question? Because he was late to class, or because there really is some kind of bet about me?

☙ ☙ ☙

When I get home, I sit at my desk and read the thirty-eight responses to Marion's poisoned pen. This is what I type. *Marion is hoping that the sort of contest she writes about here will catch on, then maybe someone will make a $20.00 bet* *and some sucker will try to get into her size 12 jeans.* I read over it twice and then slowly backspace over it. Who am I to point out that Marion has big thighs? Who am I to talk about virginity?

Besides, if I did post something, Marion would just delete it.

I think about all the ways Marion has been pulling my strings lately. She thinks she has a Parker puppet. I can feel her trying to make me dance to her tune. I had a little bit of pity for her before, but now she's just starting to piss me off.

23

Friday afternoon, three days later, my mom reluctantly says I can go to the library to work on the report about the Byzantine Empire. Raye picks me up.

"So you want to drop by and pretend you need to borrow his graphing calculator just so you can see what he's up to on a Friday night?" she asks. She's suggesting, without actually saying the words, that I'm a loser.

"Raye. I need that calculator."

"Parker, I have a graphing calculator at home. All you had to do was give me a call."

"Why do you have a graphing calculator? You aren't even in advanced math."

"Algebra two is advanced enough." Raye jerks the steering

wheel like she's totally annoyed with either me or the car. I'm betting on me. "You know that needing to drop in to check on a guy you aren't even technically going out with is borderline pathetic, right?"

"Right." I ignore Raye's tone because I don't want to think about what she's saying. "Raye, he makes me happy. Isn't that a good thing?"

"You don't seem very happy right now." Raye clenches the steering wheel. "Do you want some gum?"

"No, Raye," I sigh. She pulls into his driveway and stops to apply some pink lip gloss. She doesn't say anything, but I know there's no way she's going to sit in the car and wait for me.

I knock at the side door to the basement, like I always do, and after a few minutes, he comes to the door, halfway dressed and muttering something, like he always does. He has the phone pressed up against his ear. I follow him inside and Raye follows me.

"Look, I'll call you back later. Parker's here. Yeah, Parker. No." He hangs up without saying goodbye. He gives the phone his pissed-exasperated look. I know, suddenly, without a doubt, that he was talking to Kandace Freemont. I hesitate for a second. I could ask to use his phone and check the caller ID. But he will totally know what I'm doing because he—well, he just will. Raye will know too. And anyway, I don't need to look at the phone, because I know who he was talking to.

Still, I could figure out whether he called her or she called him. That makes a huge difference. My chest feels all tight again.

"Um, the calculator," I say in a small voice. I called him on the way here. He knows why I am, allegedly, here. Even in the dimness of his technologically advanced cybercave, I can see Raye rolling her eyes.

He goes to his desk and grabs the calculator, slides the cover onto it, and then offers it to me. Is this it? He's going to hand it to me and then we'll just leave? I feel my face getting warm.

Then he says, "Do you have to go right now? Do you want something to drink? I have Dr Pepper." He gestures at the minifridge that his mom keeps stocked for him.

"Sure," I say. Anything to get this visit back in the universe of normal.

"Oh my God," Raye says. "Is that my brother's lava lamp? The one he was going to throw away?"

I sink into the floor and disappear from sight. Um, no, that's just what I wish I could do. It's one of those weird melty goo lamps that they sell in the novelty store at the mall. I knew when I took it that it would be perfect for his room, it's totally retro, and I love the dark purple color. But even as I open my mouth to explain, the reality that I didn't have any money to buy him a Christmas present hits me, and I'm just floored.

Yeah, floored. I just figured out what that expression means. It means too heavy to pick yourself up off the carpet. Flattened. All the lame people say that with gifts it's the thought that counts, but it isn't true, not when you're taking something that your best friend's little brother was planning to throw away. And then you go and put it in a gift bag with Rudolph on it and give it to your boyfriend who went to boarding school and drives a Saab.

I can't look at either of them, and I can't think of anything to say.

"Parker, really, you need to cash that check that's in your

jewelry box. I don't understand why you're going around not even being able to buy . . ." I see her frustrated gesture, she can't think of anything specific to use as an example. That's how it is when you've been best friends with someone this long. You know what she is saying with her hands when she isn't saying anything aloud at all. "We go to the mall and you follow me around and say 'That would look great on you, that would look great on you,' and you never even buy your own cookies."

I look at my scuffed black Doc Martens that I bought because they remind me of his sexy scuffed black shoes, only smaller and cuter. I look down and imagine that I will never be able to look him in the face again. I am completely humiliated.

Raye gets it, she has put together that I gave him her brother's discarded lamp, but she doesn't *get* it. She just keeps talking. That's Raye's way of dealing with the world.

"I mean, if you didn't have any money, it would be different, Park, but you have that check. Your parents wouldn't have given it to you if they didn't want you to have it. They're probably waiting until you cash that to offer to give you more." Raye shakes her head, like I'm some kind of evolutionary riddle. She knows how bank accounts work, that you have to have money in the account before you can write checks, but she can't fathom writing a check that you don't have the funds to cover. She doesn't know that I unplugged the night-light in my bathroom to save electricity, and that every night when I set my pink and silver alarm clock I worry that the numbers won't be illuminated in the morning, that the entire house will be powerless and dark.

I am totally unable to think of a way to shut Raye up or to make this look normal, or to ignore it. I stare down.

There is a glossy travel brochure sitting on his desk. I pick it up. He takes it from my hand and clears his throat. I could be wrong, but I think he's trying to shift the focus too. He knows what's going through my head.

"My parents are planning this big trip for spring break. Scuba diving or something. I told them I thought I might have other plans, that I might stay here." I don't know what he's expecting of me. There are about a million things in his eyes, and I don't know how to react to any of them.

"We need to get to the library." My voice sounds stiff. Emotionless.

"Parker." Raye is aware now. She doesn't understand why I'm so upset, but she knows I am and is worried.

She walks toward the door.

"I'll take that Dr Pepper," I say. My voice sounds close to normal—I mean, asking-for-a-drink normal.

"I had my mom buy them because I know that's what you like," he says. I honestly prefer Pepsi, but I don't say anything. I look up to see why he's still standing by the desk and not heading to the minifridge. He reaches out and squeezes my arm. Raye is opening the basement door and looking outside, giving us a bit of privacy.

"I like the lamp," he says. I know, in that instant, that even if he talks to Kandace Freemont on the phone every night from five p.m. until seven-fifteen, I will love him forever.

There is a resigned comfort in the hopelessness of it. I recognize the fact that I no longer have control over myself. I love him, even if he will never say it back to me. Even if there is some crazy bet concerning my virginity like Marion reported? I can't even think about that. I take the drink and follow Raye, though all I really want to do is stay here and stare at him until my eyes fall out of my head. Usually I don't like feeling out of control, but I could get used to this, it's almost addictive.

Raye walks outside ahead of me. He takes my hand and squeezes it, but we don't kiss. I gesture toward Raye, outside, and he gives a little nod, and I pull myself away and walk out. I want to kiss him, but I don't want to take that step back into the relationship with Raye outside the screen door rolling her eyes. I step out and he closes the door. I imagine he's already on his computer before we take our first steps back toward Raye's car.

His neighbor's dog is barking like crazy.

"I guess they're back from vacation," I say, thinking out loud.

"What?"

"Nothing." She looks at me. She doesn't like that sort of response. "The neighbors, I guess they're back. It was . . ." I stop and look across the yard at the dog, who is throwing himself against the fence. "It was their hot tub."

Raye starts to laugh, loud, like she can't stop herself. "Look, Park, I'm sorry, I really am. Half the girls at our school would kill to be you right now, but it still sucks, you know?" She stops laughing and I can tell by her expression that her thoughts have gone serious. "Do you want to talk about this money thing?" I do not want to talk about this money thing, but before I have to force out a reply, Raye says, "Oh. My. God." With even more emphasis than when she saw the lava lamp.

"What? What, Raye?"

"Look who just came out of Erin Glasgow's house!" I peek around her and there in the driveway, getting into a gray Ford Explorer, is Kyle Henessy. "What the crap is he doing there?"

I seriously doubt I've run into Kyle two times in the last year, and now I've seen him twice this week. We just stand there and watch as he waves toward the house and drives away.

"It wasn't a break-in or he wouldn't have been waving," I say.

"Parker, your deduction skills are astounding. C'mon, we have to go see what's up." She pulls me behind her across the neighboring lawn and up the front steps. We ring the doorbell.

Erin answers the door. She is one of those cute petite girls, though, sadly, not one of the ones with short stocky legs, as I know since he has a direct view of her pool from his upstairs bathroom window.

"Hi, Erin." Raye has this way of acting like she knows everybody, even if it's just from seeing them twice between classes. I, on the other hand, always wait to see if the other person has any idea who I am and might choose to acknowledge me before I feel comfortable calling them by name, or saying anything at all. "We just saw Kyle Henessy leaving and we were wondering what he was doing here." Raye also likes to get straight to the point.

"He's tutoring me for my ACTs," Erin says. "What're you guys doing here?"

Raye ignores this perfectly good question and pushes on. "Do you have a view of your neighbors' hot tub from your house?"

"Yeah. Why?"

"Case closed," Raye says to me. To Erin she says, "C'mon, Erin, you go to Allenville. Don't tell me you haven't looked at your tutor's little sister's blog lately?"

"No. I haven't." We just stand there and look at her stupidly. "My little brother demolished my hard drive. He was downloading porn or something. I should get it back next week. Why? Is there something about me on that stupid blog?"

"No . . . just some pictures taken from one of your windows. Um, I guess we'll see you around."

I want to say something nice to Erin, something to make our visit seem a little less rude, but I can't think of anything. I'm speechless and Raye is dragging me away. "I didn't even know Erin had a brother."

"Maybe it's some kind of elaborate lie. Maybe she's got some kind of thing going with Kyle Henessy." Yeah, right. Like she would go anywhere with him. She's hot, and he's a geek.

"Raye, are we really going to the library?"

"Yep. We gotta find everything we can about the Byzantines." Raye has her driving face on, which means she doesn't want to talk.

When we get to the library I'm not surprised to see Ian Sanders sitting at a computer pretending to do some kind of intense and intellectual work. Something so important that he just closes out of it when he sees us coming through the door. Raye obviously told the cheating bastard to meet us here. I wish desperately that I had someone meeting me in the library and, since that is not the case, that Ian would go away.

Ian is a genuine blond. I'm not saying he's stupid. I'm saying he has this golden hair, like a halo. Some of the basketball players dyed their hair blond last year, but they couldn't achieve the same look. Natural, golden, gorgeous blond. I don't like Ian. He doesn't look right with Raye either. He looks all cute and boy-next-door, and she's wearing big earrings and green eye shadow today. No wonder he doesn't appreciate her.

Raye sits at the computer next to him, and they start whispering to one another. I don't use a computer. The library ones all have information filters. You can't get to anything good. In my school notebook, I flip one page past the boring notes on the Eastern Orthodox Church and make a note.

Figure out how to make a bunch of money.

Make Marion Henessy Pay.

My plan to get Kyle to do something about Marion's blog doesn't seem to have been successful. I need something better than stupid pictures of my sister.

Without even thinking about it, I start sketching lightly with the side of my pencil. What emerges is the best likeness of a person I have ever managed. Well, besides the pig nose. Marion doesn't exactly have the same nose as a pig, just a wide flat one. Marion Henessy with her flabby cheeks and her little eyes and her naturally curly-in-a-not-good-way hair looks back at me from my notebook, thin blue lines crossing her smug face. I stare at her for a minute, hating the way she has taken over my life, and then I rip her out and wad her up.

I force my hand to be still and just stare at my notebook, thinking about the things on my list. Why can't anything be easy anymore?

I hear Raye whisper to Ian that she'll meet him later. I don't hear where, and I don't guess I care. The librarian glances at us as we pass the circulation desk; then we go through the heavy doors. READ! the square sign on the door says, then right above the door handle, PUSH! I do push the door open and follow Raye to her car, where I climb into the passenger seat. Going home for another grounded Friday night, followed by a boring Saturday. I'm not even around to dreading Sunday yet. It's depressing when all you have to look forward to is school.

"Raye, are we both idiots?" I ask as I buckle the seat belt in her little blue Honda.

"Yeah. Idiots in love."

I wonder, suddenly, if Raye's continuing infatuation with Ian might have something to do with my own on-again, off-again relationship. If my crazy love madness might be forcing her to find some crazy love of her own. I mean, sure, the yearbook did a half page on Raye and Ian with the caption *Opposites Attract*. Sure, she dated him for a year before I even met my ex-boyfriend. But she seems more into him now than she ever did. And it kind of sucks to be single when your best friend is in a relationship. Believe me, I know.

But what can you do? You can't accuse your friend of something like that. It would make her sound lame, and it would make you sound like a bitch.

My dad is pulling out of the driveway in his Jeep when Raye drops me off.

"I'll e-mail you later," she says.

"Let me know how it goes with Ian." I want her to be happy, but I don't know if I'm a good enough person to want her to get everything her heart desires. And then there's that chance that Ian's going to hurt her again. I don't feel optimistic.

"Yeah." She doesn't sound optimistic either. I close the door and she drives off. My dad pulls back into the driveway and rolls his window down.

"Parker, do you need anything from the grocery?" As far as I can remember my dad has never, ever gone to the grocery store before, and especially not at eight-thirty p.m. Being unemployed has some weird consequences.

"No, Daddy," I say.

"Okay, I'll see you later, then." I stand in the driveway and blink and he pulls away. Could that envelope in his passenger seat really have said *coupons*? No way.

I look directly at the for-sale sign as I walk toward the house. I have to look at it, because my eye-foot coordination isn't that great, and as I pass it, I kick the crap out of it. Did you know that those signs are metal? It makes this high-pitched noise as the thin metal bends back and forth for a minute. Then there's nothing but a slight pain in my foot.

Paige is sitting at the kitchen table talking to Mom. I don't know what her deal is. She was never around this much when she lived here. Preston is running from one end of the hallway to the other. He yells "Marco!" at one end of the hall and "Polo!" at the other.

"Did you get any good information at the library, honey?" Mom asks. I remember after they caught me, when I was sitting in my room, my mom said that there wasn't anything about me to know, suggesting that I'm just some kind of blank teenage idiot, but I wonder, what is a person going to learn about their teenage daughter from a question like that?

"Yeah," I say.

"What, did you write it all in that spiral notebook?" Paige asks. I'll bet she thinks that I didn't go to the library at all, and this notebook is just for cover. Why does she have to try to sabotage me? I feel defensive now, like I have to watch out for an attack here in my own house. How is it fair that she's such a bitch, but her hair looks so great?

"No. I sent the research to my in-box so I could print it

here. Did you know you have to pay ten cents for every copy you make at the library?" And I emptied all the change out of the bottom of my purse weeks ago. Does Mom not realize that no one has given me any money in weeks? That I can't get a Coke from the machine after school or, well, anything?

"You girls are so smart on your computers," Mom says. As if she's a doddering old grandma who knits doilies all day. I mean, she is constantly on her computer at work. She even sent Dad an IM once. Really.

Paige smirks at me. I hate her sometimes. Actually, I hate her most of the time.

"I saw Kyle Henessy today," I tell them. When I look at my sister my eyes feel squinty and hard. We should be on the same side. I should be used to the hostility, but it hurts that she is automatically against me.

"Again?" Mom sounds worried. "Is he following you now, Parker?"

"Yeah, Parker can't even score her own stalker." Paige laughs. I glare at her. She is so full of herself. What kind of idiot is she?

"I think he's tutoring Erin Glasgow."

"Did you guys know that he's working at the computer place, that he makes over a hundred dollars an hour? They pay for his college classes too." Paige's voice is dreamy, like she's fantasizing about making a hundred dollars an hour. I think how shallow and disgusting she is. And yet the other day in history class I was fantasizing about winning the lottery, how lame is that?

"How do you know that, Paige?" Mom asks, her voice going high with alarm. She gets worried whenever anyone mentions Kyle Henessy.

"I just heard it," Paige snaps. "I wish West could make that kind of money. His parents are complete tightwads."

"Well, West is set up to inherit a good amount of money one day, and I'm sure that his father just wants to teach him the value of that money." Mom always takes up for West, no matter what. It makes her nervous when he and Paige seem to be fighting.

The pitter-patter of my brother in the hallway has gotten louder.

"Marco!" *Thud, thud, thud.* "Polo!" *Pant, pant, pant.* "Marco!" *Thud, thud, thud.* "Polo!" *Pant, pant, pant.*

"Shouldn't he be wearing his helmet?" I ask.

My mom sighs. "His head is getting to be shaped like the helmet. I thought he could go without it for a few—"

"Marco!" *Thud, thud, thud.* "Poloooooo." *Crash.*

"What's he doing, anyway?" I ask Paige as Mom grabs the first-aid kit and sprints to Miracle Child's side.

"Who knows? I brought him some of those sugar cookies he likes, but he hasn't eaten one yet, so I know those aren't the reason he's so hyper." Paige is clueless to anything that doesn't have to do with her. It seems to have completely escaped her that he has ADHD, and the *H* stands for *hyper.* It was nice of her to bring him cookies, though. Cookies with M&M's on top.

"Take one, Parker," she says, scooting them toward me. I take two. We sit there with nothing to say to each other. The only sound is Mom's voice, soothing, as she tries to console Preston in the hallway.

"I guess I'll see you later," I say. I have to step over my brother, who is getting SpongeBob Band-Aids down his leg where there is a faint scratch, and over the fourth step because it squeaks. Sometimes I feel like I don't fit in with these people. I wonder if other kids look at their family and feel a fuzzy warm sense of belonging. I feel like a cold frozen alien from outer space. I don't belong.

I really do have to write this essay. I really do want to keep my grades up. I haven't had a B since eighth-grade music class when we had to play "Pop! Goes the Weasel" on this recorder thing. I need to stay at Allenville regardless of whether we have to go live in a tiny little house or, God forbid, an apartment. I am desperate, all of a sudden, to get some sort of scholarship. Even financial aid. Security for the future would be great. Getting away from my family might be even better.

I go straight to Dad's office because I want to use his laser printer, but I get a shivery feeling looking at the leather office chair, the very chair in which I sat wearing the handcuffs. The chair in which (had things been different) I might have . . . The chair where I could have . . .

There's an ugly paperweight on Dad's desk. I made it for him at Camp Little Creek six years ago. The kind with an oak leaf under glass. Under the glass dome, beneath the oak leaf I so carefully placed there, and where my name is etched on the bottom, is a piece of paper. I pick it up.

Christopher Prescott,
Your mortgage is in default. Unless this bill is paid in full,
your home will be repossessed.

I don't read any more. I can't. I fold it carefully and put it back under the paperweight. I open my notebook. My hands are shaking. Mostly, right now, I am imagining my dad reading this letter. I can see him taking off his glasses and wiping them on his shirt and putting his head in his hands. I can imagine how this must've made him feel, and I feel awful for him. Maybe if he didn't have all these financial problems to worry about he could go back to being happy and forget about catching me in the handcuffs. At least if I could fix it I might be able to negate some of the hurt I caused him. I've always been a big fan of making things better, never like to accept that something is just irrevocably broken or ruined. I scoot the paperweight and everything underneath it back and put my notebook on the desk.

Figure out how to make a bunch of money.

Make Marion Henessy Pay.

What if I could do both of these things at once? According to Paige, Kyle Henessy makes one hundred dollars an hour. His family has plenty of money too. That's one reason our families stopped being friends. The Henessys could afford to go places and do things that we couldn't. That and our having Kyle taken in for questioning and convicted of stalking my sister. But even before Kyle started peeking in our windows, the Henessys were taking Mediterranean cruises, and the Prescotts were lucky to go to Grand Bahama Island, which isn't even as nice as Nassau.

Last year I could've asked Raye to loan me some money, but she emptied her bank account to buy her car. Since he knows how much she gets from her real dad, her stepdad is kind of tight with money, so I know she doesn't have a huge surplus. And even though everybody says my ex is loaded, after this whole lava lamp thing, there's no way I would even mention money around him, and on top of that, you can't borrow money from your ex.

But Kyle Henessy is loaded. All I need is some way to get him to give me some of that money. I guess pictures of Paige in her swimsuit won't do it. What do I have on Kyle

Henessy? The only thing that comes to mind is the restraining order. If I can trick him into violating it, I can threaten to tell someone; then the restraining order will be renewed. He's not going to want that to happen, and I'll bet he would pay to keep it from happening. He can get the money from his parents, if he doesn't have his own. He still lives with them, right? I know it's a crazy plan. I'm not really thinking that I'll go through with this. And if I do, eventually I'll find a way to pay him back. It isn't really like stealing.

I look at the letter from the bank. If we pay two thousand dollars they won't repossess the house. Two thousand dollars isn't that much. If my parents had that out of the way, then they could concentrate on paying the electric bill and whatever else they're behind on. Then maybe they won't fight and Dad can find a nice job and Mom can go back to working part-time and not hating life so much.

Two thousand dollars isn't that much money, not to most people. Not to Kyle Henessy's family. But it's enough to stop Dad from stressing out, to get him out of the house, to keep him from looking at me like I've become someone he doesn't recognize anymore. I realize with a little bit of shock that I haven't thought about my ex in nearly half an hour. Not that my thoughts have been happy ones, but still, it's better to be doing something than just worrying about everything.

I go up to my room and e-mail Raye as if nothing has happened and nothing is different, even though suddenly everything is.

25

School is the same as ever. I didn't want to come here today. I don't ever, really, but I force myself to walk out the door, get into Raye's car, and walk into the building. One step at a time. The quietly ignoring anything that might be a hateful comment thing works pretty well with the general school population. No, it didn't work with the guys in my lit class; with assholes like that you just have to endure, tattle, or wait for a knight wearing faded Levi's, a black T-shirt, and a trench coat to save you.

And now there's the story about the bet in addition to the pictures that everyone saw. They saw me with him, nearly naked, and they think he got paid, that I was a pathetic bet. It really sucks when someone has a personal vendetta against you and your family. I am so tired of taking all this crap from Marion Henessy. It seems like she's posting something about me every week now. I don't know if it's because her pseudo-pal Kandace Freemont has set her sights on my ex-boyfriend or because the restraining order is due to expire soon and her resentment at our family is boiling over, but I'm sick of it.

I'm pretty sure that posting those pictures of me violates some right of privacy or something. Only, to fight something like that you have to have lawyers, and parents who can hire lawyers. Parents who would then become aware that their beloved daughter was close to naked in a hot tub with a young man that they despise. And really, Mom and Dad don't need to see something like that, not again, not after what they saw in the study. I'm already scared that they'll never trust me again. One more thing and my dad's hair will go completely gray.

I have a horrible thought. What if the staff at Allenville saw those pics? I know for sure that Mr. Dawson and Ms. Miller read the blog, I could tell from the things they said in the melting locker-slush interrogation. Oh my God. What if they not only saw the pictures but also saw the thousand-dollar-reward story? What if they think it's true? I can't think about it right now. I won't.

I'm resolved. I'm going to go totally vigilante on their asses. If Marion Henessy thinks I'm going to let her ruin my entire high school experience because my sister didn't want to date Kyle (and who would, really?) and didn't want him peering in her window (again, no potential takers) and sneaking around following her (do I even need to say this?) . . . I'm ready to stop this BS, and to get two thousand dollars. Robin Hood style. Take from the rich and give to the, um, not so rich.

The Burbery Coffee House is about ten minutes from school and not far from the computer place where Kyle works (looked it up in the Yellow Pages). It's kind of grungy, with wooden tables that seem a little bit soaked-into, if you know what I mean. The lighting is dim, from chipped probably fake Tiffany lamps.

Kyle is sitting at a table by himself drinking what *looks* like a plain coffee. In a coffeehouse! I'm not much of a coffee drinker, but I know you're supposed to choose some exotic flavor like amaretto and get skim milk and whipped cream and chocolate shavings. I plan to add every sweet thing I can think of so that I won't have to taste the coffee. If I stay here long enough to order, that is. I have three dollars in quarters clanking around in my pocket, taken from Dad's bureau where he always empties his pockets.

He's sitting at a table for two. A tiny two-seater where, if I pull my chair all the way under the table, I imagine our knees will touch. An intimate little table. I don't like this.

Today Kyle Henessy looks like the kind of person who would sit alone in a coffeehouse. The stained glass from the overhead lamp illuminates half of his face with purple, casting dramatic shadows on his sharp cheekbones and making it hard for me to see his eyes.

"Parker," he greets me, standing and shaking my hand. He has a surprisingly firm handshake, for a deranged binocular-carrying weirdo, I mean. "It's nice to see you." He has a thoughtful voice, wistful.

I stand there flabbergasted, not sure what to say to him. We have a long history, what with our families and all, but it isn't exactly a friendly history. Prescott vs. Henessy and all that.

"I think I know why you're here. It was wrong of Marion to post those pictures of you on the blog. I've already talked to her about it, and they've been deleted." Then why did you take them? I want to say. Why give her more ammunition against me? Instead, I thank him. I mean, he did just say that he made her take the pictures down. How am I supposed to react?

I'm totally on edge. Here is this guy who used to be like an older brother to me who has been recast in the role of sexual predator. I don't know how to treat him, and it makes me nervous. I feel my leg shaking under the table, with this tip-tap reflex thing that I can't control.

"I wish—I wish you could talk to Marion about . . . these things." He stammers a little here, and for a second I can see him as a gawky overeager boy who took my sister to a dance in middle school and stepped all over her feet. I always felt a little sorry for Kyle. I suddenly remember how when I was younger I kind of wished he would forget about Paige and focus his attention on me. It seemed like a great thing, the unquestioning adoration. Now I'm not so sure.

We are the only people in this place. I can't help wondering how it stays in business.

"Well, the thing is," I begin. I feel I might need to explain myself a little bit. "Marion doesn't talk to me. She won't. She names Barbies after me and torches them. She's always writing about me. We aren't friends anymore."

"She does seem angry at you. It isn't like you had anything to do with"—he pauses and looks around—"the situation. But everything has been hard on her."

"No, I didn't have anything to do with it. I'm glad somebody realizes that," I say too forcefully.

"I don't mind meeting with you, but I'm supposed to be at work, and there's the, the restraining order." He chokes

173

restraining order out like it's a dirty word, which it certainly is in our house.

"I'm sorry that you're missing work. You must have a pretty important job."

"Not really. Why would you think that?"

Because my sister is green with envy that you make so much money? I feel bad about wasting his time, and that's dumb. Sure, I could just e-mail his sister and tell her to leave me alone, but that would ruin my plans to blackmail him. I know I'm a hypocrite; I don't want to waste his time, but I do want to steal from him. I feel guilty, but also weirdly powerful.

"I don't know. You do things with computers, right?"

"Yeah." He smiles, and the corners of his eyes crinkle up. He looks kind of old.

A waitress wearing jeans and a tight Abercrombie T-shirt comes and takes my order. At the Starbucks on my side of town you have to go to the counter to order, but this place is kind of old-fashioned.

"You want something, darlin'?" she asks.

Kyle Henessy looks at me and raises his eyebrows almost in challenge.

"I'll have a plain coffee too. With cream," I tell her, suddenly chickening out of my fancy order.

"So, um, how is your sister?" His voice is very, very soft now, and sad. I guess I would be sad too if I were a total nerd who got rejected via the police by some girl I thought I loved, even if the girl turned out to be completely shallow and self-centered. Paige kissed him on Valentine's Day when they were in the seventh grade. She told me about it too. Maybe that's when the whole obsession started, who knows? A kiss doesn't mean much to Paige, but it probably meant a lot to Kyle, with his quiet voice and sad eyes.

"West is going to trade in her car," I say. Why did I say that?

He takes a long slow sip of his coffee. So long and so slow that by the time he's done sipping the waitress has delivered mine.

"Don't ever be alone with West," he tells me, looking at me with his sad eyes. Now that I'm used to the purple light and the shadows, I can see how blue they are. I never trust people with blue eyes. So he thinks perfect West is really an asshole, I can tell by his voice. But then he'd have to think that; West stole Paige away and married her. If he had a West voodoo doll he'd totally be sticking pins in it and torching it.

I surreptitiously rip open four sugar packets at once and pour them into the glazed earthenware mug. I tip in one creamer and wonder how many I can use without looking like a lameoid. When I look back at Kyle Henessy his mouth is twitching like he's trying not to laugh at me.

"Well, Parker Prescott, it's neat to see how you've grown up. Do you remember when we went to the Bahamas? I guess that was the last time our families went on a trip together, after all the yearly family trips." He pauses, and I suppose we're both meant to be reflecting on the Bahamas. Bright sun and open air would be a welcome change from this place. "Look, I've been, um, totally over your sister for months. I mean, it's been nearly a year. In twelve days the legal order will be over. I have other things going on now." Twelve days! He knows down to the minute when the restraining order will end. This is going to be easier than I thought. He said it fast and nervous, like forcing himself to say he isn't infatuated with Paige is going to convince me. He can't even say her name. Obsession is a scary thing.

"I didn't come here to talk to you about Paige. You were the one who brought her up." I don't want him thinking of me, linking me to his obsession with Paige when he gets the anonymous e-mail asking for money.

"I know. I know. You came to talk about those pictures, but I already took care of them. So why are we drinking coffee together when we aren't supposed to be within fifty feet of one another?"

I take a sip of my coffee. It needs way more sugar and more creamer, too. And chocolate shavings wouldn't hurt.

"If you were a different sort of girl I might think you were here because you aren't allowed to be here. Because I'm a person who is forbidden to you."

I don't want him linking me to the blog, either. Because I'm going to try to get him to take it down so that my life can go back to normal. But not here and now. Later, after I have his money.

Kyle Henessy's saying this about being forbidden makes me uncomfortable, but I have to ask. "What sort of girl do you think I am?"

"Marion says you're classy. You were always a nice little girl."

Marion Henessy says I'm classy? Um, what?

"That's not what she says about me on the blog. I mean, have you seen those pictures?" Of course he's seen them. He took them—right? Still, I can't help asking and waiting for his response. Here's a guy who's in college and making big money, completely removed from the stupid artificial world of high school. What does he think about all this high school drama crap?

"Yeah, I saw the pictures."

Is he blushing? Oh my God, he is totally blushing. Suddenly my stomach clenches up. He *must've* taken the pictures. He saw me in my wet underwear, which means almost naked, without the little black boxes that Marion so thoughtfully inserted. Is he blushing because he watched me, or because he really studied those pictures? I suddenly feel like I ought to get out of this place.

"So, I have to go. Do you know what time it is? My parents are expecting me home. I'm supposed to be kind of grounded."

"Really? What for?" Like it's any of his business. Like I'm going to tell him that I got grounded for letting my boyfriend—ex-boyfriend—handcuff me to my dad's black leather office chair and then getting caught that way.

"They don't like my boyfriend," I say. Which is true. Let him interpret it how he wants.

"Parker." He puts his hand over mine as I start to put a few quarters on the table. "Hey, I'll pay for the coffee." He smiles, only now the purple light makes him look truly sinister, and his hand is still on mine. "Don't let, um, don't let your parents decide who you are going to date. They don't have very good judgment. Or that's how it seems to me."

Part of me wants to ask what he means by that; the other part wants to laugh, because either way, he's paying for the coffee. This encounter is going to cost him big-time. All of me wants to get out of here. I stand up and take three steps, wanting to be sure I can get beyond his reach before I turn and say,

"Thank you for taking care of the pictures, and for the coffee. The Bahamas, that was a lot of fun, I think." I walk really fast out into the blinding light of late afternoon. I'm so freaked out and so seriously vision impaired that I bump into a couple walking into the coffee place. I tell them I'm sorry and walk away quickly, reaching into my purse and cursing to myself because I don't have my sunglasses. Blackmailers really *should* have sunglasses.

26

When I get home the Volkswagen is in the driveway. Somebody, presumably West, has put an ugly yellow bumper sticker on it. I can't read what it says from here but I'm guessing it says something really stupid. I see West climb out of the car and walk toward the house. He stops and kicks at some rocks, so I catch up and am practically right behind him. He goes up the sidewalk and into the house ahead of me, not bothering to hold the door. It's like I'm invisible. The door slams about ten seconds before I get there and I have to fumble to open it because I have my stack of books in one hand and my cell phone in the other. I have fourteen missed calls. I don't have fourteen friends. I snap the cell shut and put it in my pocket so that I can open the door.

I try to think of something hateful to say to him, but by the time I get through the door, I'm just happy that I have good balance, because my cell phone starts ringing and I almost drop all my books and papers on the floor trying to retrieve it from my pocket and flip it open with one hand. Great, all that effort for a dropped call. I throw my stuff on the couch and head for the refrigerator.

West walks into the kitchen in front of me. He's in my way, between me and the bottled water I put in the fridge this morning. He's standing right by the cabinet looking at the newspaper that Dad left there, and I have to turn sideways to get past him. I bump the counter and bounce off him, kind of with my whole body pressed right against him for a second.

West laughs and gives me that grin. The one every girl in our school dreamed about when he was there starring on the football team and walking through the halls with supreme self-confidence. He has this smile that just won't stop, and he's big. He looms.

I look up at him and catch this weird expression. His eyes kind of widen, and he shakes his head and walks away. I get a nervous feeling deep down. Did he somehow think that I bumped him on purpose? I mean, there's no way that he thinks I'm coming on to him, right? I remember what Kyle said. But it doesn't matter. West is my brother-in-law and Kyle is a psychotic stalker.

My cell phone rings again and I'm glad for the distraction. "Hello?"

"Hey, Prescott." How can his voice saying my name make me feel so shivery?

"Oh, it's you." I run upstairs because I want to be alone in my room while I talk to him.

"Yeah. Me. Were you expecting somebody else?"

I just laugh and don't say anything. His voice makes me forget that there is anyone else on this planet, so how could I be expecting a call from anyone else?

"Parker," he says, "I can't stand this much longer."

"What?" I think for half a second of all the things I can't stand. Being so poor, the fact that our school fills six Dumpsters full of garbage every single day, the hostility that is always present when I'm in the same room with my sister, the way my dad suddenly looks old. All these things pass through my head in about three seconds, images more than thoughts. And then there is nothing but his ultrasexy voice.

"I need some alone time with you. Just seeing you at school isn't enough. Let's cut school and spend a few hours together."

I have never cut school, but his obvious desire makes all the things that are bothering me evaporate. A day with him is just what I need. All this confusion will go away, because when I am with him he is all I can think about. The other things I've been feeling are only withdrawals, only my need for him manifesting itself, right?

"I have a calculus test tomorrow. But Thursday I think I could cut." I think I could, I think I could. I can't think about my parents finding out or about the consequences, only that he wants to be with me.

"I don't think I can wait, Parker."

"I can't miss that test." I can barely hear my own voice.

"Yeah?"

"If they find out we cut it'll be an unexcused absence. And I won't be able to take the test at all, and my GPA will go down the tubes." I realize this is a lame thing to say, and so does he.

"So?" He knows this is important to me, but it's just one

of those things he blows off. Still, I have this need to explain myself.

"You know we might be moving and we might move out of the district. If I don't have the best grades they won't let me stay at Allenville." It all falls out of my mouth before I know what's happening. I don't want to think about the money problems again. I do not want pity. "Wait until Thursday for me." I hold my breath. Will he wait? Will he keep wanting me?

"I'll try." He sounds kind of exasperated. I don't want him to sound that way.

So I hear myself saying, "Bring condoms." I want to shock him. I want to keep his attention on me. I want to intrigue him.

"Yeah?" I can't tell what he's thinking from his tone of voice, and I'm starting to regret saying it.

"I don't know." Let him worry about it and try to figure out what I meant, and go over every possible interpretation of the words we exchanged, like I do after every conversation I have with him.

"Okay, Prescott, Thursday it is." There's a world of insinuation in his voice. I don't say anything because I can't seem to find my voice. "Parker?" he says. "I always carry condoms. Just in case." *Condoms.* More than one. Just in case. Why did I even mention condoms?

"I just think it would be good if we had some time together, that's all I'm saying." I struggle to get this out. Does he know I'm already regretting what I said? Does he care?

I tell him goodbye and pace back and forth across the room. I can't draw, can't study for my calculus test, can't think of anything to say to Raye.

Thursday.

27

It's been an hour and I have gotten absolutely nothing done. I cleaned my room a little and opened my textbook, but the practice problems mean nothing to me. In my school notebook, I doodle our initials all intertwined. In seventh grade we did this unit on the medieval period, and one project was making an illuminated manuscript. You know, with all the flowing lines and birds and leaves around the actual words. I remember thinking it was about the coolest thing I had ever seen. I sketch the first letter of his name. Illuminated manuscripts always start with one really big letter and then have normal-sized script. I make a little trailing vine around it. I can see the colors I would like to use, glowing colors, like these paints I had when I was younger. They were called opalescents or something like that.

I glance around the room. It's a little bit opalescent too, with all the silvery pink. I'm not ready to leave this room, or this house and all the memories it holds. I can't stand the thought of my family having to move. If I can just get that two thousand dollars, then everything will be okay. I have to set these accounts up way better than before. The other ones were just for practice.

I'm working on my secret letter to Kyle, making sure it doesn't sound like me, has at least three spelling errors, making sure it will convince him that he needs to send me some money and not tell me to go to hell like he pretty much did last time, when my door flies open and hits the wall.

"Hey, Parker!"

It isn't the loud thump or my sister's voice that makes me jump. It's my guilty conscience. Paige is standing in my doorway with her hands on her hips.

"I need you to get all your crap out of my closet."

"What?" I hit minimize. Hope she didn't see Kyle's name. She isn't a real fast reader and she wasn't standing that close, so I'm probably safe.

"I need you to move all of your stupid shorts and tank tops out of my closet."

"You mean my summer wardrobe?" She still has her hands on her hips, and she looks a lot like Mom, if Mom were thin and gorgeous.

"Yes, Princess Parker. I need you to move your 'summer wardrobe' out of my closet, so that I can put my things in there."

"Why do you need to put things in your old closet? Are you moving back in?" I follow her three feet down the hall.

Her old room isn't far from mine. So much for privacy. Going back to sharing a bathroom with the beauty queen and all her beauty products does not sound much like progress to me.

A wine cooler is open and sweating on her dresser. Fuzziest Navel or something like that. I don't say anything about it, though Mom and Dad won't like it. She sits on her bed, grabs the bottle, and downs about half while I'm pulling my short-sleeved shirts out of her closet. I feel uncomfortable because she's staring at me, and I've felt her scorn before, her contempt for having a younger sister so gawky and different from her. She takes a drink and shakes her head sadly.

Paige's room is all purple, dark purple and antique furniture that my grandma gave her when she moved to Florida. It's mahogany or something and is almost black. Maybe I should've snagged her furniture when I had the chance. Mine is all white with pink and gold accents. So girly and demure. Paige's room has some character, at least.

"I'm just going to stay here on some nights. School nights, Monday through Thursday, for right now."

"Why?" She and West just live a few blocks away, why does she need to move back into our house? She looks at me hard, but her voice is quiet when she answers.

"West and I are having some disagreements about college."

"Is staying here part-time supposed to help that?"

I try to make my voice soft too, because Paige looks sad. She takes a long swig from the bottle in her hand before she says, "It's the only way. The only thing I can think of to do. Mom and Dad say that they'd be happy to have me. They don't want to hear anything bad, so it's hard to talk to them." Great, even though Paige is married and supposed to be a grown-up, Mom and Dad want her to move back in so that they can bask in her golden perfection. I'm surprised they don't give her and West all three of the bedrooms and move me and Preston into the garage.

I mean, her life is close to perfect, she and West are playing house in their cute little apartment, and she goes to classes a couple of times a week. Why does she have to live here?

Paige frowns at me and I try to remember why my parents have always favored her over me. Because I'm uninteresting and dull? Because she was vivacious and alive and I was just a boring old ice princess? Could I have turned out any differently? We do have the same genes, after all.

I remember when I was eleven and I wanted Paige to teach me to do the electric slide because we were having this dance in the middle-school gym. I was all excited about that dance, practically jumping up and down.

"Parker, you might as well ask Mom to teach you, the electric slide is as old as Mom and Dad!"

"How do you know?"

"Because Mom taught it to me." She laughed and grabbed me by the shoulders and she tried to fold me into the dance, but I don't bend right, and I don't hear rhythm, so I couldn't do it. She tried to show me and I stumbled to follow, but I couldn't keep up with her. "No, Parker, step, step, clap, count one, two, three, four. You forgot to slide, that's the whole point. Now step to the right. Oh my God, that's my toe!" We ended up lying on the bed giggling because our toes were all mashed up and because I couldn't master the electric slide. I was, undoubtedly, the only person in the universe who just couldn't follow the steps.

Paige downs the rest of the wine cooler and drops it into the little oval metal garbage can that sits beside her bed. It chinks against another bottle. Those things come in four-packs. Bartles and Jaymes or whatever.

"Guys love watching TV more than anything else in the world. They do something for ten minutes, then sit down to stare at the screen for twenty. Get ready. A guy won't even want to have sex if something good is on TV." Is Paige jealous of the television? Is she that conceited that everything has to be about her? I'll bet most of what she's saying isn't even true. "Sex is overrated, you know," she tells me.

The khaki shorts fall out of my hands. How does she know my mind keeps coming back to sex, no matter what else I try to think about?

"Really?" I lean down to pick them up.

"Really."

I'll bet Mom paid her to say that to me. Though if anyone ought to know, it's Paige. Her reputation around school isn't just for being pretty and popular. She was also supposed to be, um, well broken-in. Easy. Guys still whisper her name with awe, and girls roll their eyes. She was way hotter than any of the girls in our class, even Zara. The kind of girl who can get away with slutty behavior and not get talked about too much.

"Did Mom and Dad ask you to tell me that?"

"Nope, I just thought I'd pass on some big-sisterly advice." She wipes her mouth on the back of her hand and makes a face as if something tastes bad, but she doesn't even slur her words. I wonder how much she drinks and how often.

I go into my room and close the door. I close it too hard,

and Paige probably thinks I'm slamming it, though I never slam doors. Paige is definitely the door slammer in our family.

My drawing pad is sticking out from under my bed. I nudge it out of sight with my toe and adjust the dust ruffle. I feel terrible thinking that my sister is across the hall again and we're still so far apart.

I sit down and work on my blackmail letter—I better not call it that, my threatening letter to scare Kyle—in between working on homework. Raye IMs me to talk about Ian for a while.

Raye: Do you think Ian was checking out Melanie D's legs today?
ParkerP: Yes, all the guys were.

They weren't checking out the skirt that was so short you couldn't see it, were they?

Raye: Do you think he'll ask me to the prom?

To this I have no good answer. What do I know about guys? My boyfriend, or rather my ex-boyfriend who is moving back toward boyfriend status, is exasperated with me. Exasperated, like fed up. Well, now he's kind of excited, but if I were to cancel Thursday and go back to being dull old Ice Princess me, he would be totally bored with me, and then he would be exasperated again.

Raye: Do U want to help me look for prom dresses just in case?
ParkerP: Um, sure, I guess I could go dress shopping as soon as I get ungrounded

Probably a month after prom.

Raye: See if your parents will let you go shopping with me
for a few hours on Sunday.
ParkerP: I'll ask. Mom's calling me for dinner now.
ParkerP signs off at 5:22.

28

"**P**arker, Preston, dinner is ready," Mom calls for the second or maybe the third time. It's really late for dinner, but my dad is back from some meeting he went to, and Mom is making a big production of cooking for everyone. I wonder if Paige is sober enough to stagger downstairs for a home-cooked meal. Surprisingly, though, she's already at the table when I get there. Helping Mom with the salad. Wow.

Mom and Dad keep smiling and reaching out to touch each other. It reminds me of the way they were on Christmas morning, before I ruined everything. It's good that they seem to be working things out.

"Honey, I don't think it was very nice of you to make Parker take all her things out of your closet," Mom says, putting a big bowl of pasta in the middle of the table. Paige glares at me.

"Did you *tell* on me?" Paige rolls her eyes. Like I would run to Mom and tattle. She doesn't slur at all, and she smells like peppermint. These tactics work well on Mom and Dad, or at least, they did back when Paige was a senior. For some reason, no matter what she did, they would look at her with stars in their eyes, in a way that they never look at me.

"Daddy saw Parker carrying her clothes across the hall. We aren't fussing at you, Paige. We just want this to be as easy as it can be, for everyone."

"Do you think this is easy for me?" Oh great, her voice is rising. The melodrama begins. This is why I so rarely play the middle-child card. Melodrama reminds me of my sister. "I'm moving back in. My marriage could be over. I'm going to lose my car, and I can't even have my entire closet? I have to share it with Parker's sandals and summer shoes?" Paige and her wardrobe and her car problems make me feel really sad, almost depressed. Preston is looking at her with this concerned expression.

"You guys are going to let West trade in her car?" I ask, surprised.

Mom and Dad look at each other. "We signed the car over to Paige, so legally, as her husband, he owns half of it," Dad says. The things you don't consider when you get married to a complete jerk.

"So if you get a divorce will he get half your stuff?" I can see stupid West sitting around with half of Paige's jewelry and shoes, with the expensive watch she got for high school graduation. He might burn them, or throw them at defenseless animals, but there's no doubt that if she left him he would take her stuff out of spite. "Wait, does this mean you get half of his stuff?" I think of the big house West's parents live in.

"He doesn't have any stuff, stupid," Paige says. "Well, just a toaster oven, three hand mixers, all that crap from the wedding." She looks down, embarrassed. My parents gave her the toaster oven, I think.

"But if you got divorced, you would get to keep all that stuff?" I ask. She could have the best dorm room ever, is what I'm thinking.

"I'm not getting divorced." She sounds like she might cry, and I feel sorry for her. I wouldn't want some idiot throwing my strappy Nine West sandals into a bonfire to see if they burn faster than a pair of Nike Shox.

"Does that mean you get half of his signed footballs? And his football cards?" Preston asks. The only nice thing West has ever done in his life was to show Preston his sports memorabilia collection. It was also a pretty stupid thing, because Preston really likes to touch things, and his hands are almost always sticky. Plus, those little plastic cubes that West keeps his collectibles in are endlessly fascinating to my brother.

Paige starts to cry. Big fat tears that run down her face. "West loves me," she says. "He won't really trade in my car, and we aren't getting a divorce."

She storms off to her room. It freaks me out when she's all dramatic like that. I can't even imagine getting up and screaming and crying and having everyone stare at me. The rest of dinner is pretty much silent. Sometimes I hate this family dinner routine and wish we could just sit in front of the TV like normal people. Finally, I mutter something about liking my mom's baked chicken and go to my room to finish my letter to Kyle.

Kyle Henessy,
You don't know me, but I know you. What happens if you
vilate your restraining order? I don't think you will like
jail, do U? I know where you were today, and I have pictures to prove it. Send $2,000.00 to this PayPal account,
or I will expose you're secret. Pervert!

I started to write it all in Internet slang, but all the *U*s
looked stupid, so I just used *U* once and then misspelled *vi-
olate*. Oh, and I used the wrong *your* for good measure. I
don't think Kyle will go to jail for having coffee with me, especially since I was lying about the pictures, but I do think
it's possible that the judge would renew the restraining
order, particularly (and Kyle and my mom gave me this
idea) if he thinks Kyle had decided to stalk me instead of
Paige. Kyle is over eighteen and I'm not. Even if the judge
just suspects him of this perversity, there he is with another
year of no Paige within fifty feet. The only way he'll see her
is through really powerful binoculars. No way he's going to
take that lying down.

My hand is shaking when I hit Send. I go to Unsend. I
wish life worked like unsending messages, wish you could
take things back and rewrite them, find the right words, and
send them again with smiling emoticons. I click the button.
Error message. You can't unsend a message that has Internet
recipients. I've really done it now.

I flash back to my parents' faces when they caught us,
when they walked in on . . . us. My stomach twists. I try to
focus on how happy Dad will be with two thousand dollars,
how this will fix the problems that I made so much worse
with my idiocy. But all I can think about now is that I've
done something really wrong. I tell myself that it's like the

bikini pics. He'll probably just tell me no, probably tell me there's no way he'll pay, tell me to go to hell. I wouldn't blame him one bit if that was exactly what he did.

☙ ☙ ☙

So, I don't ace the calculus test, but I do pretty well, considering that five minutes before Ms. Rawlins passed out the papers he slid me into an alcove and pulled me to him. The anticipation running through me made me expect more than the little kiss where he barely pressed his lips against mine, and though I found myself reaching for him, he grinned at me and headed for his algebra class. It was hard to concentrate, but I did my best.

Last night I only checked back about three dozen times to see if Kyle responded. He never did. Paige spent the evening studying for some test she has tomorrow. I had expected our house to revert to the days when she was in high school now that she's living with us again. Thought that the phone would be ringing off the hook and I would have to hear her laughing and joking with her friends all evening. But it wasn't like that. In fact, the phone didn't ring once last night. Not even West called to check on her.

Tonight I can't sleep. It would be nice, I think, to go and talk to Paige, to ask her all the questions that keep floating around in my head. I roll over, thinking how awful I'm going to look in the morning, haggard and gross from lack of sleep. I can hear my sister crying. I should go talk to her, to at least try to make her feel better. But for some reason I can't get up, so I just lie there awake for what seems like hours.

☙ ☙ ☙

Thursday morning I almost can't stand the waiting. First it's waiting for Raye to pick me up. I ask Raye to drop me off at the Minute Mart where I'm supposed to meet him, and I have to wait again. She parks the Honda in one of the three parking spaces and wants to talk.

"Parker," she says, in a voice that would sound like my mother's, except I know that Raye really knows what's going on, and her voice is deeper than my mom's.

"I know what I'm doing," I tell her. She shakes her head and runs her hand through her short dark hair.

"That's the thing. You don't. He's got you so wrapped around his finger. I know he's good-looking, but do you really think he's such a great guy?" And how can I answer this? Raye knows I'm crazy about him. She knows the good and the bad. I can't look him in the eye and think that he isn't a great guy. If I do that, it goes against everything that I feel.

I can't explain this to her because it doesn't even make sense in my head, so I change the subject.

"Do you want a croissant?"

Raye sighs. "Sure, I'd love one. Um, Park? Don't do anything I wouldn't do, okay?" We both laugh, and I feel like everything is close to okay.

I remind myself that Raye doesn't want me to get hurt. She's seeing problems where there aren't any. I'm just extra-sensitive after not sleeping and listening to my sister sob into her pillow all night.

I run a croissant out to Raye, practically skipping, I'm so full of nervous energy. Not that an ice princess would ever skip, really, but I do walk fast. I hand the croissant to Raye and she waves to me and backs out of the parking lot and turns toward school. I watch for a second, then go back inside and walk up and down the aisles. I make myself a hot chocolate from the machine just to have something to do with my hands, something to hold. I'm counting out my quarters to pay for it and a croissant when I see the Saab sliding into the parking lot.

29

"Sorry I'm late. I had to change my shirt." He's not wearing his usual black T-shirt. He's wearing a white oxford shirt with little blue stripes. His hair is still kind of damp, and I wrap my arms around him, lean close to him, and breathe him in for a second. It feels like home, comfortable.

We drive down to the park and he pulls in next to the koi pond. For maybe half an hour, we sit on a little bench and throw scraps of croissant to the fish. He doesn't touch me or say much of anything.

I've been nervous for two days, but now that we're together, strangely, I'm very calm.

"We can go to my house," I tell him. I know that his place is out of the question. His mother quit work to stay at home with his little brother and be a homemaker. When he was a little boy, his mother was some kind of killer corporate attorney—which is why they have so much money—and he never saw her. I know these things, though we have not discussed them, have not mentioned the reasons that he avoids family interaction at all cost.

His family might be cool with whatever we decide to do in the basement, but they wouldn't be cool with us cutting school to do it. They are very into his education.

"Paige has a test and classes all day. Dad is going to some meeting, and Mom and Preston are in the usual places, work and school."

He stands up, and I look back at the happy fat goldfish one last time before we get into his car. I feel oddly numb, as if somehow it's too early in the day and I haven't thawed out enough to start having emotions. It's almost scary, because I think I should be feeling so many things.

It's only a couple of minutes to my house, not even long enough to get to the guitar solo of "Cherub Rock" before he pulls into our driveway and I look up at the house, the brick, the little bit of ivy on the side, and the bare spot where Dad had the maple tree cut down after we found out Kyle Henessy was hanging out up there.

"Where should I park?" he asks me.

"Garage." I pull the extra garage-door opener out of the leather messenger bag I use for my books. We don't want the neighbors to wonder why there's a strange car in the Prescott driveway, do we?

I try not to think about the last time he was here and everything that happened. There's no reason to bring it up or even remember it. It seems like it happened a long time ago.

He pulls smoothly into the garage and I usher him into the kitchen.

"You want something to drink?" I ask, not really knowing what else to do.

"Yeah, sure." We are standing on opposite sides of the kitchen counter. I walk to the refrigerator and open the door.

"Bottled water?" I toss him an Aquafina. He takes a long drink. Is it me or does he seem nervous?

"Would you like to come upstairs to my room?" I ask him in the same voice I used to offer him the water.

"God, yes."

At least he's sure what he wants, right? He hasn't been in my room too many times. My parents are firm believers in the "no boys in the bedroom" policy. It hasn't worked too well in keeping their daughters celibate, but maybe it makes them feel better about their parenting or something. We go upstairs. He steps over the fourth step to avoid the squeak, and I realize how good he is at remembering details. It's almost enough to pull me out of the numbness. I feel the beginning of some deep-down emotion, but then it fades.

I look at my room for a second, the way I imagine he's seeing it. The bed with the silky silvery pink down comforter and the zillion pink and white pillows. The fluttery striped canopy with ruffles. The curtains are ruffly too. The only thing I can be truly relieved about is the fact that last summer I took what was left of my toys, Barbies, and stuffed animals from every corner and storage box and sold them in a yard sale. The only stuffed animal in the room is the husky, who watches us from my nightstand.

He walks over to my dresser and noses around nonchalantly. He opens a drawer. It's my panty drawer. I reach out to stop him, but then I don't. I let him look.

"What do your parents think about you wearing these sexy panties?" Thank God he pulled out a nice pair. Thank God he thinks they're sexy.

"I buy my own. I like my underwear to be coordinated." This morning I put on my blue striped panties and my matching blue demibra. I shaved my legs twice.

"Did you think about me when you bought these?" He pulls out a pair of black lacy low-cut panties and holds them out to me.

"Yeah. I bought them in September."

We look at each other. We weren't together in September. Not even close. He hadn't even looked at me in September, not that I was aware of.

"I think about you all the time," I tell him. He knows this. I know that he knows this. Admitting it feels good, like, like a confession, I guess.

"I think about you, too, Parker." He takes his wallet out and puts it on my nightstand. It's the closest either of us has gotten to the frilly bed.

"You don't have to do anything you don't want. I'll wait for you, you know that, right?" He says this now. It's the right thing to say, but it isn't exactly what he means. He doesn't want me to do something I don't want to do, but he does want me to want this, and he wants it badly. Somehow I understand this and am more trapped now than ever.

I crawl up into the middle of the bed. You know how you're comfortable in your own bed? How you can navigate it under any circumstances? I can feel my way to the right place. I touch the pillow with my hand. I changed the sheets this morning right after I shaved my legs the second time.

He follows me so that he is standing right there at the side of the bed, standing pressed against the mattress. On my knees, I am at eye level with him. I unbutton his shirt and pull it back away from him.

"Are you going to fold it?" he asks. We are so calm, calm enough to tease each other. And yet so very tense that the teasing feels forced. I do fold his shirt, properly, so that the creases will be right, and lay it on the nightstand. He's wearing one of those undershirts that boys wear with dress shirts. I put my hands up under it and lift it up over his head. Then I unbutton his jeans. My hand fumbles and for a moment it's terribly awkward.

"This isn't fair. I want to see your matching bra and panties." He sits down against the carved headboard and pulls me onto his lap. Under, over, on top of the pillows. His jeans are still on, though loosely.

We haven't kissed yet. Usually we kiss first thing. We kiss for hours. We kiss until my lips swell up and tingle so much that they feel like they are separate from me.

He pulls my shirt over my head and breathes something that sounds like "Pretty" as he leans in and kisses the tops of my breasts. I am melting. My entire body is melting.

For the first time today, he kisses me, and time ceases to exist. I cease to exist. There is just the warmth of his skin against mine. Kissing is good. I know how this part goes, and I relax. A little.

And then I hear the door open downstairs, then slam. We look at each other. Someone is in my house. He gets up and walks across the room to the window. I watch him.

"Your sister," he says. Paige parks in the driveway, so she probably doesn't even know that his car is in our garage or that anyone is here. We look at each other for a minute, and then I put my shirt back on and tiptoe downstairs. Oh my God. How can this happen? What if he wants to leave?

What if I want him to leave? Only I don't, not this way. Not exasperated by me and my crazy erratic family with their interruptions.

Paige is standing in the middle of the kitchen with Daddy's bottle of bourbon in her hand. I make a small sound and she turns toward me. Her sweater has fallen off her shoulder and there is a big purple bruise visible against her white skin. We have the same fair complexion, even though she used to go to the tanning bed a lot. She's pale now.

"Paige?"

She glances at the clock on the microwave. Figures out that I'm not supposed to be here and gives me a wicked grin. "Is the Princess sick today?"

"Paige, I thought you had a test today?"

"I'll get an excuse note from the infirmary." She splashes some of the bourbon into a cup. Her sweater is still hanging, like she's lost weight, and she's always been thin. I reach out but then can't touch it, so I just stand there with my hand hovering over the mark. She pulls her sweater up, and for a second, as I look into her eyes, she looks really old. Like ancient-and-tired-of-the-world old. It scares me, and I don't want to deal with this right now. She's probably just stressed, right?

The screech of the garage door opening makes both of us jump. Oh no. Mom or Dad? I don't want to see either of them, and I know Paige doesn't either. The door to the garage is just past the refrigerator. Paige opens it, with the bourbon still in her hand. The first thing we both see is the Saab.

"Why didn't you tell me you weren't alone?"

I don't say anything. How can I tell her that the way she looked standing there, bruised, with my dad's bourbon in her hand in the middle of the day, made me forget? Beyond the Saab is a gold Camry and some kind of monolithic SUV. I can breathe again. It isn't either of my parents.

"Oh God. It's Theresa again." Paige takes a long gulp straight out of the bourbon bottle. "Oooh, look at the closet space, ooh look at the stainless-steel range," she says in a high ugly voice. "We won't tell them that the garbage disposal doesn't work, and maybe they won't notice that there isn't a basement." She takes an even longer drink, and then sets the bottle on the counter. "Don't worry, kid. I'll get rid of them for you. Better get out of here, though. Mom is sure to hear about this, and you don't want to ruin your perfect record." Paige can't seem to get it through her head that my record isn't perfect anymore. I watch her. I can tell that something big is about to happen. She never calls me "kid." That's what she usually calls Preston. The sibling she likes.

I step back into the hallway to listen. Sure enough, I can hear Theresa chattering away about the landscaping and the two-car garage. Her artificially cheerful voice is exactly the same as the one Paige was using to mock her.

"House isn't for sale." Paige sounds drunker than I've ever heard her, drunker than she was five seconds ago. I remember suddenly that Theresa is Paige's godmother. How awful for both of them.

"Paige?" Theresa says. "What are you doing here? You know your parents are selling, that I'm showing the house."

"You're wrong. This house is not for sale," Paige yells, and she slams the door and slides the dead bolt into place. "Let's see them get in now," she says. But they don't even try. Theresa is a professional realtor. She doesn't make money by breaking into houses and showing them to people.

Paige was right. I'm sure our mom is going to hear

about what just happened. Theresa is probably calling her right now.

I turn and tiptoe upstairs. When I peer out the hallway window the Camry and the SUV are both gone. My sister works fast. The Volkswagen is pulling out of the driveway. She was faking being drunk, right? She has to be safe to drive, because there's no way to stop her now.

I push my door open. He's sitting at my computer. I absolutely hate for people to get into my private stuff. I stand there in the doorway, unsure how I should feel.

"Parker?" His voice sounds bored, but I know that the bored thing is kind of an act.

"Yeah?"

"What's all this, this folder? Are you blackmailing someone?"

This day has not been anything like I planned. I have this deal where I get something in my head, as minutely detailed as imagining what he will say to me and what I will say to him. Sure, I can take a little deviation from the script, but when everything is different and my entire day gets subsequently fucked, it infuriates me. He sees the look on my face.

"Hey, Park, it's just me. I'm on your side, so you don't have to kill me, okay? Okay?" He's laughing.

"Are you making fun of me?" I'm suddenly so angry that I actually clench my fists.

"A little bit. Are you seriously blackmailing somebody?"

"Do you think I invited you over here to snoop through my e-mail?" I start to unbutton my shirt with jerky motions. I have to distract him, to salvage this thing we've planned. To get our day back on track.

"Hey, don't get all agitated, Prescott." He stands up and

puts his arms around me and we stand between the desk and the bed for several minutes, until the trembling stops. It's because of him that it stops. That's how I know that what I'm thinking of doing is right. I'm ready for whatever comes next.

"I'm not agitated," I say in a shaky voice.

"No?" He kisses me, and then he climbs back into my bed.

Is it weird that at one point I wonder whether I will ever tell Raye or anyone about exactly what is happening? Then he distracts me and I mostly don't think about anything.

꩜   ꩜   ꩜

A little later, he goes back to my panty drawer and pulls out the black lacy panties again.

"I guess Raye told you, huh?" he says.

"What?" He's so calm, able to talk normally. This is like everyday stuff to him.

"When you bought these in September, I guess Raye had told you."

"Told me what?" I try to act calm and cool too.

"That I called her up. Went over to her house, to ask her about you, if she thought you'd be interested in going out with me." His tone is weird and I can't tell if it's because of what's happened between us or some other thing.

"No, she didn't tell me. What did she say?" He was interested in me then, asking about me? I feel insanely happy.

"She said she didn't think you would be interested, that I wasn't your type."

I am lacing up my shoes and not looking at him. Wondering what Raye thought my type was, wondering if she thought she was protecting me from him. I watch him put the panties back in the drawer and close it. I can't tear my eyes away from him. I find it amazing and daunting that another person has been so thoroughly together with me. And now we are apart, but he's right here, where I can reach out and touch him.

"If I bought you something lacy and see-through, would you wear it?"

"Yes." I hear myself answer faintly. I think I've proven that I will do anything for him.

"I have something for you," I tell him. He's standing by my door, looking in my full-length mirror. He touches his hair where it's sticking up a little, and I would laugh at him, but for some reason I don't feel like laughing. In the very bottom drawer of my desk, under the extra loose-leaf paper, are the handcuffs.

I hand them to him.

"My mom had them on her dresser for a while, I guess to remind her how bad I am and how mad she was at me. Then she threw them away last week." I was glad she got rid of the reminder, but somehow I couldn't let them go.

He puts them in the pocket of his jacket. Doesn't ask about how I rescued them from the garbage, even though as I was fishing them out I was totally thinking about what a great story it would make. Guess I was wrong. He doesn't ask about the key, and I don't tell him that I put it on my key chain, with my house key and my key to the Jeep. Just in case I ever need it again. His casual acceptance of this thing, this item that, with his help, threw my life so completely out of whack, feels like a slap in the face, like he's ignoring all that I've been through. I bite my lip and look down as he puts his hands on my shoulders. He pulls me close and presses his lips against my forehead. I want him to stay.

I know he has to leave, his mom is expecting him home right after school, but I don't want to stay here alone. If I weren't grounded I could go and hang out at his house, but I'm trapped here, and my mom won't be too pleased if she finds him here, so I just have to say goodbye to him, awkward as hell, and watch as he drives away. It sucks.

☙ ☙ ☙

In my room, I find the e-mail I've been waiting for. Nearly two thousand dollars are now sitting in my new anonymous PayPal account. Two thousand dollars minus PayPal fees. How am I going to get this money to my parents? I feel strange and, well, honestly, kind of hormonal. You know how sometimes when you have PMS you want to laugh and cry at the same time and in the end, you just feel nuts? That's how I feel right now.

I can't think about the ex because I have to figure out what to do with the money. Obviously I can't just hand it to them. I have to be sneaky.

Raye is shopping online for prom dresses and filling out precollege applications. I can't help thinking how different our days have been. She e-mails me an essay to ask if her commas are in the right places. I'm good with commas, with all punctuation, really.

I go over it on autopilot. She has two comma splices and a fragment that doesn't make a damn bit of sense. I fix it and e-mail it back to her. She doesn't ask how things went. I am disappointed and relieved. Are we still not talking about intimate things? Does that mean our friendship is disintegrating? I wonder. I worry about things like this.

Two thousand dollars. Why am I suddenly picturing a beach and the sky over an ocean, palm trees? Are there palm trees in the Cayman Islands? I could tell my parents, I could convince them that the trip was school related. You know, with two thousand dollars I could get Paige to go with me as my chaperone. If she would go. After the way she covered for me today I feel like maybe she would.

As if she knows I'm thinking about her, Paige pushes my door open. I didn't even realize she had come back home. "Raye is on the phone." I glance at where it's sitting mute and useless on my dresser. It's like Raye knows I need to talk to her. Am I becoming psychic or something, both Paige and Raye know when I'm thinking about them? I didn't even hear the phone ring. Paige hands it to me.

"Hurry *up*, Kyle is on the other line."

What? I stare at my sister. Is she insane? Did I hear her right? I put the phone to my ear because I can't ignore Raye forever, and say, "Hello?"

"Hey, Parker. I got your e-mail. I just wanted to see if you needed to talk," Raye says.

I did. I do. I want to talk. But now that she's listening I'm not ready, and what Paige said about talking to Kyle is freaking me out.

"Raye, you aren't going to believe this, but my sister just told me that she's on the phone with Kyle Henessy."

"What? Why?" She sounds almost scared, which is a big deal for Raye.

"I don't know. She's crazy lately. I'll call you back later on my cell phone."

"What about the restraining order?"

"I don't know." Maybe she doesn't care anymore—but I should. Right? I can't stop thinking about the money he just paid to protect himself. Surely a phone call to my sister is worse than coffee with me. "She's been acting weird."

"I don't think she should be talking to him."

"I know. If I don't call you back later, call the police or something."

She laughs. Then her voice gets all serious. "Really, Parker?"

"No. I'm joking." There's a long silence. I know that didn't sound like me, and she's thinking it over. I don't feel like me.

"Okay," she says finally. I can imagine her running her hand through her hair, how it'll stick up and then after a few minutes lie back down. I tell her goodbye and sit at my desk imagining what it would be like if the police showed up here again. I can still remember watching out the window when they picked Kyle up for questioning. It was pretty awful.

I tiptoe downstairs. My bedroom is making me claustro-phobic, and I'm seriously worried about my sister. I scan the kitchen and am surprised to see Dad sitting at the table reading a newspaper. I didn't hear him come in. He's wear-ing his wire-rimmed reading glasses and he looks like he just got his hair cut. He must've had it trimmed today. When he had a job, we could expect Dad at five-thirty every single day. Now he just shows up. Kind of drifts around the house and the neighborhood, I guess.

Paige sits down by Daddy and smiles at me. Dad frowns at her, and she moves slightly away from him. I watch them, wondering what they are thinking. Dad knows something is up. Paige doesn't have him completely fooled like she does

Mom. Or else maybe Theresa already called Mom and Mom called Dad. It doesn't matter—Mom is the one she has to worry about. I'm the only one who worries about Dad—and that's because I hate to disappoint him—not because he'll ground me or anything.

"Your mother will be home in a few minutes" is all he says.

"Why were you talking to that person?" I ask Paige. "That one person from school?" I glance at Daddy. He's looking at the help wanted ads, not listening to us.

"I didn't have anyplace to go after I left here. So I went to the place where that person works." For the first time in my life my sister and I are speaking the same language. It's the language of vague hints and lies, but still it makes me feel weirdly happy for a minute.

Mom comes through the door just as I'm trying to figure out how to ask Paige why she felt compelled to go see that person, her ex-stalker. Kyle. And why she would have to call him afterward.

Mom looks stressed. Her hair is a mess. There's a run in her panty hose. There are creases on her forehead that I don't think are ever going to go away.

Mom sits down. Dad looks at the table. Paige scoots her chair back.

"Sit down," Mom says. Paige wasn't actually standing, but she stays put. "What the hell happened today? How could you attack Theresa like that?" Mom's face is red. I feel bad for Paige and glad that Mom isn't glaring at me for once.

"I just couldn't stand the thought of those fat losers living in our house," Paige says.

"Honey, somebody else is just going to have to live in

our house, because we can't afford to live here anymore," Mom tells her, flat-out. Dad makes a tiny movement that neither of them notices, and I know he thinks this is all somehow his fault. I can feel his shame and it leaves a bad taste in my mouth. "So why weren't you at your class, and who were you meeting here?" Mom asks.

"What?" Paige's surprise is as genuine as my own. For once she's innocent, and she almost doesn't know how to react.

"Theresa says there was a strange car in the garage. An import. A nice car, and that woman recognizes quality cars. So it wasn't West, everyone knows his car, and if it wasn't your husband, who were you meeting here when you should have been at school?" Oh God, this is really bad. Both of the parents are getting worked up now. Parental indignation is the thing that gets you every time.

"A friend, just a friend," Paige says. She's protecting me, keeping my secret. Right now, I love her. And not just because she's my sister and I have to. But I have to say something. This has already gone on long enough.

"It was my boyfriend's car," I hear myself say. I think my parents forgot I was here. They both turn toward me, more surprised than I am. I truly hadn't planned to tell them, it just kind of came out of my mouth. "I cut school today and brought my boyfriend here," I say. Now the dreaded indignation is focused on me, and Paige can escape. Except they don't let her.

My mom and dad both look stunned. "I am so disappointed in you," Mom begins. I keep my head high and try to maintain eye contact with her because I don't know what else to do. I sense, rather than see, Paige sliding back from the table, and Mom says, her voice rising, "Don't you go anywhere. We aren't done with you yet." There is this in-sanely long pause, and then she says, slowly, "We must be really bad parents."

Paige and I don't say anything, because it's hard to know what to say.

"Tell your little sister about you and West," Daddy says all of a sudden. What is he talking about?

"Why? Why does she need to know?" Paige asks.

"Because she's your sister, and if nothing else maybe she can learn from your mistakes," Mom says.

What is going on?

"Oh, Mom. This is Perfect Parker, don't you remem-ber? She's the one who's always in control. She doesn't need my help." Perfect Parker? Yeah, and she's the one who just looks perfect, the one with the perfect self-confidence, the perfect friends, right?

"She isn't the first girl to cut school and bring a boy home, is she? I think she needs to hear what happened with West," Mom says.

"Paige, you expect to come here and live in our house. You expect us to help pay for college, but you won't even talk to your sister. You help her cut school, but you can't give her some advice?" Dad sounds pissed. I sit across from Paige with my hands in my lap and feel uncomfortable. I was trying to take the heat off her, and somehow everything has gotten turned around.

"There isn't anything to tell, really." Paige sounds like her pouty self again. "Just that I thought I was in love with him. I was in love with him," she corrects herself. "But things don't seem so good now."

"You were too young," Mom says.

"I wouldn't say—"

"You did say. You said those exact words last week when you asked to move back in." Daddy completely calls her out. She looks shocked and hurt, but also a little bit confused, like she's believed her own lies for so long she can't understand the truth. So what does this mean, that things are screwed up between Paige and West? That my parents think I'm going to get married in a couple of years, that I'll be just like my sister? Get a big wedding and then move back home less than a year later? Do they realize that big white dresses and sugary cakes don't appeal to me in the least?

Paige stands up and Mom and Dad don't say anything to stop her this time. A few minutes later we hear her bedroom door close softly. Poor Paige.

"That may have been a little hard on her," Mom says to Dad. "What with her and West separating so suddenly." She stands up, but she doesn't go after Paige, just stands in the doorway and looks up toward Paige's room. I think she's feeling sorry. Mom has always favored Paige. Her first child, her golden girl.

"I'll go upstairs and talk to her," I suggest. Anything to get out of here.

"I told you I didn't want you to see that boy anymore." Mom hasn't forgotten my confession. Of course not.

"I know." She doesn't say anything, so I blurt out, "I'm in love with him."

Mom laughs a bitter, ugly laugh.

"Paige thinks she was in love with West too. Maybe they can work things out, but she's struggling, lost. Not even done with her first year of college, and she's twenty. I wish I knew where it went wrong. We've always had such high hopes for her and now it's hard to figure out how she can fix things. Parker, you have to be yourself. Don't change yourself, don't remake yourself and let some boy use you."

This could be pretty good parenting stuff, but what Mom doesn't understand is that I am myself when I am with him. I am myself plus more, a new and improved version.

"Are those people going to buy our house?" I try to change the subject.

Mom gives me the exasperated look that she usually reserves for Preston. "I doubt it, honey." She opens the refrigerator.

I go into Paige's room to thank her for what she did for me today. There is a two-liter bottle of Pepsi, nearly full, on the nightstand beside a half-full bottle of vodka. In the metal garbage can there is an empty tequila bottle. Wow. A person would have to have destroyed their taste buds to drink like that. I would have had to down the entire Pepsi with just one shot of the vodka. Alcohol makes my stomach want to curl up and die.

"I didn't tell on you," I tell her.

"What?"

"When I was twelve and you were making out with Brett Sanders. Mom looked out the window and saw you."

"Why would Mom look out the window? She never does that."

"Yes, she does. She's always craning her neck to look out when Preston is in the yard. Anyway, I didn't tell on you." I turn to leave, and then I stop. "How much did you like Brett Sanders?"

Paige shrugs. "At the time I liked him a lot. He broke up with me after that. You know, the humiliation and all. The Sanders are a fine upstanding family and all that."

"My friend Raye is going out with his brother, Ian." If it were me dating Ian would Paige respect me? I've always wondered that.

"How come you can't find yourself a fine outstanding Sanders of your own?" The truth is that I really wanted to go out with Ian Sanders our sophomore year, just because his brother used to go out with Paige. Like some of the magic dust would rub off on me or something. Stupid, huh? I don't even like Ian very much.

"What do you mean humiliation?" I ask. "What exactly were you doing?"

"You don't want to know. Go on, go to your room, good girl." She says *good* like it's a crime and *girl* like it's the world's worst insult. I am completely tempted to say something that will shock her, to make my big sister look at me differently, but I don't trust her enough. Does she know what I did today? Does she suspect? No, she's only thinking about herself. She's walking all around her room, like it doesn't fit her right anymore, touching things and moving them around. She turns the sheets back on the bed and says, "Sleeping alone is really weird now."

I don't know what to say to that, so I just quietly go back to my room and turn down my own sheets. I kind of know how Paige feels. When I look around this room, it doesn't seem to fit me anymore either. But I want to grow out of my room and my parents' house, not get forced out of it by the stupid mortgage company. I want to come back here when I have a break from college and remember things that were good, even if there weren't so many of them.

I don't get into bed. I walk over to my desk and spend a couple of hours wasting time, messing around on the computer, not really focusing on anything. Then I put on my purple pajamas from Victoria's Secret. I kind of hate the way the flannel feels against my skin, and I kind of like it. Warm, comfortable, fuzzy. Is it possible that stubble is already popping out on my legs after having shaved them twice today?

I click on the blog. Today there's just an announcement that one of Marion's friends, Ellen, was asked to prom by some senior, followed by all of Marion's friends and readers congratulating Ellen on her good fortune. Yeah, the prom is such a big freaking deal.

I get out the sketchpad and my yellow pencil. But I can't draw anything. I take the drawing I did of the front of my dream house, and I fold it back and forth, back and forth, until I can tear it out of my sketchbook. Then I shred it into tiny little pieces and drop them one by one into the pink princess garbage can. What good is a house with an ice-skating rink in the basement if you can't even make the windows look right?

So, the thing is, I don't feel bad about the sex, I feel bad about not feeling bad about the sex. I can't remember why I didn't want to in the first place, or what I was waiting for besides that look in his eyes. But in having lost those things, am I forgetting something about myself?

I watch the clock, and I keep watching even after I lie down and try to go to sleep. It doesn't seem like I could have slept even a little bit, because every time I see the clock only a few minutes have passed.

I'm thinking now that distracting a guy from the fact that he's dating an extortionist is not a valid reason for having sex. I know I brought him here and told him to bring the condoms, but after Paige and the realtor and everything . . . I pull the blankets around me. I don't know why I tuck them in so tight when I make my bed in the morning. I like them wrapped around me at night.

I wish we had just laughed and then watched a movie or something.

☽   ☽   ☽

Friday morning feels like any other morning. I feel like the exact same Parker, only, my eyes are gritty from not sleeping enough. I walk into school just as the bell rings. Mason, the office aid who helped me after the ice thing happened, is walking toward me.

"Hey," I call to him, "I've been wanting to talk to you." He stops, holding his books in front of him, that pause where you know the person is in a hurry, just stopping to see what you have to say. I had wanted to thank him, had thought about him a couple of times. "I just wanted to thank you—"

"Hey, Parker, how was yesterday?" Raye interrupts from nowhere, elbowing me in the ribs.

I turn slightly to say hi, but before I can respond, I see him. I never see him before lunch, yet there he is, sauntering down the hall alone. He sees me but he doesn't acknowledge me. He doesn't speak to me. He walks past, a cryptic little smile twisting his lips. I can't breathe. I feel my face flushing. I want him to speak to me, to greet me, to look happy to see me. I want all of this so badly that it is beyond desire, it is a need.

As we lose eye contact, the world comes slowly back into focus. I can hear the voices of my fellow students again. I can hear lockers slamming and girls laughing. I feel my eyes tearing up; the frustration of wanting him is too much for me this morning.

"You had sex with him," Raye accuses. "Oh, Parker. I was just joking, I didn't think—"

"Where did Mason go?" I ask, ignoring Raye's question.

"Who?"

I look around. I didn't get to really thank him, but he's gone and I guess it doesn't matter.

"Raye, when did we stop talking?" I look at her, at Raye, my best friend. Her dark eyebrows come together. She's quizzical, but deep down she knows what I'm talking about.

Raye bites her lip. "Let's go, the office goons are watching us." I follow her. I have for three years. When I was little I followed Marion Henessy because she was my neighbor and I thought she was my friend. Raye is a million times better. She's a real friend. I'm not ever going to get dropped again. I can't take wondering about our friendship when this thing with him is overwhelming me.

"C'mon. Look normal, not like you saw a ghost."

"What?" We walk past where I should've turned to go to my class.

"Your face is white. Just come with me, and don't cry in the hallway."

"I'm not going to cry," I tell her, even though I'm not completely sure about this.

We go into the band room. Raye is an aid for Mr. McClusky, the band director. She has no musical talent, so rather than general music student, she gets to be the general music paper grader. There are all kinds of little rooms behind the band room, where they practice instruments or whatever. Raye pulls me into one.

"Tell me what happened." She stares at me, her dark eyes intense. It feels great to be the focus of her attention. It feels great to have her here with me.

"Really, when did we stop talking, Raye?" I need to fix this gulf that is between us before I say anything else. I need to be sure of something in my life. I want to be sure of several somethings, but right now all my energy is focused on Raye.

At first I don't think she is going to say anything.

Then she says, "When you stopped believing that a guy like Ian Sanders could love me." I open my mouth to speak, but she grabs my arm. "I know you're right. I'm glad you're honest with me, even if it's just in your eyes and your voice. I'm glad you don't lie to me. But since you and I both know that I'm living a lie and that my relationship is a lie, well, it doesn't bear discussing, does it?"

Have I mentioned that Raye is one of the most perceptive kids at Allenville? She sees things clearly and is close to brilliant. If her family lost all their money and had to move to the projects, this school would still beg her to attend.

"Raye, it would be nice if Ian loved you, and if you loved him back, but you're only sixteen. I mean, are we going to get married and stay with these guys forever? This is high school. If you're happy with him, I'm happy for you. Ian's hot." Even though it's true and Ian is reasonably hot, it's hard for me to say this out loud. Ian is hot. Sigh.

"Yeah, but you *are* in love with your boyfriend, ex-boyfriend, whatever, even if he is the world's biggest jerk." Is this what she thinks? I mean, obviously I am or I wouldn't have invited him over yesterday, but saying so would not be cool at this point, and who even knows what's going to happen, whether things are going to be different between us now.

"Raye, why didn't you tell me that he called you in September? Why didn't you tell me that he was interested in me?"

"Did he tell you that? I was wondering when he would. Asshole." She sees the look on my face and her voice gets softer. "Oh, Park. I really didn't think you'd be interested. He's so different than the other guys you've dated. I just didn't. It wasn't much of anything. He called me and he asked how long I had known you. Then he asked a few questions about you, whether you were dating anyone. Even though he was asking about you he seemed disinterested, bored. I guess that's just the way he is, but it hit me wrong. He sounded like he could care less, and so I didn't say anything to you, it was just weird. I told him you had just started going out with someone—remember that guy James you went out with twice? He said thanks and that was that. A month later when you were hot and heavy with him I was as surprised as anyone else."

Hot and heavy? I guess. After he ran the freakazoids off, he just looked at me and said, "So, you want to have dinner Saturday?" After all that stuff about thawing me, I wasn't sure quite how to respond. What came out of my mouth was "Yes," I remember that.

He leaned forward and wrote his e-mail address on my notebook. It was the first time I smelled the scent that was him, his shampoo, his soap, whatever else makes up a guy's smell. I felt like I was going to faint.

He said, "E-mail me and let me know what time to pick you up, directions to your house and stuff. What you like to eat." It was the first time in my life that I forgot to breathe.

Isn't that sort of thing supposed to happen naturally, where your body just takes over? It doesn't happen when I'm with him. At the beginning I felt awkwardly moronic having to gasp for breath every minute or so. Now I'm kind of used to it.

He picked me up at seven. Was wearing black jeans and a Led Zeppelin concert T-shirt with a navy blue corduroy jacket. He came in and met my parents, just walked into the living room where they were watching TV and shook both of their hands. They didn't know what to make of him. I saw the look that passed between them right before we left. I think they hated him already.

He took me to a nice place, with candles and a guy playing the violin. I couldn't eat a thing, I was so nervous. I kept imagining that my sleeve would catch on my tiny glass of Coke and that it would spill everywhere, or that I looked terrible and he was wishing he had never asked me out.

I guess none of those things showed, because he didn't treat me like a nervous little girl. I have lots of practice being cool and calm, remember? He treated me like I was beautiful. He kept watching me. He always does that, just looks at me, as if he can't get enough, as if he could just stare into my eyes forever. Sometimes we talked and sometimes we didn't. I can't remember anything we discussed.

Between the appetizer and the elegant little steaks, he reached over and casually rubbed my hand. Sparks shot through my body.

"So, you mostly go out with smart guys, huh?" he said.

"Smart guys are the only ones who ask me out." We smiled at each other. I relaxed a bit, though there was still an ache at the pit of my stomach, the nervousness I was so trying to ignore.

He's the only guy who has ever taken me out and paid

with a credit card. He put the card in the little book they brought and put the tip of the pen in his mouth for a moment, then filled out the total and signed. I saw the tip of his tongue for just a second as he took the pen out of his mouth.

Then we left. We got back into the Saab and sat. It should've been awkward, as nervous as I was, but I don't remember it being awkward at all.

"I'd like to get your opinions on a few songs before I take you home, would that be okay?"

I agreed, though it made me even more nervous when he pulled into the parking lot behind the skating rink that had closed three years earlier. A world-famous make-out spot. He pulled way over to the side, by a line of trees, and turned the key to where the car was neither off nor totally on. He hit a button on the stereo and kind of leaned back, and we listened. He watched my face intently.

"Creep" by Radiohead.

"It's about infatuation and longing," I said. In a weird way it was the most beautiful song I had ever heard, but some part of me hated it, because I had felt those things, I felt them about him, the longing and the wondering. Knowing I'd never be good enough.

"And self-loathing," he said.

"Yeah, self-loathing. Have you ever felt that way about a girl?" I couldn't believe I asked him that, and yet, I found I needed to know.

"Yeah." Long pause. "Listen to this one." He played a song by the Ramones, then one by the Clash. He didn't say anything. I liked his car. It felt exciting and comfortable at the same time. Like good things could happen there, but they weren't guaranteed. Does that make sense? The car was a good place, being beside him was perfect, and yet it didn't mean that I would necessarily be happy. But right then, being near him was enough.

He took me home. He did not kiss me. I was so ready. My body was aching. I almost leaned in for it, but he never made a move.

"I'd like to take you out again," he said. Some stupid voice inside my head was yammering that I would always remember this moment, that it was the greatest moment ever, and though I wouldn't want to admit it, I was so happy that in a way it was.

"I'd like that." My voice came out a whisper. When did I get so lame?

"I might send you some more songs. See what you think about them, since I have your e-mail address. Is that okay?"

"Yeah." Absolutely the weirdest date I've ever been on. First a fancy white-tablecloth restaurant, then a crash course in his favorite music, and no kiss, even though my heart was hammering its way out of my chest.

I didn't even know how to begin telling Raye about it. That same night this guy Ty took her to a pizza place and a horror movie. She was using him to get over Ian, we both knew it. There wasn't any way I could share the experience with Raye. Telling would diminish it.

The next weekend I visited the basement for the first time. He put on some music and we lay together, not touching, on his floor on the striped comforter.

"This is the first time since I got kicked out of Penbrook that I'm glad."

"Glad?"

"That I got kicked out. That I'm here now."

"I'm glad you're here too." The music swelled, guitars and drums and a throbbing urgent need that I understood at last. He kissed me then. Our mouths came together, and for the first time I understood the magic of kissing, understood the movie-star kiss that lasts for minutes and has to be seen from four different camera angles. Before, there was this awkwardness with various boys, a certain vague feeling that someone wasn't doing something right. With him, it was crazy intense emotion just rushing through me. Little to no fumbling.

He never asked me to be his girlfriend. He never introduced me as his girlfriend. Everyone just eventually realized that we had become a couple. Everyone except Kandace Freemont. Marion did a whole page on her blog about it.

He kept looking at me with that hungry look. When we were alone, when we were in a crowd, when we were in bed, when he slid me over onto his lap as we sat in his car and listened to music. I was always afraid that I would do anything for him. Now I am sure of it.

☙ ☙ ☙

"Raye, your bank has a regular ATM, right?" She goes to her bank whenever her dad sends a check to her mom—like for her senior ring or whatever. They have a really complicated custody thing going on. I don't really understand it, but I need the use of an ATM as quickly as possible.

"You aren't going to tell me what happened?" Why does *it was amazing, tho* pop into my head right now? Stupid, stupid Kandace Freemont. If only it could've been smooth, like kissing him.

"Not yet, Raye. Maybe you can tell me how things were with Ian?" I'm stalling because I don't know how to talk to her about this.

"Yeah, maybe. I wish we could go someplace. Are you still grounded?"

"Honestly, Raye, I don't think that my parents care anymore. Why don't you pick me up at about five tonight? We can go to the mall. That way they can stop me if I'm still under house arrest. Will you take me to the bank on the way?" I want to go with her, to forget about the butterflies devouring my stomach and maybe have some fun. To prove to myself that I can still have fun, even when he isn't around.

"Sure." She kind of shrugs. "Cute Cookie Guy has been seriously missing you. He says all the M&M cookies are getting hard and moldy waiting for you to come and buy them."

We smile at each other, and it feels good.

"I've almost gotten the Sbarro pizza out of my system. It's time for a big slice of pepperoni."

"Okay, it's a date."

"Raye? Do you think that maybe he doesn't want me anymore, now that he got what he wanted?" It's hard to say this, to even ask.

The bell rings before she can answer.

32

It's almost time for fifth period, and the concert band is filing into the band room. Raye goes out into the main part of the classroom and I try to slip out the side of the band-practice-room door. I've missed all of my history class and I need to make it into advanced British lit without Mr. Leonard spotting me. You would think that with all the years of being quiet and unobtrusive I could slip unnoticed from one place to another, but no such luck. Standing right in front of the door that connects the auditorium to the rest of the school is Marion Henessy, holding a clarinet.

She looks so awful that I almost laugh. She's wearing tight flared jeans that accentuate the fact that her thighs are dumpy, and a little tight short sweater that accentuates the fact that her chest is flat and her stomach isn't. It's almost enough to make you feel sorry for Marion. Almost.

"Parker Prescott." She brandishes the clarinet like a sword and then points it at me. She sounds pissed. "I've been looking all over for you. Have you been avoiding me?"

Yeah, like we've talked even once in the last year. How am I going to avoid that? She walked out when I walked into the Gap. I imagine myself saying, *No, I've been in a sex-induced daze, write about that on your blog, you bitch,* but of course I don't. I don't even have to answer because she keeps talking.

"You tell your sister to stay away from Kyle. She already ruined his life once. You tell her not to call our house because I will hang up the phone." She's actually waving the clarinet now. I take a step back to keep it from connecting with my face.

"Since when is being the object of a freak job stalker's obsession ruining someone's life? Just leave us alone, Marion." She wants to blame Paige, and by extension me and the rest of the family, because Kyle screwed up. I'm so unbelievably tired of this.

Marion's mouth drops open. Because I stood up for myself? I shake my head; half of that response didn't make a damn bit of sense. I stomp out of the auditorium. Sit through advanced British lit even though being this close to him makes me fear I will spontaneously combust.

I don't talk to him. Ms. White is lecturing and I don't have a chance. I want him to say something perfect and wonderful to me. I'm afraid that if I talk first I'll say something reprehensibly stupid, so I just take notes and glance over at him once in a while. Several times he catches my glances. The second time he smiles. He leans toward me just a little bit, and then Ms. White turns around and he stops, jots something down on his paper. Class goes on. After class I have to hurry to meet Raye. He knows this, so we don't really have any time for more than this blissful thirty seconds where we look at each other.

"I'll e-mail you as soon as I get home, okay?" he says. Um, sure, that's okay, that's perfectly, perfectly, wonderfully okay. After an entire day of waiting, just hearing his voice is enough.

Raye drops me off at home a few minutes earlier than usual. She's driving straight over to her dad's because he wants to talk to her. They'll go the deli down the street like they always do and Raye will just eat chips. I wonder how weird it would be to have one parent living way across town. One parent actually hating the other. At least we haven't had to go through that.

"Good luck," I tell her as I climb out of the car. She's hoping to ask her dad some questions about college, but she's nervous that he'll be a jerk about paying, just to make her mom mad. Uncomfortable stuff.

"Let me know if he calls or anything." She's all concerned about my nonrelationship and the possibility that I will get hurt.

"Okay." I give her a tight fake smile and walk up to the house. I go in the front door, walking just a little sideways so that I don't have to look directly at the Century 21 sign. Paige is sitting at the kitchen table.

"What're you doing here?"

"I live here, retard." Oh God. She is totally hungover. I can see the signs now that she has raised her face from where it was pressed against the table. Red eyes, skin that looks bruised, stretched, thin. Before, she was always like this on the weekends after a big party. If she wasn't too grouchy sometimes she would tell me about how great it was, all the funny jokes and the guys who flirted with her. Now it's just kind of sad.

"Sorry," I say, and start to tiptoe my way out of the kitchen.

"No, I'm sorry," she says, and puts her head back down. My parents never realized how often she was like this. They used to play tennis on Saturday mornings before we let our club membership lapse. Leaving me alone with the monster who had had too many tequila shots. Only, now I'm not as intimidated by her as I was when I was younger. I'm actually very sorry for her; she looks like hell.

My brother is sitting in the hallway outside my door. He knows better than to bother Paige when she's hungover.

He hands me a rumpled piece of paper. It has a sticker on it that looks like an award. *Excellent* is written in blue block letters underneath.

"My spelling test," he says. My brother, he's just sitting there, waiting for me. This is exceptional because he can't sit still for more than like thirty seconds, honestly. I feel bad. It's like with all the chaos in our lives, he just gets ignored. You would think it would be hard to ignore him, but really, after a while, the hyperactivity just sort of becomes constant movement that blends into the wallpaper, and you don't notice it anymore. I wish I had more time to spend with him.

He's a cute kid, when you can focus on him. He didn't get the cold husky eyes. He got Dad's warm brown eyes and dark hair. He's small. I've seen him with other boys his age and they are so much bigger than him, so much bulkier. I guess that all the running and jumping burns a lot of calories.

"Did you get all the words right?" He nods and smiles. I mean, he's in a special kind of class, so they might put *excellent* on it regardless, how would I know?

I crouch down in front of him, the spelling test still in my hand, and for a minute I want to wrap him all up in my arms and hold him. I remember how little he was, how I used to sit and watch him when he was a baby, to see what he would do. It's amazing how sweet a kid he can be when he's still for a minute. I want to grab him and keep him here, but then he starts to bounce. We look at each other. He can't help himself. He starts jumping up and down, like a little pogo boy. A Mexican jumping bean. You can't even tell the kid is reasonably cute when all you can ever see is a blur. He takes off down the hall, leaving me holding the paper, sticker, excellent comment, and all.

In my room I sit down with the big notepad. It has a few drafts of my house plans. These are the very last ones. Between the slush in my locker and my temper when I wadded the last one up, I'm down to just three of them. I smooth the pad with my hand and feel weirdly remorseful over all the ones that got destroyed. I get the pencil from my desk and add an addition to the back of my dream house. It's a big play area with padded walls and lots of drums and sliding boards. If possible, it should have soundproof walls. It's a dumb thing to do, but it makes me feel good to think that Preston will feel at home when he comes to stay with me someday in my imaginary house.

Mom and Dad come home. I hear them talking to Paige, and I feel a little nervous. I'm still grounded. The one grounding has just kind of morphed into an ongoing punishment. They didn't address my cutting school with a specific punishment, because there is nothing left to take away. Did I overstep? Was I wrong to think they wouldn't stop me? Will they make a fool of me in front of Raye, with Paige laughing at me? I'm starting to wish I hadn't been so confident when I told Raye that I could get out tonight.

At four-thirty, I put on my favorite jeans and a pink Old Navy perfect-fit T-shirt, layer it with a white cashmere sweater, pull my hair back into a casual knot, and put on just a dab of lip gloss. Raye and I have nothing but disdain for people who dress up to go to the mall. Girls who put on red lipstick complete with lip liner to stalk the mall for boy-prey.

Raye pulls up at exactly five. I walk downstairs. My parents are in the kitchen, sounds like they're fighting again. I clear my throat a couple of times. This won't work if I sound nervous.

"I'll be home by ten," I call in to them.

"Have a good time, honey."

Okay, my feelings are mixed about this. Relief that I'm getting the crap out of here, confusion, disappointment that I didn't try this earlier. Was getting out of being grounded as easy as walking out the door?

33

In my pocket, I have my cell, the bronze lip gloss, and one of Mom's deposit slips, carefully folded. In the other pocket, I just have my house key. I ought to carry a purse, I guess.

Raye doesn't even ask me why I need to go to the bank. She just pulls up and starts fiddling with the radio before I've even opened the door to get out.

I go up to the ATM and try to remove all of Kyle's money. The machine will only let me take out five hundred dollars. That means I'll have to come back to the bank three more times. The cash comes out fast, crisp. I hold the bills in my hand. All these twenty-dollar bills. I have never had this much cash in my possession before in my life.

I hold it for several minutes. Mostly nobody in the bank

notices me, though the young guy who was behind me at the ATM is kind of staring at all the money in my hands.

The deposit slip is already filled out, so I have to scratch out the $1970 and write in $500. I don't have to sign it because I'm not withdrawing any money.

I hand the cash to the teller. The line is long because it's Friday night, so lots of people just got their paychecks, but that's actually good, because nobody pays any attention to me.

"Do you know that your account is overdrawn?" the teller asks.

"I'm sorry," I tell her. I don't know what else to say.

Raye is on her cell when I get back in the car, but as I'm buckling my seat belt, she snaps her phone shut and puts it in her purse. "Campbells Lane Mall, here we come," she says.

I look out the window at an empty field that will soon be a row of stores. Someday when I'm old I might tell my children how I remember how the whole area around the mall was just fields and barns and stuff. And they won't care.

Despite the Friday-evening traffic, we arrive fairly quickly and get a magically close parking spot.

"Any luck with your dad?" I ask her.

"No, he just wanted to talk about spring break. I'm supposed to spend it with him, and he wants to take his girlfriend to Europe or something."

"Oh. Did you ask him about . . . ?"

"No. Maybe after his dumb spring break trip he'll feel guilty and want to donate to the Rachel Tannahill college fund. You never know."

We walk into the mall and toward the food court.

"Raye, I need to go to Victoria's Secret," I tell her.

"Good lord, Parker. You don't have to have a matching bra for every single pair of panties you own. Really."

"I don't need panties or a bra."

I remember the way he looked at me when he asked if he bought me something lacy and see-through if I would wear it. Should I wait for him? I know I should wait. But if I buy something on my own, he'll give me that surprised look, that slow appraisal. I want that.

"Okay, well, you don't have to have a different pair of pajamas for every night of the week either, especially with Paige cutting your closet space in half."

"I don't need pajamas, either."

Raye looks at me. "All right, then, but I reserve the right to veto your purchase if it's too sleazy. No fishnet, no mesh, and no edible panties."

"Um, Raye, I think you're thinking about Frederick's of Hollywood. I don't think Victoria's Secret sells edible panties."

"Whatever." She makes a face at me, and I laugh.

☺ ☺ ☺

Most of what they have in Victoria's Secret are bathrobes and white lingerie appropriate for a wedding night. Not exactly what I was looking for.

"Maybe I do need to go to Frederick's." I hold up a purple see-through nightie with matching G-string panties. "At least these match."

I know Raye is rolling her eyes, even though she is standing behind me shuffling through the panties.

"Oh my." I look up into the always-admiring gaze of Zara Thorpe. "Oh my, Parker. Wow. I've got to say I'd put my money on you over Kandace any day."

"Are we in competition?" I ask in my coldest voice. Zara blinks at me. I feel Raye behind me.

"So you guys aren't going to the party tonight?" Zara says.

"We aren't really into the party scene." Raye glances at me. The party scene was Paige's scene. It turned her into someone who drinks Jack Daniels straight out of the bottle in the middle of the day. She had more fun in high school than I'll probably have my entire life, but I know when I don't belong.

"What party?" I ask.

"Some girl from school whose parents are out of town," Raye says.

"Were we invited?" I ask.

Zara shrugs. "I wasn't officially invited. Don't know if it's that sort of thing. I do know that there were whispers among Kandace's friends about something big planned for tonight."

"Aren't you one of Kandace's friends?" Raye asks.

"Kandace and I are friendly"—Zara smiles—"but that doesn't mean I can't be friendly with you and Parker. It isn't like we're dating or anything." She smiles at me. She has dimples. "I think Kandace's whole trying-to-get-a-guy-who-isn't-into-her thing is just pathetic, especially when the guy is in a relationship. But she can't seem to let it go. I hear Ellen and Marion are staging some kind of intervention. Should be funny, if nothing else. She would absolutely die if you were there to witness her humiliation."

"I don't know."

"We're heading over there as soon as I'm done here." Zara takes the purple negligee from my hands. "Are you going to buy this? Because if you aren't I think I'll take it."

"There's a whole rack of them over there." My voice is

237

still cold. I want Marion and Kandace and all of their friends out of my life.

"Yeah. I think I'll take this one." She gives me a lopsided smile and takes the ensemble to the checkout girl. A couple of minutes later Zara saunters out of the store, giving us a little wave.

"What, does everyone in school have the hots for you now?" Raye sounds bothered. More than that, she almost sounds jealous. "Ian called and told me about the party. I didn't tell you because I didn't think you'd be interested."

"Your opinions about what and who I would be interested in have been a little bit askew lately." My voice is still cold. I grab another little lacy number from the rack, double-check that it's really a size XS—sometimes they put them on the wrong hangers—and hand it to the cashier.

"Wow, did I see crotchless panties on that number?"

I laugh. "Get your mind out of Fredrick's of Hollywood. You know they don't sell crotchless panties at Victoria's Secret." The ice is still between us, but it's cracked a little. "You know where this party is?"

"Ian's there. I can get directions."

"Let's go."

"No mall pizza?"

"You want to eat it in your car?"

Raye sighs. There is no way she's letting mall pizza be eaten in her car.

"Okay, we'll just grab a few cookies."

In the car, loaded with cookies and iced cappuccino, I turn to her. "Raye, I hope we can get things back to where they were before, that we can talk about anything and everything again. The worst part about being grounded is never getting to talk to you." She doesn't say anything, and there is silence for a long time. She takes a drink and puts the cup back in the cup holder.

"It's all so stupid, isn't it?" she says finally.

"What?"

"Oh, high school and everything. The first day I met you, you were almost crying because those guys were teasing you, and it was just because they thought you were cute. You hate attention, that's a given. But I like it, okay? I like to get some attention at school and when we go out. I'm kind of jealous of you, Parker."

"Why would you be jealous of me? You have cool hair. You can dance in public. You can say anything to anybody without the fear that you are going to freeze up and look like a moron."

"Yeah, and you got the hottest guy in school."

"You don't even like him. I mean, if we broke up would you even want to go out with him?"

"No. I can't stand him. Smug little prick. But I do know that since you have him, the entire school is fascinated by his fascination with you. You are suddenly the most interesting girl at Allenville, and that's just a little different." Raye turns sharply, and though she's the outgoing one, I can tell this is hard for her, painful, maybe.

"I hate all that stuff. I just want to be with him, to be your friend, to drift along under the social radar. Same old Parker Prescott."

"You may be the same old Parker Prescott to you, but not to anybody else. He's done things to you and to your reputation that even I don't understand."

I look at her. The interior lights in the Honda make a greenish glare. What things? What has he done to me?

"Look, Parker, it's my fault, the jealousy thing. I'll deal

239

with it. We'll go back to being Raye and Park, the girls who go to the mall every Friday night."

"Except this Friday night we're going to an Allenville party."

"Yeah. Who would have thought it?"

34

Allenville has a *very* active party scene. It goes with the frenzied-rich-kids-trying-to-pretend-they-aren't-in-a-school-for-dorky-smart-kids kind of vibe we have going on.

I went to a party once with Paige, when she was a junior and I was a freshman. It was before she started hating me for being the good one. In fact, I was hopeful that night. Here we were, Paige and Parker Prescott, in high school together, and here Paige was taking me to a party with her. I know, pathetic, right? It isn't like I made her bad, or it was my fault she was so wild. But I couldn't change from being a nervous freshman who stood in the corner and sipped her drink and wished she had something to say, just because my sister was laughing and everyone at the party wanted to get close enough to talk to her.

That party was the first time I ever saw two people having sex. I mean, really doing it. They were in the corner. Most everyone was drunk, but I wasn't, and I took in everything. I usually avoid the party scene. Not because I'm a prude, just that as an official ice princess, I don't really know where to look or how to react when I have to step over two people locked together in "the act of love" to reach the restroom.

Plus, drugs and alcohol are pretty much staples at these parties. I have a fear of drugs and alcohol that I suspect stems from my inability to lose my self-control. I don't like puking or drooling or dancing around looking like a fool. I don't particularly like people who do puke, drool, or dance like fools either.

It's not inconceivable that he might be at this party. He goes to most of them. When we were together we often just spent Saturday nights at his house. He never really pushed me to go to parties, and it just became one of those things we didn't share. One of many things, possibly. There have been rumors lately, stupid rumors about him and about Kandace, and he's been distracted. Ever since . . . well, he was exasperated before, now he's distracted. I know it's barely been a day, but what if I'm not good enough and he just doesn't want me anymore? Could I be any more pathetic? I try to keep my brain focused, but it's really hard.

"Where is this stupid party?" I ask, trying to distract myself from the thoughts that won't stop going round and round in my head.

"I don't know. This neighborhood sucks," Raye says. We've left the affluent suburbs behind. The houses here are rectangles and squares, the cars are older, the shrubs need to be trimmed. This doesn't look like any Allenville party I've heard of. The ones the kids talk about are usually at big places with swimming pools and wine cellars and stuff. Raye is making a face, and I wonder if she will react this way if I have to move to some dumpy neighborhood with square shrubs.

"This must be it. Now, where to park?" There are cars everywhere. Cars upon cars upon cars. Raye pulls into a neighboring yard, and we walk toward the music.

I knock on the door, because that's what I always do before I go into a place. The girl who answers has serious dental issues—her mouth is full of braces—and her brown hair is sort of wispy and falls all around her face. She looks familiar. I know she goes to our school, but she looks even more familiar than that, like I should know her.

"Hi," I say.

"Hi. I'm Alicia."

"This is your party, right?" Raye asks.

"Yeah." Alicia doesn't look all that happy.

"C'mon, let's see what's up." Raye pulls me inside. Four girls are sitting at a cheap Formica table in this little square dining area. I can hear people laughing in the living room, but Marion's group have the kitchen all to themselves.

"Oh no." Ellen Birch glances up, sees us, and makes a face. "Look who's here." The horror on their faces would almost be comical—well, I guess it is comical, except that my heart is beating really fast and I feel nauseous. It might be a bad idea to eat mall cookies and drink iced cappuccinos when you're a passenger in Raye's car. Sometimes I get a little sick.

"Don't trust your man, huh?" Marion Henessy must really hate me. Real true hate. But her saying that proves that he is here. This makes me happy and worried at the same time. Happy because I can't wait to see him, need to see him. Worried because, well, he's here.

"I don't know what you're talking about." Is he messing around with Kandace Freemont? Is that what's happening? Do not throw up mall cookies, white chocolate macadamia nut vomit all over the floor, no way. I take a really deep breath and squint at them through the smoke.

"Right. You show up at the one party of the year where we have this thing planned for your boyfriend, and you don't know what's going on."

"Zara Thorpe told us we should get over here." Raye can sound really tough when she wants to. I'm glad she's on my side.

"You want to make a wager, Prescott?" I'm looking into the eyes of Ellen Birch, Kandace Freemont's sleazy-ass best friend. "I'm betting that Kandace gets what she wants before tonight is over."

"How much?" I ask. Did I say that out loud?

"One thousand dollars," she says.

I hesitate. I know they don't have a thousand dollars, and neither do we, and just the idea of this kind of a bet makes me feel sick. Plus, I suspect that they are becoming aware of my money problems and that if they find a way to twist this so that I owe them money, I will never live it down.

"She doesn't trust him," Marion says.

"No, she doesn't have a thousand dollars. Have you seen the for-sale sign in her yard? Her family is broke. Pretty soon she'll be living in some dump like this," Ellen says. I flinch for Alicia, the girl who lives here, but she's hovering in the background. She actually seems glad to have these bitches here.

"I'm good for the money. We'll take your wager," Raye

says. One thousand dollars. That's how much they said he got for being the one, the first one. These guys aren't overly creative.

"Okay. Alicia, go downstairs and open the other basement window." Alicia moves quickly to obey the great and obnoxious Marion.

"If you guys say anything or do anything to mess this up, the money is forfeit," Marion says. She and her friends go over in the corner and whisper for a few minutes. Raye picks up a Coke and a plastic cup. She splashes a little bit of Coke, and a healthy dose of whiskey, over a couple of ice cubes.

"You want something, Parker?" a girl asks. I don't recognize her.

I shake my head.

"Everybody take your places!" Marion herself grabs my arm and nearly wrenches it out of the socket.

"Why are we going outside?" I ask. All the girls make shushing noises, they're like a flock of stupid chickens. I swear, Marion's little group of friends are the most annoying people I've ever met.

The great one, Marion herself, leads me to this little rectangular window.

"You can watch through here," she says. "Stay down where they can't see you." I kneel in the mud. "This place is just crap," Marion mutters. She kneels beside me.

There are maybe thirty kids in the basement. He's sitting on the couch, with his ankles crossed loosely, smoking a joint.

He's wearing gray pants that are a little baggy and a black shirt. He turns to another guy, says something, laughs, then passes the joint on. He looks delicious. Watching him, I can't believe that I felt let down or that I hated the way it felt some of the time when he was touching me. He is so perfect, and I'm so lucky to have him. And these things get better, right?

Somebody—Alicia?—turns off the music. Several people stand up and walk off, probably to get more beer. A girl spills something on the floor and somebody hands her a roll of paper towels.

I'm staring so hard at him that I barely sense that Marion has turned toward me, that she's looking at me instead of in the window.

"You weren't supposed to be here tonight," she says, and I can't tell if she's angry or apologetic or what. "I didn't really mean for you to be here to see this," she says. This is probably the closest thing to an apology I will ever get from Marion. She didn't even apologize when we were in preschool and she gave my favorite doll a makeover complete with a new punk hairstyle and permanent-marker eye makeup. Even though her mom made her apologize, she still didn't, not really.

In the smoky basement Kandace Freemont appears through a door. She was obviously already there, waiting. She's wearing this tiny little skirt, and this tiny little sweater, and though you can't see any details through this tiny little basement window, several guys turn to stare. My guess is that Kandace looks pretty hot. She's an attractive girl. I can admit that. I know she's heading for my boyfriend. He's like a magnet to her. I wonder what he feels for Kandace? There has to be something, even if he's not showing it. Would she keep throwing herself at him with no encouragement at all?

She walks toward him very slowly. He turns toward her, and I can see him take her in, from head to toe. His gaze is slow. He's so relaxed, so comfortable in his own skin. I'm having trouble breathing again. I strain forward, trying to hear what she's saying, but I can't make it out. His voice is louder.

"Jesus Christ, Kandace. Can't I go anyplace in this town without you showing up?" He stands up. She reaches for him, puts both arms out, like a supplicant, a beggar. He pushes her away. "What part of 'I don't want you' don't you understand?"

I stand up. They may want to keep watching, but I don't. My leg aches from the way it's been bent, and my palm is grooved from holding myself up on the concrete. I didn't want to see this. I didn't want to witness this. It's disgusting. I am singing inside, dancing on air. I maintain my air of disdain, though I want so badly to smile.

"What was the point of that?" I ask Marion as I pry a tiny rock out of one of the grooves in my hand. "I thought Kandace was your friend."

"We were hoping he would throw her down on the couch." Marion looks straight at me as she says this. "We had the camera set up just for you, so you could watch later. If that didn't happen, we were hoping to get him out of her system once and for all. That's why we we're calling it an intervention. Kandace needs to move on. The whole thing is annoying." She can say that again.

I see Raye with Ian on the couch. He's trying to get her to kiss him, nibbling at her, but she's too interested in the unfolding drama to get wrapped up in him.

Marion commands her minion, "Get Kandace up here. This won't be effective unless we confront her immediately."

"How do you know about this intervention stuff? From your creepy stalker brother?"

"Do you know how many times my brother drove your sister to the hospital when she drank too much?" Marion's voice is all shaky and weird. I would feel sorry for her, but that would be pretty stupid when she seems so determined to ruin my life.

"My sister would never get in a car with your brother." Why does she always try to make Paige the bad one?

I really should just ignore her. She shakes her head at me, but then turns away because someone has dragged a bawling Kandace up the stairs. The girls gather around her, patting her, giving her hugs, consoling her. I suspect I'll never hear another word about the thousand-dollar wager. It was all just Marion's crowd acting tough.

I slip unseen down the dark, creaky basement stairs.

The basement is smoky. Somebody cranks the music back up, and people are talking, laughing, socializing. He's turned away from me, and there's a frown on his face. He shifts, and my heart jumps into my mouth. *What if he's planning to get up and go after Kandace?* I find myself picturing them in an embrace and it makes me physically sick. I put my hand on his shoulder.

He turns quickly, almost angrily, as if he's offended by being touched. Then he sees me, and a slow smile spreads across his face.

"I thought you were grounded, Prescott." He takes my hand in his. I yank my hand away. I didn't mean to, I just, for some crazy reason, did. "Parker?" He pulls me down on the couch. He's such a flawless kisser, and I just relax and let him kiss me.

I forget where we are. I forget about our audience. I forget that Marion straight-out told me there was a video camera in this room. His thumbs are hooked into the sides of my jeans, pulling me into him. This could be much better than things were before, much, much better. Everything feels so perfectly right between us all of a sudden. Not awkward or forced or anything. Not like it was. The whole interruption thing and the realtor, and knowing that Paige could come home any time, it was too much. We should've just watched a movie.

His mouth is all over mine, and it feels wonderful, but there is this distracting snuffling sound. I break away and make sudden jarring eye contact with Kandace, who is standing across the room crying into something that looks like a kitchen towel. Looks like she has broken away from Marion and was maybe pretending she wanted a beer, just to see him again.

"C'mon, Kandace." Marion is behind her. She sounds pissed. It isn't often that one of her little lackeys doesn't do exactly what she says. Believe me, I know.

"Let's get out of here." He pulls me to my feet.

We go upstairs. I don't see Raye anywhere. As I walk into the kitchen, holding his hand, Marion's friends watch me from the Formica table, which seems to be the base of operations for all their evil plans.

He walks away from me, into the living room, where some guys are drinking beer and arm-wrestling. He leans against a wall and looks bored. Can't he see I need him right now? I thought we were leaving. I stand in the doorway behind him, awkward and alone.

I can see that he has totally tuned out, turned off by all the drama. He gives a little head jerk, telling me to come on in and sit with him, but for some reason I can't. I open the screen door and walk out onto the narrow front porch.

Raye and Ian are still in the basement, I think. I walk

outside. If I walk down to where Raye parked, I can get some Tylenol out of Raye's glove compartment. Did she lock her car? I can't remember and I'm just kind of turning circles in the driveway, not sure what to do, when I see my dad's Jeep pull up. There's no doubt that it's his; I can see the way the left headlight kind of wavers, and I can see the stupid air freshener he hangs from the rearview mirror, and I can even see the glint from his glasses.

What is my dad's Jeep doing in the driveway of this house all the way across town from our neighborhood? For a second I'm sure my dad has come to rescue me. I open the door and get in. I see myself reflected back at me in his glasses for a second before I realize it isn't my dad driving the Jeep at all. It's Kyle Henessy. He has his cell phone against his ear.

"Oh fuck," I say.

"I'm right outside in the green Jeep," he says into the cell.

The back door opens. "Kyle?" Marion climbs into the backseat. "What're you doing driving this? What happened to your car? You were supposed to be here ten minutes ago."

"I had a flat tire, at the Prescotts' house."

"Oh no." Marion puts her head into her hands.

"It's okay, Marion. Paige and I have been talking. She's not going to have me questioned by the police or taken to court again."

"Oh, no no no," Marion says. I realize with surprise that she's crying. "You already let Paige Prescott ruin your life once. Why would you give her another chance to hurt you?" This is a good question. Another good question might be, why would Paige Prescott give Kyle Henessy the time of day? She only speaks to her own sister when she wants to taunt me or make fun of me, what's up with her suddenly wanting to talk to him?

"I'd like to get out of the car." I try to say this calmly.

"I'll drop you off at your house, Parker. I want to tell Paige goodnight, anyway."

He says this like it's reasonable. Like running out of a party and getting into my dad's Jeep only to discover that it's being driven by a guy under a restraining order, my sister's stalker, no less, who just borrowed said vehicle because the stalker-mobile has a flat in the Prescott driveway, and he (Kyle) needs the car to pick up my worst enemy (Marion) from this party, where she just tried to sabotage my love life and my self-esteem, is reasonable.

He says to me, "I'll give you a lift."

Yeah, this is normal. To him. And I'm totally entering his world. Hell, I'm already here.

We drive across town in silence. The only sound is Marion's annoying snuffling from the backseat. I try to understand what is going on with her, why she is so freaking upset, but it just doesn't make sense to me.

We pull into my driveway and everyone just sits there.

"Well, thank you for the ride," I say. Is he going to park my dad's Jeep or just drive off in it? Marion is all hunched over with her arms around her knees.

We aren't in the driveway five seconds before my sister runs out the door.

"I'll take Kyle and Marion home. Bye, Parker," she says in a rush.

"I'm going with you," I tell her. There is no way she's driving around with these freaks alone. No way. This is all so crazy, if I go with her, maybe we'll both make it back to our house alive and everything.

"There's no reason—"

"I want to know what's going on here," I tell her.

"Nothing is going on."

"Then it won't matter if I ride along with you."

I stay in the front seat because I don't want my sister near Kyle. Even though he's been pretty benign, being around the object of his obsession may not be the best thing for him.

The Henessys live about ten minutes from our house. They moved into the nicer, newer subdivision before Kyle started hanging out in our tree. My parents took it as an enormous insult, because they had been sharing our backyard with the Henessys since before I was born, having cookouts and things like that.

"You'd better make sure your alcoholic sister is sober enough to drive," Marion hisses. The only other sound for nine and a half minutes is the hum of the Jeep's tires skimming over the back roads as we drive through three interconnected subdivisions to reach the Henessys' great big well-lighted house, where there is no for-sale sign anywhere in sight.

"I didn't know you knew where I lived," Kyle says to my sister. For a stalker he's awfully vulnerable.

"I remember," Paige says.

"So do I," Marion says. "You passed out in our living room."

"What're you talking about?" I ask no one in particular and get no answer at all.

Paige puts the Jeep in park. Kyle gets out, walks around, and opens the door for Marion, who practically falls out onto the sidewalk because she's trying to keep her distance from Paige. Confident, bossy Marion is sure different when she gets away from her disciples at school. Of course, she used to completely worship Paige when we were little. Kyle doesn't say goodnight or slobber on my sister after all. He stands in the driveway looking confused and lost for a minute, and then he follows Marion inside.

Paige and I drive home in silence. I spend the whole trip trying to think how to ask her what the heck is going on, how to break the ice, and before I say anything we're pulling past Kyle's Explorer with its flat tire and into our garage.

35

Before I go to bed, I leave messages on Raye's phone and on his. I wish I had just stayed at the party, but I don't know. I really needed to get out of there, though I won't be able to explain it to either of them. I know I won't be able to make them understand.

I draw an all-new house plan. Something smaller and without the ice-skating rink. I imagine an ice rink would make it expensive to heat in the winter, anyway. That guy Albert from the electric company would probably call and tell me off for wasting energy.

When I'm done I pad down the hall and borrow my brother's Crayola markers and start coloring my illuminated manuscript. It isn't as beautiful as I wanted it to be, what with the bright primary colors, but it keeps me from screaming, or pulling out my hair, or stealing one of my parents' vehicles and driving back to the party to see what's going on. He could have at least called to check on me. I try not to ask myself why I am always hoping for him to call and then being let down.

        ᵔ   ᵔ   ᵔ

Saturday is uncommonly confusing because I don't know whether to press my luck. Should I consider myself officially ungrounded or lie low for a while? I'm thinking that maybe Paige's bizarre behavior will take the heat off me. That's the way things have worked for the sixteen years up to this point.

I slip downstairs to swipe something to eat and test the waters. Mom is on the phone, wandering around the kitchen.

"So, Theresa, I would really appreciate it if you would get me some estimates for houses in Florida. Yes, Chris was offered the job he applied for on Tuesday, and I could always transfer. I think Florida would be great for Preston. With the beautiful weather he could spend so much time outside." I was reaching for a Pop-Tart, but now my hand is frozen in midair. "Yes, I know it'll be Parker's senior year, but to be honest with you, we haven't been that impressed by the education she's getting at Allenville. And Chris and I would love to get her away from her boyfriend." Mom turns and looks directly at me. She knows I've been listening.

I take the Pop-Tart and head back to my room without a glass of milk. I figure I had better lie low for a very long time.

Florida. I can't even contemplate it. The fact that they

would go to such extremes to ruin my life makes me want to ram my fist through something. What have I done all this work for, getting money from Kyle, if they're just going to move us away from here?

Mom calls me down less than an hour later. My sister is sitting on the couch, appearing sober, and talking to Dad. They want to take us all to Red Lobster. This kind of thing doesn't happen much. What with my brother's inability to sit still and my sister's nonstop social life, we never went out even when my dad had a job and we could afford to. The last time I went to a restaurant with them was for the rehearsal dinner for Paige's wedding.

I wasn't even supposed to be in the wedding. I've always had this secret desire to dress up and be a bridesmaid, but Paige didn't want me. Not until one of her bridesmaids couldn't make it home from college. So I got drafted to wear a too-big dress and carry a bunch of purple geraniums. It was the first time I ever tasted champagne, the first time I danced a slow dance on a dance floor, and the last time I danced a slow dance on a dance floor. For one thing, ice princesses simply do not dance, and for another, one of West's best buds was looking down the front of the hideous purple dress that was too big for me, the imposter bridesmaid. I was wearing purple satin panties and a matching bra, but I wasn't particularly interested in having some Neanderthal check out my underwear.

❧ ❧ ❧

"I have to have dinner with my family tonight," I tell him on the phone. "At Red Lobster." I just keep talking, like he cares. I couldn't stand it, I had to call him, but I haven't mentioned the party, or Kandace Freemont, or me leaving abruptly.

"What time?" That's a weird question. Is he pretending to be interested or something?

"Supposed to be six, but Paige will be running late, so probably closer to seven. Why?"

"We'll be there."

"What? Who?"

"Me and the folks, little brother. We'll share some calamari and talk about where they want me to go to college. See you at seven." He hangs up.

That was weird. I call Raye. She shows no interest in taking her family to Red Lobster, but she has plenty to say about everything he and I did not discuss.

"Why did you run out?" she asks.

"I'm not cut out for the Allenville party scene," I tell her. How else can I explain?

"That's a real surprise. You have to be an alcoholic slut to enjoy an Allenville party. That or an extrovert."

I laugh. "I don't think I qualify as either."

"I changed my mind," she says. "If you two break up, I totally want him." Her voice is light—is she joking?

"Too bad. You can't."

"Why not?"

"Universal rule of friendship."

"But you asked me last week if I would want him."

"And your answer was no."

"Now it's yes."

"Why?"

"I don't know. I liked his style last night. Pushing Kandace away."

"Raye, he didn't have any style. He was kind of a jerk. I left because he just walked away from me." I've spent so much time beating myself up for walking out, for possibly messing things up again, that this is the first time I've let myself feel irritated with him. And just because I'm talking Raye out of wanting him, which I know is really just her teasing me. I remind myself that he gestured with his head, that he was waiting for me to join him, but somehow it wasn't enough. And then there's the thing with always waiting for him, always being on edge. Sometimes I wonder if it's worth it.

"Yeah, I guess you're not the only one who's attracted to jerks. Ian is being a complete jerk too. He went and comforted Kandace Freemont, you know. Totally ignored me the rest of the night." Her voice is low, bitter.

"What, why?" God, poor Raye.

"He said he felt so sorry for her, it was the least he could do." I can't tell if she's sarcastic or sad or what. That's what sucks about cell phones, you can't always tell how the other person is feeling. "It's all screwed up, isn't it?" Raye sighs.

I hate all this freaking drama so much.

Dinner at Red Lobster. I'm wearing a black skirt and a red sweater, more because he said he'd be there than because I care how I look at a seafood chain. Preston sits by me. I don't know what's up with his recent liking for me. He keeps asking me to draw things for him. It's kind of flattering. I feel pretty fond of him right now too. Dad sits on his other side. Mom and Paige are across the table.

"So what classes are you taking this semester, Paige?" Dad asks. Paige mumbles something about public speaking. What a joke. She straightened her hair and it's silky and wispy. I wish I were cool enough that she would talk to me instead of rolling her eyes at me.

I see him. I feel him. I hear him across the room. A

hostess in a black vest is seating him and his family at a booth. He looks at me.

"Parker, your father asked you a question," Mom says.

Dad repeats himself for me. "It's okay, honey. I just wanted to know what your favorite class was this year."

"Advanced British lit," I answer.

"Oh yes, Shakespeare and *Beowulf* and all, right?"

"I guess."

"I can spell *salamander*," my brother says.

"That's a pretty long word for him," Mom tells Dad.

It turns out my brother has no idea how to spell *salamander*, and on that depressing note, the appetizers arrive. We spend ten minutes trading dipping sauces, and the waitress brings my brother a refill of what appears to be Coke but is really Diet Coke, and when he takes a big drink, because he doesn't like Diet Coke, he spits it out all over the place.

Mom mops him and the table off with a stack of napkins, and Dad fondly remembers the days when Red Lobster had cloth napkins rather than paper. The food comes.

I see him stand up. A young waitress checks him out, but I don't feel anything. He didn't come here to Red Lobster to see her, did he? He stops and says something to her and she smiles. I'm sure it was nothing.

I excuse myself, though I have a bad feeling that all my fried shrimp will be gone when I return. That's one of the hazards of sitting by Preston.

I slide into an alcove beside him. There are tons of people waiting for tables, but somehow there is just enough space for me to press myself next to him.

"Oh, Prescott, you have made my parents so happy."

"They like the family dinner thing?"

"They lap it up."

I could lap you up, I think. Oh my God, where did that come from? I can feel my face getting hot.

"Good, I'm glad they're happy." I think about my parents fumbling for something to say, about his parents jumping to spend an hour with him. It all makes me a little depressed.

I start to ask him what he said to the waitress, what was so funny, but I don't.

He kisses me. I know there's a family with two young kids and an elderly couple with a full view, but there is nothing in me, no part of me, that cares at all. In fact, I wouldn't mind if the entire staff of Red Lobster were watching. My heart beats faster as I realize people probably are watching, rolling their eyes or whatever. I'm not completely comfortable with this after all.

"I'll have to get back soon." We come up for air, and I open my eyes.

"I know." He nuzzles my neck a little. I have about a million worries about where this is going and where he's been, but right now all I can think about is that after everything he still likes me. He wants to be with me. He brought his family to Red Lobster and here we are.

"About the party," I say.

"I know, Park, I should've taken you home."

"I wanted to tell you why . . . ," I begin, even though I don't know why I left, exactly.

"Well, well, well." All of a sudden Paige is standing right over us. "What's he doing here?" she asks.

"Eating dinner," he says. The look he gives my sister is not friendly. She doesn't notice, maybe because the lighting isn't so good in Red Lobster. Maybe because she doesn't care.

"Mom sent me to see if you were sick or climbing out the window. Wait until she hears you were making out with him in the waiting area."

"You would tell on me?"

"You know what, Princess Parker? I've hit rock bottom. I have nothing better to do than tattle on you and Preston." She gives a little smile, and I don't know if she's joking or not. The rock bottom part sounds about right.

"I hate you," I tell her. I turn back to him. "I hate her." He nods as if this is reasonable.

"I guess you'd better go, I don't want you to get grounded again." Feeling insanely happy that he cares if I am grounded again, I give him a quick hug and follow Paige back to the table. I don't know why she has to act like such a bitch. It isn't like I ever really told on her.

"Parker, have you done something new with your hair?" my dad asks.

"No." There is an awkward silence. Really, I haven't done anything different. Haven't even changed the part or anything.

"You look different. I don't know what it is."

I've lost my virginity, Daddy. That's the difference.

Why does that pop into my head? What is the matter with me? I glance over at Paige. She raises her water glass at me in a mock salute. Is she going to tell on me or what? The lemon wedge falls off of her glass and she stares at it like she isn't quite sure where it came from. I don't think she's going to say anything, and I feel very relieved. The absence of extra drama will always be a relief, for me.

My brother is trying to color his coloring placemat with a piece of shrimp. Mom watches him for a minute, then sighs and asks for the check. It doesn't add much in the way of color (the shrimp), but it does give the ocean-view picture a nice glossy sheen.

Dad hands the waitress a credit card. I hold my breath. What if it gets declined? What if it's declined and we don't have any way to pay?

She brings back the credit card slip and Dad signs it. When he thinks no one is looking he slides the pen into his pocket.

"I guess it's time to hit the road," Dad says. He stands up. Mom fumbles for her purse under the table. Getting five people out of a restaurant can be a ridiculously slow process. As we walk past his table I stare at him but try not to show recognition. His mom looks up and sees me and gives a little half wave. I smile at her and follow my sister out the double doors to the parking lot.

We pile into the Jeep and head home. I stare out the window and remember when I was little and going out to dinner was the highlight of my week. I thought it was so fun to sit between my brother in his high chair and Paige and order grilled cheese or chicken fingers and share a dessert with them. Things have changed and it makes me sad.

My parents go into the kitchen to make after-dinner drinks, exclaiming about how expensive the drinks are at Red Lobster. When did they go from making me feel safe and secure to making me feel so sad and worried?

꒜   ꒜   ꒜

I leave my parents, and their silly drinks, downstairs and go to my room to call Raye. When she picks up it sounds like she's been crying. I knew after what she told me that she was most likely staying home tonight.

"I broke up with Ian, again."

"What? Why?"

"I just got tired of his not being in love with me."

"What about prom?" I know I often castigate prom, have even been known to call it the most overhyped night of a girl's life, but Raye seemed really excited about going. She already picked out a strappy little black dress and matching four-inch heels. It was a hot ensemble, not foofy or frilly or sequiny in the least.

I go to the computer and click over to the stupid Social Siren. There's a little sign that says UNDER CONSTRUCTION. Interesting. Marion must be too screwed up worrying about her brother to spew any venom, even about her so-called intervention for Kandace Freemont. I've got nothing in my anonymous account from Kyle H. I wasn't expecting anything, but I checked just in case. It's kind of a relief to see an empty in-box. I feel pretty vile. I can't even think how I'm ever going to repay him.

"Parker?" Raye's voice is quiet. For a second I got so distracted that I forgot I'm still on the phone with her.

"Raye, will you come over and spend the night?" I ask, needing to make things better.

"Do you have any chocolate chip cookies?"

"No."

Loud sigh. "Okay, Parker, I'll stop and get some on the way."

It seems like hours before she arrives, and I'm lying on my bed trying not to get sleepy. The aftermath of too much family time, I guess.

Raye picked up the kind of cookies you have to bake, so we head down to the kitchen. With the smell of baking and the warmth and the softness of the recessed lighting, our kitchen is probably the most comforting place on earth. I can't imagine some other family sitting here happily. Of course, I can't really picture my family sitting here happily either. Not anymore.

Paige comes in and sits down at the table. House rules state that I can't make her go away. Rules established by yours truly, when Paige and her high school friends thought they *owned* this kitchen, and the living room, and the den, and the telephone, and the big-screen TV, and the computer. We only had one computer back then, if you can imagine.

She helps herself to a cookie. Raye's eyes meet mine over the plate. She doesn't have much use for Paige, and neither do I, I guess.

"So are you two going to the prom?" Paige asks. Here we go again. The things Paige thinks are important.

"No, my boyfriend is a junior, like me," I tell her, in case she forgot. Or doesn't know. Or gives a damn.

"I was going to go, but I broke up with my boyfriend just a few hours ago." I don't suppose I've given Raye appropriate sympathy, especially if she's trying to get it from Paige.

"I went to the prom every single year of high school," Paige tells us, as if we don't know. It was probably buying all the prom dresses and jewelry and shit that caused my parents to go into all this debt.

"The guy who took me my sophomore year was such a loser." Oh great, it's the loser-date story. I remember this guy. He drove a white pickup truck. "Yeah," she continues, as if we are showing some interest. "We had to stop by a grocery store on the way to prom to buy contraceptives. Like, here he was in a tuxedo, and I was in that really hot silver dress, do you remember it, Parker? And the people checking us through had to know exactly what we were doing and why."

"Why didn't you go through the self-checkout?" Raye asks her.

"I don't know, I told you that guy was a loser." Should I tell Paige that it sounds suspiciously like it takes one to know one? No, something else comes out of my mouth. Something that sounds surprisingly friendly, like sisterly gossip.

"Well, at least he didn't tell you how much he likes to fish."

"What?" Paige and Raye in stereo, something to remember in my old age.

"Remember that guy Droopy that you set me up with, the one who wouldn't pay for my movie ticket?"

"*What?*"

"Josh's friend, the one who couldn't stand up straight and who kept staring at my chest?" Raye obviously has no recollection of anything besides Josh's tonsils on that date, so I launch into the details. Before I get to the attempted kiss, she and Paige are laughing so hard they're almost crying. I think Raye might actually be crying.

Then Paige says something I don't know how to interpret.

"When did you grow up, Parker? And why didn't I notice?"

"I think it was Thursday," I say, still in the mood to joke around. Except I forgot that they both know what happened on Thursday. And they don't agree with my whole not-diminishing-the-experience thing. They want the gritty details. It starts with Paige.

"What happened?" she asks. The way she is looking at me, all wide-eyed and attentive, is the same way she always looked at her popular pretty friends. No wonder they liked telling her stuff.

"Yeah, you never really told me, exactly . . . ," Raye jumps in with Paige, trying to wear down my resistance. She knows I don't want to talk about this.

"Where are Mom and Dad? Do you think they're listening?" I stare at the doorway that connects the kitchen to the living room, as if they're lurking around. I kind of hope they will show up so we can change the subject. No luck.

I sigh, really loudly. I guess I'm going to have to talk about it sometime.

"It was just, you know, not perfect. I thought with him, it would be."

They both look at me. And nobody says anything.

"I wasn't frigid," I say to Paige. It's a dumb thing to say.

Paige shakes her head. "Parker . . ."

"Of course not." Raye gives Paige a dirty look. "I've seen you with him, you know, kissing or whatever. There's no way you're frigid. Why would you even think that?"

"You know, the whole Ice Princess thing."

"Yeah, what is that, Parker?" Raye hands me a cookie. "That Ice Princess thing is just Marion Henessy garbage. You need to stop listening to that crap. Would I be best friends with some kind of stupid Ice Princess?" She gets up and walks over to the oven, opens it, even though you aren't supposed to, and looks in. "Hey, do you have any M&M's? We can make these into Cute Cookie Guy–worthy cookies."

"You just set your expectations too high," Paige says slowly, like she's really been thinking about it. "It's like the way you put things or people on a pedestal. Nothing ever lives up to your expectations."

There's a crash from the living room, and Preston comes into the kitchen, followed by Mom and Dad.

"I know I never could," Paige says. "Live up to your expectations." We stare at each other. I'm not sure what she means, exactly. When did she ever care about what I thought? I want to ask her, but now our parents are standing in front of the kitchen counter with the glasses from their cheap after-dinner drinks.

"You guys want some cookies?" Raye asks my parents. I get up and pour Preston a glass of milk. He can never manage it without spilling half of what was meant to be in the glass all over the counter. I give him a straw. Same theory; without one he spills as much as he drinks.

"What're you girls talking about?" Dad asks.

"School," I say.

"Prom," Raye says.

Paige doesn't say anything.

☙ ☙ ☙

In my bedroom, Raye unzips her backpack and hands me my Victoria's Secret bag.

"Let's see how it looks," she says.

In the spirit of feeling slightly warmer than I was last week, I strip off my jeans and sweater and hesitate only for a second before I slither into the little nightie and matching panties.

"You're lucky, having skin like that. When I'm pale I look all blotchy and sick. You have Snow White skin."

"Thanks, I guess. I mean, it could be worse, but a nice bronze tan wouldn't hurt any of us." Raye laughs. I change into an oversized T-shirt and boy shorts for sleep. The way she's acting is weirding me out. I mean, it's almost, but not quite, like flirting.

Although, if you think about it, a friendship isn't that much different from a romantic relationship. I mean, you get together because you have things in common. You stay together because you're compatible. The only difference is that unless you're some kind of freaks you don't ever make out.

I take the pillows off the bed and put them on the window seat.

"Do you do that every single night?" Raye always asks this, since the first time she ever spent the night.

"Yes." What else would I do, throw them on the floor? Raye laughs at me, not with me, and things are back to normal. We are definitely not going to make out.

"Did he like the pink canopy?" she asks. I switch off the light and get into bed, underneath the pink blankets and the silky sheets. She's way over on the other side of my bed fluffing up her pillows.

"Yes," I say, feeling that smile I can't control, "he liked it very much."

We don't say anything else for a long time. Then she asks, "Parker, you did change the sheets, didn't you?" I pretend I'm asleep.

The next morning I get up earlier than Raye. She's a late sleeper, and I'm not. This is no big deal as long as we aren't spending the night at her house. Her stepfather, the dentist, is always in the living room watching reruns of this army show and he smokes a pipe. She has a TV in her room, but if you turn it on in the morning, she pulls her pillow over her face and moans and groans.

I tiptoe over to my dresser, open my jeans drawer, and get out my favorite jeans and an Allenville hoodie that I never wear in public. I wouldn't want to chance an uncharacteristic display of school spirit, but it's soft and comfy so I do wear it around the house.

I glance over a few times to see if Raye is going to wake up, but no such luck.

I go downstairs, glad for the warm clothes because it's cold down here. Preston is sitting in front of the TV eating the center of a frosted strawberry Pop-Tart.

"If you eat the sides first, then you can save the middle part for the last few bites," I tell him. He sticks his fork into the very center, in what appears to be blatant defiance of my words.

Then he says, "Here, Parker," and pops the fork into my mouth. The hot center of a frosted Pop-Tart. Is there anything better in the world?

"What're you watching?"

"People jumping."

He's actually watching people jumping on a rerun of *Fear Factor*, which is a very poor selection of programming for Preston since his ability to make good choices is severely underdeveloped.

Speaking of poor choices, while I'm standing there, watching to see if this heavily muscled guy can walk across this beam that's suspended way up in the air, West walks in. Of course, his eyes go straight to the TV and he says,

"Damn."

"How did you get into the house?" I ask West.

"Little guy let me in. You got any more of those Pop-Tarts?" Preston gets up to go fetch breakfast for our vile brother-in-law.

"Does Paige know you're here?"

"She will." When he says this he looks sinister. Usually he looks bad natured and sometimes a little bit stupid. Last week he looked kind of hot. Right now, he looks dangerous.

"Preston, run upstairs and tell Paige that her husband is here. While you're at it, tell Mom and Dad."

"Mom and Dad went to play tennis. They said you

would watch me," Preston says. Crap. Sometimes now they go on Saturdays and play at the high school tennis court, and it usually takes half the day because they have to wait until the court is open. I would have liked West to think that our parents are here, that they might wander into the living room at any time. He's making me nervous, and I know if my parents were here he'd be on his best behavior.

Paige comes downstairs. Some part of me, some romantic part, maybe, expects West to beg and plead for her to return to him. He doesn't, though. He just says,

"What the hell are you doing hanging around with Kyle Henessy?"

"Just hanging out," Paige says, like she doesn't care.

"After all the effort we went to, to keep that filthy perv away from you?"

I can kind of see his point. I mean, it doesn't seem really smart for Paige to be dating her ex-stalker, especially while she's still married to West.

"You need to come home with me," he says, glancing over her shoulder to see if the girl wearing the tank top is going to get across the beam faster than the muscular guy. The clock is ticking the seconds away.

"No," Paige says. I'm seriously getting ready to exit the room—my sister's marital problems are not really my business—but then West hauls off and hits her in the face.

I guess I've seen people hit each other in anger before. Even though Allenville is a great magnet school, we still have fights once in a while. Usually some guy pushes another guy and they say things to each other, and then they start whaling on one another. It happens, but not like this. Paige kind of stumbles backward against the wall.

I never saw a guy hit a girl before. I never saw a guy hit

my sister before. I sit down. Not for any reason, just my legs stop holding me up and I fall onto the couch beside my little brother. I stare at them, speechless, but they don't seem aware of Preston or me.

West stomps down the hall and Paige follows him. He doesn't say anything to us, though he usually pretends to be so friendly. Paige's face might be turning purple, or that might be some kind of shadow I'm seeing. Yeah, I think her left cheek is turning purple. I can't really tell, because her hair is hanging in her face. If you want to know the truth, I'm not so good at telling what Paige is thinking, and I never have been. Is she sad? Scared? Completely freaked out, like I am? As she passes me, she pushes the hair back and her hand is shaking.

West slams the front door, and then we hear the car doors. Why is she going with him?

I know I should have stopped her, should have told Paige not to leave with him, but I couldn't say anything. Not to Paige, or to West, or to Preston, who is sitting completely and totally still. My voice has disappeared.

☙   ☙   ☙

It's been ten minutes.

"Are you okay?" I ask Preston, finally.

"Yes." His eyes are big and dark. I don't know if he's answering my question, really. I don't know if he knows I mean emotionally and not just physically. He doesn't look okay.

"Let's get the phone and call Mom, all right?"

"Okay." He gets up and I walk behind him. The doorbell rings. I walk to the door. I hear Preston pattering after me, like he doesn't want to be alone. I don't blame him.

"Where's Paige?" Kyle Henessy is standing there

wearing these baggy gym shorts and a shirt that says GEEKS NEED LOVE TOO.

"She left," I hear myself saying. "She went with West. He hit her." I sound like a little kid, like I'm saying things my brother might say. Kyle pushes his hair back from his face.

"What am I supposed to do?" he says, almost to himself. "I'm not even supposed to get near her. She has the restraining order, remember?"

"What's going on?" Raye comes downstairs. She looks tired and her hair is flat on one side. I think in my crazy overheated brain that if anyone else tries to stand on our tiny little decorative porch, Preston, being the smallest, will be knocked off into the yard.

"Do you mind going home?" I ask her. It sounds rude. "Paige and West are fighting, and I need to deal with him." I gesture toward my brother. Raye nods. She knows a little bit about fighting. I was at her house once when her parents were going at it. I think that's why she's cool with this, even though I didn't explain things very well. I just can't talk about it right now. About my perfect sister being hit in the face.

"Call me if you need anything. I'll just get my bag and let myself out," she says in a quiet and un-Raye-like voice. I want to say thanks, but Preston is pulling on my shirt. I turn to him and he starts to cry. I take the phone out of his hand.

"Look," I say, "I'm calling Mom. She'll go get Paige, and it'll be okay. Okay?" He wraps his arms around me and pushes his face against me as if he's hiding. I pat his back, then wrap my arms around him and hold him for a really long time.

I stumble into the foyer with Preston still attached to

me. "Mom? Mom? West came and took Paige, and he hit her, and Preston is rubbing snot all over my favorite shirt." I can barely hear Mom, she's talking to Dad, but I get that they're coming home and that they're going to fix everything. I hope.

"I'll call you if I hear anything," I tell Kyle. He kind of nods and starts to walk away, following Raye, who is pulling out of the driveway.

"Do you have my cell phone number?" He takes my phone and puts his number in. I think that doing something makes him feel better, even something as small as programming his number into my phone. He doesn't really say goodbye, he just kind of walks away and gets into his mom's Volvo.

39

It's one of those days when the sun never really comes up, so time just seems to drag on and on. After what seems like forever my parents come home. They're trying to act calm in front of Preston.

"Should I drive over to the apartment and see if she's there and not answering her phone?" Dad asks Mom.

Mom sighs. "I'll call West's parents again and see if they know anything." Dad has his keys in his hand and he keeps walking back and forth, picking up his coat and putting it down.

We're all sitting in the kitchen waiting to see what will happen. My mom puts a plate with chicken fingers in front of Preston, even though we all know he won't eat them.

"You should eat," she says to me. I shake my head.

I reach over and pat Miracle Child—I mean, Preston's leg. I tell myself that no matter how screwed up our family is, I will try to be there for him. Maybe tonight I'll play Monopoly with him, or one of his stupid video games so he can beat me. I know he'll like that. It makes me happy when he laughs. He has a great laugh.

The phone rings. Mom answers and we all hold our breath. She nods a couple of times. "Yes, we'll see you in a little while," she says, but she's worried—the line between her eyes is more pronounced than ever.

"That was Paige. West went to his parents' house. She's coming home," Mom tells us. "It's going to be all right, everything is going to be all right." My mom sounds all teary. I think maybe it would be good for her to let some emotions out. Maybe it would be good for all of us.

Preston goes out onto the porch to wait for Paige. I sit at the kitchen table, voluntarily in the same room as my parents for once.

"I got another job offer, right here in town," Dad tells me, with a sad little smile. "Not as much money as before, but it could turn things around."

"That's great, Daddy." I smile at him across the table.

"Mommy, Dad, there's a police car in our driveway!" Preston calls through the open front door.

"Now what do you suppose . . . ?" Mom's forehead creases again with worry.

"She said he left, didn't she? You don't think he came back . . . ?" Daddy stands up and they walk to the door together. I peek out around them.

They think the police are here because of Paige and West, and I don't know whether to hope that's true or not. I don't know what to think. If they are here because of Paige that might mean something bad happened, and I don't want that, but if they aren't here because of Paige . . . My stomach clenches and I take a step back, thinking that I'm actually truly going to throw up.

"Mr. and Mrs. Prescott?" the police officer asks.

"Yes." My father's voice sounds quavery.

"We need to ask you a few questions."

"Of course." One police officer, who is tall and heavyset, falls into step beside my father and follows him into the house. The skinny one stands and watches us—well, not Preston, who's sticking close to my side, but me.

Skinny Policeman takes a couple of steps up the stairs. The fourth stair squeaks loudly and he looks surprised. He looks like a normal guy, like a teacher or a parent or whatever, except for the uniform.

My mom walks after him.

"Is this about my daughter?" she asks. "Has something happened?" The police officer looks at me. I am so scared that I feel my legs getting trembly. I wonder if it would look suspiciously weird if I sat down right here in the hallway. Skinny Policeman frowns and walks up the stairs and directly into my room. He's facing my canopy bed with the pink stripes and the frilly pillows. The princess room. My room. I follow him.

"This is it," he calls to the other policeman. "This computer could be the one."

"How do you know?" The skinny one clicks something and both of the officers loom over my tiny seventeen-inch monitor.

"Can we take this computer?" the fat policeman asks. My dad is in the doorway, and I can tell he's struggling with what to do.

"Don't you need a warrant to take something from my daughter's room?"

"Not if you give us permission."

"I think we need to know what's going on before we allow you to take anything," Mom says.

My mom is holding on to Preston as if he might float away. I wish she would wrap her arms around me and hold me the same way.

"Is this your room and your computer, young lady?" The skinny policeman doesn't look so much like a teacher now.

"Yes." I feel my mouth move, but I don't have a voice. I reach for my mother but she's too far away.

He comes toward me, and I see his handcuffs dangling from his belt. Real handcuffs.

He puts them on me. They're cold. They don't feel sexy at all. Mom's mouth drops open and Daddy's face is bright, bright red.

"Parker Prescott, you have the right to remain silent," he begins.

"How do you know her name?" my mom asks. Something about the way she says it sounds unfamiliar, and I'm afraid to raise my eyes and see how she might be looking at me. "You can't take her outside in those handcuffs. The neighbors might see." She puts her hand on my shoulder. I want to throw myself into her arms, but I'm frozen, turned into an icicle with the cold metal handcuffs holding me in place.

The police officers whisper to one another, and after a couple of minutes they take the cuffs off and the skinny one escorts me to the police car without them. The other officer stays back to talk to my parents. I want to hear what is being said, but I don't want to see the looks on their faces.

When we reach the police car, its lights still flashing, the fat police officer opens the door for me, even though I could have done it myself since my hands are free. I stand beside the police car for several seconds. Long enough to make the skinny cop frown. Finally, I force myself to climb into the backseat. The vinyl makes a squeaky sound as I sit back and put my head in my hands.

I don't think or feel anything as they drive me downtown. Sure, there is an occasional stab of fear, a bit of shame, but overall I am only numb. Empty.

The police station is a big dingy building. A lady comes out and whispers with the officers who brought me in, and then she takes me into a room. There's a rough orange couch made out of some kind of woven material, a couple of chairs in the same rough weave, only yellow, and a rug over the concrete floor.

I expect them to fingerprint me and take my picture. For some reason I imagine a hideous mug shot plastered all over Marion Henessy's blog. I clasp my hands and unclasp them over and over, wipe the sweat on my jeans, try to focus on something besides the fear that is building up in me.

"We don't know yet if charges will be pressed. Sit in here, honey. I'll be back in a few minutes."

Is that good news? She called me "honey," is that good? Does it possibly mean she likes me or feels sorry for me, or does she call everyone "honey"? Can I start feeling hope now? The little glimmer of hope just makes me that much more aware of the fear I'm trying to keep under control. I had American government last year, why can't I remember the difference between a misdemeanor and a felony? Where does two thousand dollars fall? Am I going to jail?

There's a noise, a creaking footstep noise, and I look up so quickly that a sharp pain twists its way through my neck. Kyle Henessy is in the doorway. The security in this police station must be pretty lax if they'll let my sister's stalker come into this room. I mean, there *is* a restraining order requiring him to stay fifty feet away from each and every member of our family. I take a gaspy breath. Me and Kyle both at the police station—that means I'd better start figuring out how to talk him out of pressing charges.

He sits down in the yellow chair and turns toward me.

"I knew it was you," he said. "I found the picture on your computer when I was visiting Paige last week. The one I assume you tried to sell me the first time?"

I stare at his eyebrows. For a guy's eyebrows they are fairly neat, not bushy or anything. If I stare at them, then I don't have to meet his eyes, and we'll never have the deeper connection that comes from looking into another person's eyes. My own eyes feel weird, like they're made of plastic, like they could burn right out of my skull. I stare at Kyle Henessy, with his wire-rimmed glasses that are exactly like my dad's.

"How old are you?" he asks.

"Sixteen."

"Old enough, I guess. If you're old enough to blackmail me, I guess you're old enough to hear some ugly things about your sister."

"I know some things about her," I say for some idiotic reason.

"You probably know more than you think. I noticed you never went to parties with her, after that first one."

"No."

"I guess you were aware of the big stupid crush I had on her."

"Everybody knew," I say. It was pretty obvious.

"Before the restraining order and everything, even when we were kids."

"Yeah, everybody knew," I repeat.

"Paige is nearly a year younger than me, and she's probably the first thing I remember. Before you or my sister were born, I just remember playing with her in our backyard. I can't remember a time when I didn't think about her, though when we were little it wasn't so much attraction as regular friendship. I had a thing for her in middle school, and I took her to my very first dance. My mom drove, and Paige ditched me for some other boy almost as soon as we walked through the door."

"I never knew she ditched you," I say. He looks down at his ugly Timberland boots.

"Well, that was about the time the intense feeling started. I call it love, my parents call it obsession. By the time she was a freshman, your sister was extremely, um, notorious on the party scene. It was terrible, Parker. I hated myself for the way I felt and for not being good enough for her and just for being alive.

"I can't explain to you why I started going to all those

parties. At first it helped me to feel more popular, more in touch with other people. Then there was Paige. She was like an angel, the same angel who kissed me on the cheek when I had my tonsils out and signed all over my cast when I broke my arm.

"Sort of. We were older, and Paige was different. Like part of her was gone. The sweet part that I remembered from when we were kids, it seemed locked away." If I hadn't been so close to hypnotized by his quiet, stumbling voice, I might have agreed, might have told him that it seemed the same to me.

"Then the thing happened." He stops and looks at me quickly, and then his eyes dart away again.

"I was at a party, and I went down to the basement to pick up some more beer, and there was Paige, completely passed out. I went to get a blanket. She was just sprawled there on the floor, but when I got back West was lifting her in his arms.

"He took her upstairs to one of the bedrooms. I thought he was probably just going to put her in somebody's parents' bed, make sure she was breathing, but still wanted to be near her. I wanted to be the one to save her. So I followed. He took her shoes off. I thought that seemed normal, because a person can't sleep with their shoes on. I came in the room and I asked him if he needed any help.

"He started laughing, and said something that I won't repeat to you. Then some of the other football players came and forced me out of the room."

I start to stand up. I suddenly feel deeply afraid. "What're you telling me? What did the football players do to her?"

Kyle touches my arm. "No, no, I'm sorry. I didn't mean

for you to think that. Just West. He was proprietary, but she was his girlfriend. He had this hold over her. The other guys knew she was his. I was the only one who didn't pay attention when he staked out his territory.

"I followed her everywhere, trying to help. Trying to save her from herself and from West. She drank way too much, not like she was trying to get a buzz, like she was trying to forget herself, like she didn't care about being conscious. Three different times she drank so much that I called the hospital and had an ambulance come for her. It made her furious, and she was supposed to go into an alcohol program, but your parents signed for her to get out of it.

"I watched her on the way to school, I watched her on dates, and I watched her through her bedroom window. It was all to try to protect her. If I had wanted sex, I could have just done what West did. She was passed out so many times and in so many places, it would have been easy enough." He clears his throat again.

"I thought I was some superhero guy, but I wasn't supersneaky, and I started to seriously freak her out, and she knew that one more trip to the hospital would mean a rehab stay, or some counseling, that there would be consequences. That's when she got your parents to get a restraining order."

Kyle takes his glasses off and wipes them on his shirt. Just like my dad does sometimes. What I want more than anything is to get out of this room with the orange couch and the nubby yellow chairs and to go home and curl up in my frilly canopy bed for about a week. It isn't that I don't care about Paige and what happened or that I don't all of a sudden feel sorry for Kyle, it's just that this is a jail, and I want to go home to my parents.

"So are you going to press charges?" I ask. Because what

else *can* I say? I knew he was obsessed with my sister. I knew she liked to party, I didn't know it was a big problem. I don't know what to think, really.

"No. No, I'm not. I reported the original blackmail, but once I figured it was you I was prepared to drop everything."

"Um, Kyle, if you were just watching Paige to protect her, what were you doing taking pictures of me? You know, the whole hot tub thing?"

"I didn't take those pictures. Marion has convinced some moron to supply pictures of you. She keeps a counter on the blog, and apparently the entries about you get lots of hits. The hot tub pictures and the ice in the locker were done by the same guy. He was planning on taking your picture when you opened it, but you came to school late."

"Oh." What do you say to something harsh like that? Being treated like that. "So you don't know who did it?"

"No, but I can promise you that she won't be posting any more of that garbage." Kyle looks at me quietly for a second, then changes the subject. "So, Parker, what did you do with the money?"

"I put it in my parents' checking account."

He laughs. "Seriously? Why?"

"To keep the mortgage company from foreclosing on our house."

He just kind of sits there and looks at me. "Marion's right. You are different from your sister."

"Marion hates me."

"Yeah. This whole thing has been hard on her. She always looked up to Paige, and she's crazy about me." He smiles here, the way a nice older sibling might smile when thinking about his little sister. It makes me feel a little left out or something. "My parents had a hard time dealing with everything, and Marion had to be the go-between, trying to smooth things over. She was too young for all that pressure. Plus, she lost her friendship with you, and that was important to her, even if she won't admit it."

"Don't you want your name cleared?" I ask him. It seems like he would.

"Of what? I guess I am a stalker, really. I sat outside your house for hours, sometimes in the rain, sometimes in the cold, just to get a glimpse of your sister. What does that make me?"

A stalker? And yet, if he was doing it for a good reason . . .

"You still want to go out with her, after the way she treated you?" I can't help asking.

"Yeah." I knew he was lying whenever he said he was over her.

"You're crazy," I tell him.

"Yeah, but see, I think she felt the same way about West that I felt about her, which means that she would do anything to keep him. I understand her."

"I don't know why she had to stay with him and why she needed to get drunk all the time."

"Your parents seemed to think it was just regular teenager stuff, but I think she needs help. With the drinking and maybe with getting away from West."

"And then she's going to go out with you?"

"I hope so," he says quietly.

"You and Paige are both crazy, and maybe you deserve each other." Except that he's nicer than my sister, but maybe her hotness makes up for not being nice, who knows?

"Parker, I hope you are much happier with your current obsession." I wonder what he knows about that. Probably just what he's read on Marion's blog. I think he means it, he isn't even being sarcastic. Wow.

"Do you think Paige is happy?" I ask him.

"No."

"Do you think Paige was happy in high school?"

"No."

"Not ever?"

He shakes his head. "She smiled a lot, but it hardly ever touched her eyes. I don't think she was happy."

That's the part that's a revelation. I knew she drank sometimes, and it's becoming clear that she probably should've stayed away from West, but I thought that behind all that partying, she was happier than I would ever be. I thought she was bubbly, happy, alive.

"I never wanted to press charges, but since I filed a complaint the officers wanted to bring you down here, to scare you," he says, his voice apologetic.

Kyle walks me out of the police station. My dad is there waiting for me. We walk silently to the Jeep and get in. Mom is sitting in the passenger seat. She looks like she's been crying. I get in the back and buckle my seat belt.

"You put the money into our bank account," he begins.

"Yes."

"But she stole it," Mom says.

"I know, but she was trying to help."

"I stole the money, Daddy. It was wrong," I say. I'm tired of excuses.

"I know it was wrong," he says, "but I am aware of why you took it. It does make a difference to me." I look up and see his eyes in the rearview mirror. For the first time since the handcuffs incident he is looking straight at me. We smile at each other. I can almost hear my mom's eyes rolling.

She sighs. It's okay. She has her favorite golden princess, and Daddy has me.

"I guess I need to pay Kyle Henessy back the two thousand dollars," I say.

"I already gave him a check," Mom tells me. I can't help wondering if we have enough money in the account to cover that check, but I don't ask.

Dad drives up to our house. Even though I was kind of hoping that it would have disappeared, the for-sale sign is still in the yard. I go into the house and straight upstairs to my room.

My mom comes upstairs and sits on my bed.

"Your sister's going into rehab tomorrow. She wanted me to tell you something. Let's see if I can get this exactly right. She wanted me to tell you that it's hard to focus on other people when you are completely focused on yourself, and when you're drunk."

Mom had to memorize that? Really?

"Why didn't Paige tell me this herself?" My voice always sounds abrupt when I talk to my mom, and I don't know how to change it.

"I don't think Paige knows how to talk to you, Parker. You're so different from her friends." Yeah. None of us knows how to talk to each other, only at least Mom's trying.

I lean forward and press my face into her for a minute, and she has her arms around me before I'm even all the way forward, like she was just waiting for an excuse to touch me. I don't think about what that means, because it feels good.

☽   ☽   ☽

I lie down and try to relax, to hide under the pink comforter for maybe half an hour, but then I can't, and I realize that it isn't even late, not even late enough for Preston to be in bed.

So I get up and plod downstairs. My parents are sitting on the couch. The recliner seat part is broken where Preston kept pumping it to make it pop out over and over, so Dad is sitting kind of slumped over with his elbow against the armrest. Preston is sitting at the coffee table with a big piece of notebook paper. On it he has drawn five stick figures and labeled them, *Mom, Dad, Parker, Paige, Me.* His Preston stick-boy is only slightly shorter than the one that's supposed to be me.

"You want me to help you with that?" I ask him.

"You don't ever draw people," he says.

"People are really hard, 'cause it's hard to get all the little details right. Sometimes you don't even notice the details, but I think we can do better than that." I jab my finger at the corner where he has drawn and labeled Mom and Dad. They look like identical stick-twins except Dad is wearing enormous glasses.

"Do you want me to go get your special pencil?" he asks.

"Yeah," I tell him, "that would be cool."

We're back at the nice place, the place he took me on our first date. Things are almost like they were the first time, except some things have changed and I'm not so nervous. I'm watching him over the linen tablecloth, around the lighted candle and the white rose in a cut-crystal vase.

"I've never had dinner with an ex-convict before," he says.

"I'm not . . ." I make a face at him and pretend to study the menu. It's been exactly one week since I, um, went to jail.

The violinist approaches and stands right in front of us, which seems strange because usually violinists ignore teenagers in fancy restaurants. He begins to play, a sweetly familiar tune followed by a screeching chorus that is strangely familiar. *I don't belong here.* The violin fades away. I see a fifty-dollar bill exchange hands. Fifty dollars.

"You paid the violinist to play 'Creep'?"

"Our song. He liked playing it."

"He was, um, enthusiastic."

"Infatuation and longing, remember?"

"And self-loathing."

"I would have found the money for you."

"Yeah?"

"I could have. Why didn't you tell me you needed it?"

"I was ashamed." The waiter brings a basket of bread.

ᔅ   ᔅ   ᔅ

Earlier this afternoon I went downstairs to look for my favorite jeans.

Gasp, Kyle Henessy was on the couch holding my sister's hand. I just looked at them.

I know they think I am just like her, that I have latched onto my version of West. My parents can't tell the difference, you see. They barely understand the difference between Paige and Parker, the daughters they created. How could they possibly know the difference between the things we desire? Or—and this is the thing that feels like cold water seeping into my reality, and it's becoming something like a flood—what if we really are alike and I just don't see it?

ᔅ   ᔅ   ᔅ

"Parker . . ."

"You don't know what it's like to see your whole life changing because of money."

He kind of shrugs at me. "My parents worry about

money. My mom is always worried she'll have to go back to work. She hated being a lawyer."

"Really?"

"Yeah, but don't tell anybody that I listen to anything my parents say. Honestly, Park, they were thrilled when I flunked out of boarding school. The tuition at that place was astronomical."

"Flunked out. I thought you got kicked—" He puts his finger against my lips to silence me.

"Shhh. Not so loud. There were rumors about one of the guys sneaking a girl into the squeaky-clean upperclass dormitory, but I officially got kicked out because of my grades."

"Do I want to know?"

"No." He takes a drink from the delicate little water glass. "Self-loathing, remember?"

"Do I make you?"

"You make it all better." The sweet smile, pure evil. "Do you want to guess what I have in my pocket?"

I know what he has in his pocket, and he knows that I know.

ᗡ   ᗡ   ᗡ

There was this loud knock at the door.

"Can you get that, Parker?" Does Paige not realize that I'm running late? I hope she wasn't making out with Kyle in our living room. Yuck. I opened the door and kind of swallowed my heart. The little creepy twerp from advanced British lit was standing on my porch. The guy who accused me of . . . the guy who said I liked to . . .

"Is Kyle Henessy here?" he asked. "I'm supposed to drop off this essay for him to edit for my stepsister."

"Who's your stepsister?"

"Erin Glasgow."

Pieces started falling into place.

"If you live right next door to my boyfriend, why haven't I ever seen you there before?"

He sneered. Same little perverted creep I shouldn't waste my breath talking to.

"I've seen you plenty of times." Gag. Then, "I live with my mom. I only visit my dad a few weekends a month."

"I'll give your sister's paper to Kyle." Knowing for certain that Kyle didn't take seminaked pictures of me makes him a little easier to take as a potential new member of our family. Plus, he didn't press charges against me; plus, he's sticking with my sister through all this crazy shit.

"You know what I'd like to give you?" Erin's brother moved closer on the little porch, breathing on me, same rotting-meat breath as before. I breathed in (through my mouth), braced myself, and shoved him right off the porch. Down the same set of stairs that I rode a skateboard down when I was seven. Preston falls off our porch three times a week. Falling off our porch won't kill him, but I guess a girl can hope.

♪ ♪ ♪

"So about this bet. I think I figured it out."

"Yeah?"

"There was a bet, right? The guy in advanced British lit was the one who started it. I didn't even think it was real. I thought Marion made it up."

"I think she did, along with Erin's stepbrother, yeah. He took the pictures too. I think he was trying to get in good with Marion. It wasn't a real bet, like he had any takers or was offering anybody cash. He's a loser. I um, kind of hit him. You know, in the face. A couple of times." He looks embarrassed. Why does it make me happy that he hit some-body for me?

"So he's your neighbor?" I ask. "I never knew."

"He's over there on the weekends sometimes." A girl in really high heels clomps past our table. We look at each other and kind of smile.

"It's a good thing your parents dropped that plan to move to Florida, Prescott. I was having a hell of a time find-ing a good boarding school there." He's obviously trying to change the subject, but that's okay, I let him.

"You were going to follow me?"

"I'm not a stalker, if that's what you're thinking." He laughs, but I don't.

I look at him across the table. I'm not my sister, and I'm not my mother. How desperate am I to keep him?

We stare at one another through the flickering of the single candle. There are crazy insane thoughts going through my brain over and over. I should probably go home and lie down or something.

"I love you."

An hour passes. There is echoing silence. I know that there should be conversation and forks hitting china and the music of a violin, but it's all gone. He's looking at his hands, and his plate, anyplace but at me.

I've been waiting for him to say this for a long time.

I bring my chin up, catch his eyes.

"I think that we shouldn't get back together," I say. In-side, some part of me is shouting over and over, I love you too, I love you too. It isn't like he doesn't know this. But with all the things that have passed between us, and all the words that have and haven't been said, I think I'm going to keep these to myself.

"So do you want me to take you home, or what?" He looks hurt.

"After dinner, maybe." I tell him. "I'll send you some music that I like and you can tell me what you think." This doesn't have to be the end, I'm thinking. I don't want it to be the end.

"You have pretty good taste in music," he says, and cuts into his steak. For the first time ever, I'm able to sit across from him and eat a few bites of my meal without being sick from nervousness.

43

"Do you think he meant it?" Raye asks.

"Yeah," I say. "Maybe. Maybe like you would say 'I love that shirt,' or 'I love mall pizza.' He loves me like that."

We both laugh, but she looks a little bit worried.

"Are you okay with that?"

I break my last glorious mall cookie in half and push it toward her. We're sitting at my kitchen table, and it's close to midnight. My entire family is asleep, and Raye is here with the things I accidentally on purpose left in her car earlier. A bag from the Limited with my new jeans and my three new shirts.

I start to laugh. "You know what? I've broken up with him twice, and I don't even know if we ever had a relationship to begin with. I just broke up with a guy who wasn't even my boyfriend."

"Parker, are you crying?"

I'm laughing so hard I'm almost crying. Or maybe I'm just crying, I don't know.

"Does that mean you won't go out with him again?" she asks.

"Oh, I'll go out with him. But he'll have to ask me. I'm not going back to his basement without some kind of commitment."

"Like a diamond ring or something?"

"Um, no. No rings here." Paige and I had a little ceremony earlier. It was very satisfying. Normally Raye would ask me what the hell I'm talking about, but she's focused on other things right now. Raye has an enviable ability to get completely focused on something.

"So we're both single. Are we happy?" Raye is full of questions. I don't think I've ever seen her so unsure of things. She's downright hesitant.

"I'm happy. It feels like a cease-fire from all the relationship trauma. Now I can relax for a few days before I start worrying again."

"You've had a lot to worry about. I can't believe you blackmailed Kyle Henessy. I'll bet Marion nearly had an aneurism."

"I nearly had one myself. Especially when they took me downtown." I say this, the "took me downtown" part, like I'm a complete badass, but we both know better.

"I really didn't know, you never told me what was going on."

I shake my head, and we don't look at each other. "It was stuff that I couldn't talk about."

"Well, next time you have stuff you can't talk about, be sure to tell me about it, okay?" I nod, and she continues. "I guess now that you have these things you left in my car." She scoots the bag toward me. I finally cashed the check that I got for my sixteenth birthday. Mom and Dad pretty much made me. And Raye took me shopping so that I could get something to wear for the big date. The date. What could realistically be the last date. And we also got the pink shirt from the Gap—which is in the bag.

"Thanks for bringing them."

"Ah well, it's not every day your best friend breaks up with the hottest guy in school, or whatever."

"Or whatever," I agree.

I walk her to the door. Stare out into the empty yard. The Century 21 sign is gone now. My parents decided we could stay here, at least for the rest of the year. It doesn't look like the house was going to sell anytime soon anyway. And they're going to have to replace that garbage disposal.

There's a pair of handcuffs down there, and an engagement ring. It happened after he dropped me off. I walked into the house and found I didn't know what to do with myself. I was standing in the kitchen, trying not to cry. Paige came into the room.

"What's up?" she asked. "I thought you were on the big date?"

"Yeah." It was a big deal. I had to beg forever before the parental units would let me out on parole, and then beg again until they let Raye take me shopping. And here I am, home early. And she's home too.

"Didn't you have a good time?" she asks. Not sarcastic or anything, although for a second I wonder if maybe she is looking for some ammunition so she can make fun of me.

"I don't know. Until I figure out what constitutes a good time for me, maybe I won't go out anymore. With him or anyone. Maybe I'll just stay in the house and watch TV, or something."

She sighs. "I wish I was as smart as you and just stayed home for a few weekends. Maybe my life wouldn't be so . . . well, you know."

"Did Dad ever fix the garbage disposal?" I ask her.

She raises her eyebrows. "I don't think so, why?"

I pull the handcuffs out of my pocket. "I got these back tonight."

"And you're going to . . ." We walk together over to the sink. I look down into the opening that is supposed to grind up food and stuff.

"I don't think they'll fit." I guess it was a stupid idea. I feel somewhat moronic now.

"I know something that will," she says, and she takes off her diamond ring.

"No way. Paige, you can't put that—"

But she does, she drops it, and it hits the side and rolls around and around.

"Turn it on," she tells me. I stand there with my hand on the switch. It's like a light switch on the side of the counter.

"Do this for me, Parker?" She says it like it's a question, like she's begging, and she's looking at me like I've never done anything for her in my life.

"Wait." I open a drawer and get the square mallet that has weird ridges on the hammer part. Mom says it's for tenderizing meat, but I've never seen anyone use it, ever.

"I got one of those for a wedding present," Paige says.

I almost say something about hitting West in the head with it, that maybe she could improve him, but I figure things are rough enough without giving her murderous ideas. So I hold the handcuffs sideways and hit them. Once, no change. Twice, nothing. But the third time the cuff part bends in enough that I can fit it through the hole in the sink. The second one crumbles more easily than the first one. I drop it in with my sister's diamond engagement ring.

I take a deep breath, shrug, and flip the switch. The garbage disposal comes to life. It makes an unholy god-awful racket, like a monster with metal teeth eating cookies with lead chips.

"Paige!" I'm about to have a heart attack. It's suddenly becoming real to me that she dropped that great big diamond in there. I can't believe I just ground it up.

"Don't worry about it, kid. It wasn't a diamond. It was a fake, and not even a very good one. Just like my marriage. West's mother told him I was too young and silly for a real diamond, and hey, maybe she was right. I jumped up and down when I got the ring and I agreed to marry him." She turns and walks out of the room, stopping for just a moment to admire her reflection in the decorative mirror Mom has hung in the dining area. Some things will never change, I guess.

☙ ☙ ☙

"Parker!" Mom yells. It's morning. I know because the sun is up. I'm trying to decide if I'm feeling any different. He finally said it. Is loved-by-her-ex Parker any different than yesterday-morning Parker? How about broke-up-with-her-kind-of-boyfriend Parker? I do feel different, but I can't quite explain why.

"Hmm?" I say this to my mother, but of course she can't hear me because I'm talking into my pillow. I struggle out of bed and smooth the blankets. I'm putting the last pillow in place, folding the pink comforter over so that the pink and white striped sheets show just a little, when Mom comes into my room. She sits down at my desk. She has her makeup on, and her businesswoman outfit, even though it's Sunday morning. She just dropped Paige off at rehab. It isn't really rehab, they say, just a counseling center so she can try to get her crap together. I wonder what the counselors would think about Paige dropping her engagement ring into a garbage disposal.

"She says she wants the divorce," Mom says. I can't tell if she's sad or just tired.

"Did West show up?" I ask. Paige called him and was hoping he might come for some counseling thing her doctor set up.

"No." Mom runs her hand over the big empty space where my computer used to sit. It's in the kitchen now. Yeah. I have to check my e-mail in the kitchen, where they can watch me and make sure I'm not doing anything illegal.

"Paige is stupid," I say. Saying it makes me feel like crap, and I realize how mad I've been at Paige for screwing up her life and for not being perfect.

"Sometimes people just get an idea in their head."

"You mean like Paige thinking West was so great?"

"Or like me thinking that a perfect family had to have three children."

"What?"

"Well, you know, I was an only child, and I thought to have that perfect family we had to have this big brick house with a white porch and three children. Do you have any idea how hard it is to raise three children?"

"Not really."

"If you had been half as difficult as Paige and Preston, we would have never made it. We thought we were lucky to have one quiet child."

Yeah, it's really great to be the quiet one. It's totally fucking awesome. Wait, what did Mom just say?

"You mean it wouldn't have mattered if Preston was a girl?"

"Well, of course it would matter. Can you imagine a girl collecting all those gross things, and the plastic snakes and playing those sumo wrestling video games?"

"Um, I mean, you didn't feel like you had to have Preston because I was a girl, and you really wanted a boy?"

"Three boys, three girls, whatever combination. I was just determined to have three perfect children."

I start to say something terrible like, Well, then you really screwed up, considering her last chance at perfection just woke up and is now crashing into my room. It's a good thing Mom didn't close the door all the way, because it looks like he entered headfirst. Like, he hit the door with his head, and then it slams into the wall and bounces back to hit him on the other side of his head. Ouch.

I could also tell her that I know something about getting ideas in your mind that won't go away, but I'm not ready to talk to her about stuff yet. I'll just let her stay here and feel like she's being a good mom. Everybody deserves a little confidence boost, especially when they're trying so hard.

"Honey, where's your helmet?" Mom asks Preston.

Instead of answering he jumps up onto my bed and rolls around in the pillows, like a crazy puppy with ADHD.

"C'mon, let's go get your medicine and a Pop-Tart." Mom takes him by the arm and drags him away. She looks over her shoulder and says, "I guess that middle-child stuff isn't all baloney, huh, Parker?" almost like she's a real person and she's recognizing me as a real person too. Weird.

I stand up and smooth out the comforter where I had wrinkled it. I rearrange the pillows and pick up the one Preston knocked to the floor. It takes a minute to get them all in the exact right spots, but it's worth the effort. Looking at my perfectly made bed makes me happy. I like this stupid princess room and this house, and sometimes even this family.

It's been almost two months since Christmas, and over a week since I last made my mom cry. I guess I might be improving or something.

ACKNOWLEDGMENTS

I would like to thank the following people:

Maya Rock for totally "getting it" and loving this project, sometimes even more than I did.

Krista Marino for her enthusiasm and insight.

Lee Faith for being the love of my life and supporting my writing even when it seemed like a crazy dream, and even when it meant feeding and bathing the kids almost every night.

Ezra and Noel for keeping me sane through rejections and revisions and life in general.

My mom, Vicki Griffin, for teaching me to love to read.

Stephanie Hale and Carmen Rodrigues for being the best critique partners and friends anyone could ask for.

Jamie Sobrato for reading everything, telling me I could do it, and then reading even more.

My Eastside readers—Missy Wood, my number one never-critical reader, as well as Lana Yeary, Kathy Price, Kevin Vachon, Trish Priddy, and Kimberly Thompson.

And finally, each and every one of my students, but especially the eighth graders of 2006-07, many of whom will presumably be my tenth graders when this book is released!

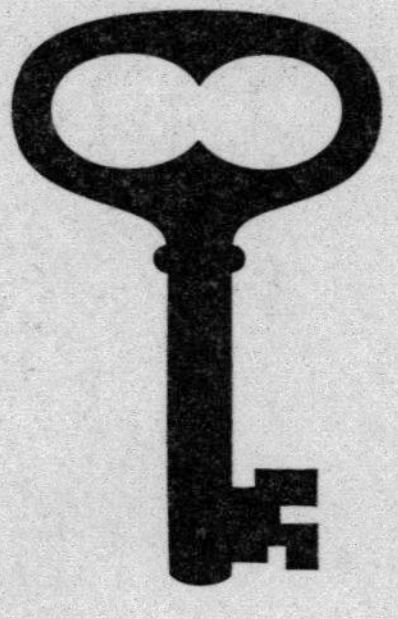